ALFHEIM ACADEMY

ALFHEIM ACADEMY: BOOK ONE

S.T. BENDE

Alfheim Academy
Alfheim Academy: Book One
Copyright © 2019, S.T. Bende
Edited by: Antonella Iannarino and CREATING ink
Cover Art by: Melissa Stevens of The Illustrated Author Design
Services

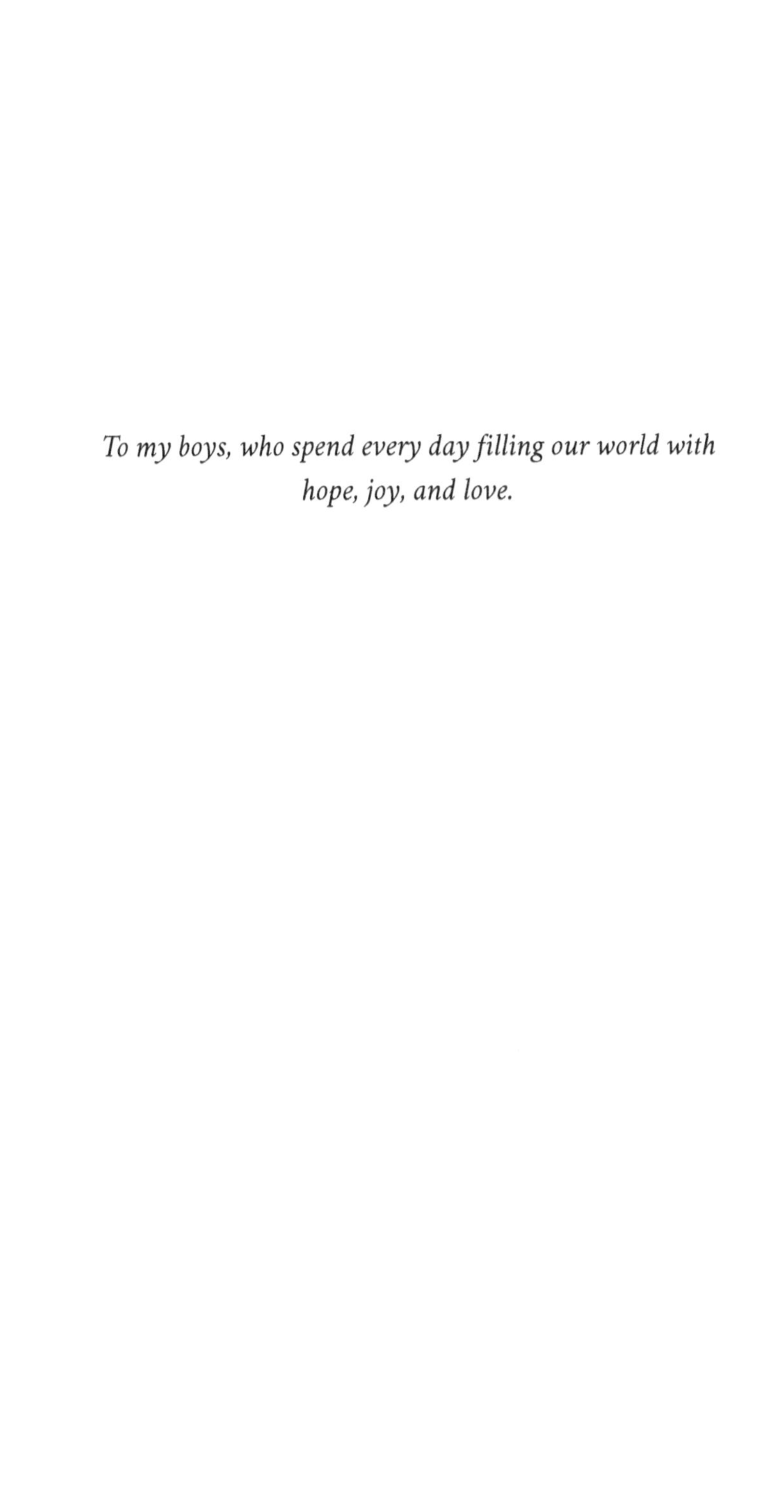

*To my boys, who spend every day filling our world with
hope, joy, and love.*

CHAPTER 1

THE FACT THAT I nearly died on my sixteenth birthday was pretty much my own fault.

I knew better than to go that deep into the forest, just like I knew better than to go *anywhere* by myself. But I'd spent my entire life in hiding and hadn't seen so much as a hint of a threat so . . . I took a chance.

And it almost cost me everything.

The day started out well enough—I aced a chemistry quiz, avoided getting called on in English Lit, and scored a sweet birthday gift from my best friend.

"Here." Elin Eklund slammed her locker shut before handing me a rectangular package. She'd drawn anime-inspired caricatures of the two of us on every inch of the wrapping. "It's that valkyrie graphic novel you wanted to pre-order, but the idiot in the comic shop couldn't figure out how to submit the form."

I laughed. "You're supposed to let me open it before you tell me what it is. Though maybe I should just frame the paper instead—this is some of your best work."

Elin waved off the compliment. "Happy birthday, Aura."

"Thanks. Uh-oh." I pulled Elin closer to the lockers as Britney "Bitch-Face" Blomgren and her dance-team disciples sashayed down the hallway, cheering loudly about the impending homecoming rally.

"Didn't want you to get trampled on," I said by way of explanation.

One corner of Elin's mouth curled up in a snarl. "I'd like to see her try."

"Oh, she's tried plenty of times." I shrugged. "We're just faster than her. You know she always skips out on our martial arts lessons."

"That's because she's lazy. Speaking of Bitch-Face, do you still have to tutor her this afternoon or do you want a ride home?" Elin shouldered her backpack and walked toward the parking lot.

"I'm tutoring. I'll be at the library for at least an hour—two, if she hasn't grown any new brain cells this week." I sighed. "Thanks for the offer, though. See you at dinner?"

"Your birthday dinner? Wouldn't miss it." Elin leaned over and gave me a hug. "Hang in there. You won't be tutoring that cow forever. Two more years and we'll leave Earth for Alfheim, and then—"

"Shh!" I hissed. I glanced over both shoulders to see if anyone was listening. In the grand tradition of Granite High, everyone was too into themselves to notice the *extremely foreign* foreigners blabbing right beside them.

"Oh, come on. Nobody's figured out we're faeries yet." Elin stepped forward, her loose tunic swishing around her thighs.

"Light elves," I corrected. "Faeries have wings. We have mean right hooks."

"Says the girl who reads comic books." Elin dug her keys out of her backpack. "Okay. If you're tutoring, I have time to finish that painting I'm working on for my mom's birthday. See you at six. And try not to catch the dumb from being around Britney."

"I'll do my best." I bumped my fist against Elin's, shifted my new book to the crook of my elbow, and turned on one heel toward the library.

I was two hours away from a seven-layer chocolate cake, four different kinds of ice cream, and a Netflix queue packed to the brim with superhero movies. The only thing standing between me and the weekend of my dreams was one teensy little tutoring session with the dumbest girl in the history of Granite Ridge, California. *Two short hours.*

How bad could they be?

"Gods, Aura, are you seriously wearing combat boots?" Britney planted one manicured hand on her waist, and positioned herself directly in front of the library window. The mid-afternoon sun shone through the pine trees outside, lighting Britney's obsidian locks so her hair appeared to glow. As she flicked an errant strand over one shoulder, the dappled light caught the sparkles in her smoky silver eyeshadow. On the outside, Britney was the picture of Midgardian teen perfection.

On the inside, she was mean as a fire giant.

Snort.

"Aura! Are you even listening to me?" Bitch-Face jutted her hip. Her pleated dance team uniform swayed against her thighs.

"Huh? Sorry, right. Don't dress like a boy. Got it. Anything else, or can I get started teaching you basic math *again?*" I pointed to the empty chair across from me.

"Gee, I don't know." Britney placed her hands on the table and leaned forward. "I'd teach you how to be less of a loser, but I honestly don't think there's any hope for you. Still no date to homecoming this weekend? Or to anything, *ever?*"

I narrowed my eyes. "I have better things to do than get felt up under the bleachers, like some people I know."

"Jealous, much?"

"You wish." I shoved an algebra worksheet across the table. "Let's just get this over with, already."

"Fine by me." Britney dropped into her seat with a hefty eyeroll. "My mother's paying you good money to make sure I pass, so shut your stupid nerd-face and do your job."

Some days, high school was literal hell.

The next forty-five minutes unfolded in typical, tortuous fashion. By the time we'd finished what should have been an easy ten-minute algebra lesson, the only equation I wanted to see ever again was *me squared* plus *storming-out-of-the-library squared* equaled *never having to tutor Bitch-Face again, ever. Squared.* But Britney was right—her mom did pay good money. Plus, she was friends with my aunt, which meant I was stuck with the gig until we graduated. Or until Britney flunked out, whichever came first.

I was seriously hoping for the latter.

"Are we done now?" Britney closed her workbook and shoved it into her backpack.

"With math, yeah. But your mom asked me to cover, uh . . . Government, before you, me, and Elin take that homeschool quiz next week."

"Look, I know you're a dork and all, but I'm not taking Government until I'm a senior. So, I'm out of here." Britney pushed her chair back.

"Not U.S. Government." I lowered my voice to a whisper. "*Alfheim* Government."

"What? Why? We're not going back there for two more years."

"I know that, but the adults want us to be prepared. And they're giving us a quiz on Tuesday. Remember?"

"That's Tuesday-Britney's problem. Friday-Britney has to be at the homecoming rally in"—she checked her phone—"half an hour."

"Fine, then I'll make it quick." I glanced over my

shoulder to make sure the library was still empty. As predicted, the rest of Granite High had better things to at four p.m. on homecoming weekend.

"I'm waiting." Britney drummed French-tipped fingernails on the tabletop.

I pulled a thin binder out of my backpack, then scooted my chair around so I was next to Britney. With my back to the window, I'd be able to see if anyone entered the library . . . and pull the plug on our inter-planetary civics lesson, real quick.

Nobody at Granite High could know that Elin, Brit-ney, and I were different. We'd been hiding on Midgard —the planet humans called Earth—since the day Svar-talfheim assassins killed my parents and set siege to our realm. Our guardians never let us forget that the dark elves still hunted us. But in the sixteen years since we'd left home, we managed to avoid detection. Our little group settled in a tiny mountain town outside of Los Angeles, and did our best to live as humans. The adults *never* used their magic, and since the rest of us wouldn't come into any powers until we turned eigh-teen, staying off the grid was easy enough.

"Twenty-eight minutes." Britney tapped her phone. "Chop, chop, nerd."

Tutoring Britney, on the other hand, was *so not easy*.

"Fine. We only have to review the Keys since we covered the Queen's Cabinet on Tuesday. Quick recap, what are the names of the two political parties back home, and what do each of them stand for?"

Britney just blinked, her chestnut eyes revealing the window to her uncomprehending brain.

"Seriously? We *just* went over this."

"Seriously, can you *still* not figure out how to wear eyeliner?" Britney sneered.

You're making good money. You're making good money. You're making good—is any amount of money worth dealing with this?

"Okay." I exhaled slowly, releasing as much anger as inhumanly possible. "The two parties in Alfheim are the *Kongelig* and the *Opprør*. The *Opprør* are the current minority party, and they believe in equality for all. The *Kongelig* gained control of the Queen's Cabinet after the Svartalfheim attack sixteen years ago, and they use fear and intimidation to further their agenda of purifying Alfheim—prohibiting off-worlder immigration, and deporting all non-full-blooded light elves. Right now, Alfheim's a fear-zone; the place that once spread light through the cosmos is being torn apart from the inside."

"I still don't see the problem with what the *Kongelig* believe." Britney fingered the ends of her hair. "The purer the elf, the better she can serve her purpose of channeling light to the realms. That's what Mother always says."

"Well, your mother's a bigot," I said honestly. "Sorry, but it's true. The cosmos is a scary place, and there are plenty of perfectly good beings who had the misfortune of being born on dark realms. They deserve the chance to build a good life for themselves, same as you and me."

"Whatever. Are we done?" Britney picked up her phone. "Twenty-five minutes."

"Done with the recap," I said through gritted teeth. "But not with the Keys. And that's going to be half the test—so you should really understand it. Who are the Key Daughters of Alfheim, and why were we hidden across the realms?"

"Uh, the Key Daughters of Alfheim are . . ." Britney glanced down at the binder, where I'd written *extensive* notes. "Right. Light elves destined to perform functions vital to the survival of the realm, acting as military leaders, healers, prophets, whatever."

"Correct. And why were we hidden across the realms?" I prompted.

"Because, uh . . ."

I tapped the binder. Britney wasn't the only one who wanted this tutoring session over with.

"Um . . ." Britney scanned the page. "There. We were hidden after the Svartalfheim Attack, when the dark elves ordered the execution of all known Keys. Three of us were hidden on Midgard, and the rest are scattered across different realms—nobody will tell us where."

"That's a precaution—in case we get captured, they can't torture the info out of us."

"I really don't care." Britney stood and shouldered her backpack. "Listen, it's been real and all, but I have better things to do with my Friday than learn stuff I'm not going to need to know for years."

"We're being tested on it in four days," I reminded her.

"Yeah, but so what if we fail? It's not like they can un-Key us." Britney rolled her eyes. "It's a life sentence, remember?"

"Don't you care about what happens to Alfheim?" Gods knew I did. I'd been furious when I first learned about the things the *Kongelig* did to non-full-blooded elves, the crimes the queen's ministers covered up, and the way Queen Constance did nothing to stop any of it. As scared as I was to leave Midgard, I knew the minute I set foot on Alfheim I'd do everything I could to bring light back to the realm. I was bound not by duty, but by basic *decency* to do everything I could to make my world a better place.

How did Britney not see that?

"Nope. I don't care." Britney pushed the binder across the table, and waltzed backward toward the door. "Later, Aura. If you need me this weekend, try *all* of the homecoming events. I'll be the one wearing the crown."

She left the library with a perfectly executed twirl, her glossy locks flowing gracefully behind her. And I stifled *another* sigh at her inability to think of anyone outside of herself.

As I packed up my books, I wondered for the hundredth time what would happen when Britney, Elin and I were sent home. No doubt Britney was a high-kick away from being crowned Queen of Granite High. But would she be able take on an actual queen . . . and the entire corrupt government who came along with her?

And, for that matter, would I?

I USUALLY STUCK TO the main road when I walked home. My aunt, Signy, was obsessed with safety, and I could count on a few cars per minute trekking up the hill from the high school to the entrance of Little Big Bear Forest. Signy *really* didn't like me walking alone on the trail that went from our cabin to the school—it was one of countless activities she deemed 'too risky' for a light elf in hiding.

But the fact was, the hiking trail was shorter than the main road. It was also prettier, quieter, and didn't require me to walk through the staging area for the homecoming rally . . . where, in all likelihood, I'd run into Bitch-Face and her butt-kissing minions in all their dance team glory.

So, I'd be taking the trail today.

It only took me three minutes to clear the back of the school and hit the base of the hiking path. Late blooming wildflowers lined the edge of the dirt, and I took mental snapshots of the different species as I scaled the steep base of the hill. *Wild rose. Fireweed. Corn lily. Lemon lily.* By the time I reached the top of the hill I'd catalogued no fewer than fifteen types of flowers. I'd also been reduced to shallow breathing. The trail may have been shorter than the road, but it was definitely more taxing.

I shifted my focus as I neared the cathedral of pines that was the halfway marker between school and home.

Okay, now on to trees. Douglas fir. Coulter pine—huh, that one looks different. Darker. Maybe because of the drought?

A loud snap from behind sent my pulse into overdrive.

Oh, gods.

My chest clenched as I drew my fists to my face and bent my knees. If I was about to face a human attacker, I could take him. But if it was something else . . .

I whirled around, prepared to punch, kick, or claw my way out of whatever situation I'd landed myself in. But when I saw the massive, grey bobcat perched atop a too-close branch, I dropped my elbows to my knees and doubled over in relief.

"Oh, my gods!" My heart thundered in my ribcage as the cat jumped down from the tree, landed neatly beside me, and sidled to my side with a jubilant purr. "Bob, that is seriously not cool. You have *got* to stop sneaking up on me."

Bob nudged my hand with his head. My pulse still pounding, I begrudgingly scratched his ear and wondered for the hundredth time why a fully grown bobcat showed up every time I went into the forest. And also, why he never tried to eat me.

Maybe he was a vegetarian?

"Yeeooowl!"

Bob's purr morphed to a growl the second the screeching howl pierced the forest. Goosebumps ripped from my forearms as my pulse shot up again.

"What was that?" I whispered.

Bob stepped in front of me while I dropped to a ready position and scanned the trees for threats. But everything seemed completely normal, from the pines to the moss to the angry deer charging through the low-lying ferns.

Wait. What?

With its silver, spiked antlers, beady red eyes, and a set of extended canines I'd never before seen on an herbivore, the animal racing toward me was the bizarro version of the woodland critter I always hoped to see on my walks. Before I knew what was happening, the deer had launched himself over Bob to bear down on me with his freakish fangs. I threw myself out of his path, landing in the dirt with a thud and scrambling to my feet as my attacker slammed into the base of a tree. He shook his head, rose on hoofed feet, and charged at me again.

What the hell is happening?

Bob jumped back up and barreled toward our assailant, knocking the monster off course in a blur of fangs and fury. He yowled, then pulled back with a hiss as the deer sunk those sharp canines into his front leg. Without Bob to restrain him, the beast changed course to fling himself at my ankles. His antler nicked my bone, eliciting a level of pain so excruciating that it made me drop to the ground. He seized the opportunity and leapt on top of my ribcage, driving his head toward my neck. A chill shot up my spine as his goo-covered fangs began to elongate.

The monster was going to eat me.

Bob's furious growl distracted our attacker long enough for me to grab hold of his antlers, wrench him into a nearby trunk and jump to my feet. I bolted across the dirt with every ounce of strength I could muster.

Then I felt the burn.

"Arugh!" I dropped to my knees as a searing heat pummeled my back. Agony laced the skin between my shoulder blades, the sickening scent of singed flesh punctuated by the intense humming of . . .

Did the deer have a blow torch?

My vision blurred from pain, and the forest shifted from vibrant green to faded black. I blinked back tears that *so weren't invited* to this death match, then curled into a ball and rolled on my back to put out the fire.

When the smell of burning skin gave way to a residual char, I pushed myself up and braced for another hit from whatever torch was aimed my way. But the flicker of a fluorescent green flame stopped me cold.

That is no blow torch.

The deer's jaw popped open a second before a fiery green stream shot from its mouth. The flame landed at my feet, igniting the pine needles on the forest floor in a fierce, green bonfire that created a firewall between me and Bob.

What. The. Actual. Helheim?

I jumped behind a tree, careful not to brush my still-aching back against its rough surface. But the trunk trembled as another fiery blast struck the bark and I dove, quickly rolling out of the path of another shot. The deer had somehow cleared the green firewall and was coming for me—*again*. If I didn't outsmart him fast, it'd be lights out.

Think, Aura. How do you kill a fire-breathing beast?

Said beast shot off another fire stream. This one missed my head by inches, landing at the edge of a low-hanging branch and sending its leaves up in blazing green flames.

That's it!

I raced to the crackling branch and ripped it from the tree. I'd turn my assailant's weapon around on him —literally fight fire with fire.

Gods, I hoped this worked.

Without dwelling on the consequences of getting *even closer* to the fire-breather, I charged at the monster and waved the blazing stick in his face. The flame reflected in his wide, red eyes as he tried to run behind a boulder. But Bob, who'd somehow cleared the fire-wall, intercepted the deer. He pinned him to the ground, allowing me to drive the stick into our attacker's torso. A growl ripped from the deer's throat and he turned on me again, firing off a stream that turned my stick to ash. He forced Bob back with a shot that singed the bobcat's ear, before turning his attention back to me.

Skit.

Weaponless, defenseless, and utterly terrified, I turned my palms out, raised my hands to my face, and waited for imminent incineration.

But as the deer opened his mouth to fire, my palms trembled. Vibrations rocketed up my arms as a blinding white light shot from my hands. The light engulfed my attacker in a shimmering orb that somehow contained not only the monster, but also the stream of fire now shooting from his mouth. My palms shook harder, and in one inexplicable surge the orb imploded, destroying the fire, the deer, and any concept I had of my own sanity.

As black ash rained down on the forest, I raised my shaking hands and blinked at their now-shimmering skin.

What the hell just happened?

Bob limped to my side, using his slightly charred head to push me in the direction of home. I stumbled beneath the canopy of still-falling ash. A thousand questions filled my head, ranging from *what was that thing?* to *when did I get laser hands?* But Bob's urgent growl kept me moving forward. By the time I reached the little cabin I shared with Signy, my brain was a fog of confusion.

Bob started to slip back into the woods, just like he always did when we reached our property line. Before he could slink off, I dropped to a knee and held out my hand.

"You okay?"

Bob stepped closer, allowing me to examine the still-smoking fur on his ear, the bloodied gash on his leg, and the tar-like goo coating his back. Bizarro deer had gotten him good.

"Let me go inside and get some things to clean you up. It'll only take a minute, and—hey!"

Bob's thick skull bumped against my chest. He pushed so hard that I nearly fell backward.

"Don't you want me to help you?" I asked.

Bob chuffed, nudged me again, then disappeared into the tapestry of greens.

"Fine!" I called after him. "But if you need anything, you know where . . ."

I didn't finish. Bob never had trouble tracking me down. He'd come and get me if his injuries got worse.

I hope.

With a shaky breath, I made my way across the dirt and onto my porch. I wrenched open the kitchen door to find Signy leaning over a nearly frosted birthday cake. Flour dusted her brown pixie cut, and she bit down on her bottom lip as she piped icing along the confection's edge.

"Nearly done," she sing-songed. "And . . . *ferdig!* Happy birthday, my sweet, beautiful Aura. I can't believe it's been sixteen years since your mother promoted me from best friend to honorary aunt." She looked up with a tearful smile. "If she and your father were still alive, they'd be so proud of the intelligent young woman you've . . ."

The smile slid off her face as she registered my torn shirt, muddied jeans, and the faint trickle of blood along my arm.

"My gods, what happened to you?"

"Why can my hands shoot light beams?" I blurted.

Signy's freckled face paled. "What?"

"My hands," I said shakily. "They shot light beams and destroyed the deer who tried to kill me with his fire mouth. What the Helheim, Signy? Am I going insane?"

Signy dropped the icing and rushed to the kitchen window. As she peered outside, she fired questions over her shoulder.

"The deer, did it have silver antlers?"

"Yes, but—"

"And was the fire green?"

"Yeah, and it—"

"And your light beams." Signy finally turned around. "Is that the only power you developed today, or did the others manifest simultaneously?"

"It's the only power that—wait, what? My powers aren't supposed to show up until I'm eighteen! I have two more years!"

"That's what I thought, but . . . they must have come early because you're—" Signy's hands flew to her mouth.

"What? Because I'm what?"

Instead of answering my question, Signy crossed to the freezer and retrieved an ice pack. She pressed it lightly against my back before running from the room.

"Hold that to your wound," she called from somewhere down the hallway. "And don't leave the kitchen!"

"Wasn't planning on it," I muttered. Then, slightly louder, "Are you going to tell me what's going on?"

Signy backed into the kitchen, her arm at eye-level. It took me a minute to register the now-familiar—but still completely crazy—white beam shooting from her palm. It coated the tiny living room in its shimmering light, encasing the space in an orb that quickly shrunk to the size of a golf ball. Signy directed the ball into a tiny case she held in her other hand, and when I looked back at the living room all of our furniture, books, and blankets had disappeared.

My gods. Signy was using her magic. I'd never seen her do that before. This meant things were bad. *Really bad.*

Also, my white light was . . . magic? I had magic now?

Breathe, Aura. Just breathe.

Screw breathing.

"Signy, I am about to lose my ever-loving mind so if you don't fill me in *right now* I'll—"

"It's not safe here anymore."

Well, obviously.

"Are you too injured to travel?" Signy's pale green eyes bored into my sky-blue ones. She stroked a loose strand of my hair, and offered a sympathetic smile. "I know your back hurts, but we need to get to the drop site as quickly as possible."

"Drop site? Signy, what is happening? Where are we—"

"Shh." Signy typed quickly on her smartwatch. When she'd finished, she opened her palm behind her. "I forgot the kitchen."

A white beam streamed from her hand, encasing the room in another orb and shrinking its contents into a golf ball which she tucked into her pocket. Then she wrapped both arms around me, held tight, and whispered, "The Bifrost."

In one dizzying whirl I was pulled from the cabin through what I could only assume was an invisible portal, shot across the forest, and deposited atop Granite Ridge. There, an enormous rainbow tunnel streamed from the sky, positioned to beam us up to gods only knew where.

"Signy!" I raised my voice to be heard above the windstorm whipping off the rainbow. "You'd better start explaining *right freaking now*."

"That rainbow is the Bifrost," Signy said. "We studied it in the Prose Edda, don't you remember?"

I remembered my aunt reading the Viking bible to me just fine. But never for a minute had I thought I'd actually *be traveling by rainbow*.

Despite what I'd always told myself, I did *not* want to be the badass valkyrie from my comic books. I just wanted to go back to being the junior class nerd.

Signy took my hands in hers. "We don't have much time. Your powers manifested two years early, which means that none of you girls are safe here anymore. We have to evacuate to Alfheim immediately."

"No," I whispered. "I'm not ready."

"Whether you're ready or not is irrelevant. As your *Protektor*, it's my duty to keep you safe. My regiment is sworn to protect not only the realm, but also the crown."

"The crown? What does that have to do with . . ."

Lead landed hard in my gut. Was Signy saying that I was . . . that my mom had been . . .

"Sweetheart, look at me." Signy lifted my chin with one finger. "First and foremost, you are my Aura. My family. The girl I would protect with my own life. And if I could keep you here any longer; if I could shelter you from the fight ahead for even just a few more months, I absolutely would. But that thing that attacked you in the woods was a Svartalfheim tracker. The dark elves know that you're here, and they remain determined to eliminate the crown. With Midgard— Earth—no longer safe, it's my duty to bring you home."

"You said 'the crown,'" I whispered. "Twice."

"I did." Signy held my gaze. "You're more than just my charge, and my best friend's child. You are Aura Nilssen, the granddaughter of Queen Constance, and the crown princess of Alfheim. And . . ."

"And?" I squeaked.

Signy drew a slow breath. "And it's time for you to claim your throne."

CHAPTER 3

"**S**HUT THE FRONT DOOR. I'm a princess?" I was a comic-reading, combat-boot-wearing, STEM loving, card carrying nerd girl. There was no world in which this was possible.

Not even one accessible *by actual rainbow.*

"Yes. But that *must* remain a secret. Nobody on Alfheim knows your mother had a child—she ran away with your father two years before the Svartalfheim attack, and stayed off-realm throughout her pregnancy. After she was killed, the queen and I decided not to tell anyone who you were—not only for your safety, but to ensure the realm had an heir in case . . ."

In case the queen was assassinated, too.

Like my parents.

"Wouldn't the barrier keep the queen—uh, my grandmother—safe?" I knew from our Alfheim lessons that around the time I'd been born, the queen had authorized construction on a barrier to keep all off-worlders out of Alfheim. She'd done it in part because my father wasn't from our realm, and she didn't think he was good enough for my mom. But she'd also done it in the hopes of keeping her people—and herself—alive, as rumors of an impending dark elf attack grew.

"The barrier should have kept her safe, yes. But once it went up, things on Alfheim got very dark. The *Kongelig* took control of the queen's cabinet, and convinced many of our citizens to fear those who were different. Internal conflicts flourished, which meant the queen's safety was no longer guaranteed—not even from her own citizens."

Gods. What kind of backwards planet was Signy taking me to?

Pop!

I jumped at the loud burst from the other side of the rainbow tunnel. "What was that?"

"Oh, good." Signy released my hands to wave across the Bifrost. "The others are here. We can leave."

Right. Others.

Must keep princess-hood a secret. Must not disclose I'm descended from a bigot. Must not—

"Larkin, Elin," Signy called. "Hurry—we need to go as quickly as possible."

Liquid relief coursed through my veins. I may have been fleeing to a world run by zealots, but at least I'd have my best friend at my side.

Elin charged around the rainbow to envelop me in a fierce hug. Her ombre-blonde hair whipped around my shoulders, the blue tips a perfect complement to the late-afternoon sky. "We get to move to another planet *today*," she squeaked. "This is so freaking cool!"

"Not the sentiment I was going with."

"How do you not think this is cool?" Elin pulled away with wide eyes. "It's straight out of a movie!"

"Yeah . . . a horror movie." I warily eyed the Bifrost of Terror.

"Or a super cool adventure movie," Elin countered.

"Hi, Aura." Elin's mom and *Protektor*, Larkin, approached from behind with a tight smile.

"Hey," I offered. "So, I guess it's time."

"Are you holding up oka—"

Another pop interrupted Larkin's question.

"You dragged me away from the rally to get inside of *that?* Oh, hell, no. Absolutely not. I am *not* going anywhere near that thing. Not when homecoming's *this freaking weekend*, and everyone knows the dance captain's a shoo-in to win Queen."

Oh, gods. I'd know that high-pitched, nasal voice anywhere.

I whirled around to face Elin. "If Britney wants to stay, we should really let her stay."

"Yeah." Elin turned to her mom. "What Aura said!"

Larkin and Signy narrowed their eyes as Britney stormed around the Bifrost, followed closely by her mother and her *Protektor*. Bitch-Face stopped in front of Signy and jutted her hip, her dance skirt swishing with the movement.

"Mother tells me you're in charge, and I'm here to inform you that I am not going on your stupid rainbow. I was promised two more years here, and I am *this close* to being crowned Queen of Granite High." Britney's lip curled as her eyes grazed over Elin and me. "You two losers can go. I'm staying here."

"You don't have a choice." Signy placed her hands atop Britney's shoulders. She gently guided her back to her *Protektor*, who gripped Britney's wrist and held tight.

"Let *go,* Ivy!" Britney tried to wrench her arm away, but Ivy must have been a master of the mom-grip. Bitch-Face got absolutely nowhere.

"Signy, your communication said a tracker found Aura in the woods?" Ivy frowned. "How did the dark elves figure out where we are?"

"I have no idea," Signy said. "But we'd better not waste any time. Britney, step into the Bifrost."

"No." Britney glared at my aunt.

"Sorry about her." Ivy locked a second palm around Britney's arm and muscled her into the Bifrost. Britney's mother entered the transport next, and the three of them were sucked upward. They disappeared into the rainbow wormhole, Britney screaming all the way up.

My artsy best friend ran a hand through her multi-hued curls. "Any chance that rainbow will spit Britney back out?"

A snort escaped my nostrils.

Beep!

Signy and Larkin glanced down to study their

smartwatches. When they looked back up, their faces were pale.

"What?" I glanced nervously at Elin. "What is it?"

"The Council of *Protektors* just sent an update," Larkin said. "Two days ago, on the eve of the Ministry vote to determine whether only full-bloods would be granted admission to Alfheim's best educational institution—the one that feeds all top government posts—the high-ranking *Opprør* ministers disappeared. With only the *Kongelig* in office, the vote passed almost unanimously, which means the next generation of leaders will be exclusively native-born."

"And the missing *Opprør*?" Elin asked.

"They haven't been returned."

My stomach churned. "What's the queen doing to fix it?"

"Nothing, so far. The *Kongelig* control her cabinet, so that majority can block any action she proposes. By the time our next ruler takes the throne . . ." Signy avoided looking at me. "It may be too late to repair the damage our world's incurred."

Ice danced along my spine. I didn't want to be the princess of a place like that—or a princess at all. I barely knew how to manage my own life, much less an entire realm. And given the legacy my newly discovered grandmother was creating, I had zero desire to pick up her reins.

"Enough talk. Larkin, Elin, go ahead." Signy gestured to the rainbow. "We'll be right behind you."

With a nod, Larkin and Elin stepped into the

Bifrost. They flew upward without so much as a whimper.

"Our turn," Signy said softly.

Right. It was time to move to an entirely new planet. As a secret princess. *No big deal.*

"To be clear, this isn't optional, right?"

"No." Signy wrapped me in a tight hug. "But whatever happens, I will be with you every step of the way. No matter what, I am always on your side. And I will *always* have your back."

My eyes pricked and I hurriedly pressed the heels of my hands to my face.

"I love you," I whispered.

"I love you too," she replied.

With great reluctance, I withdrew myself from her embrace. "Guess we'd better go."

The only parent I'd ever known stepped inside the rainbow and held out her palm. I took in the feathery tops of the evergreens, the sharp peaks of the mountains, and the soft glow of the afternoon sun. A deep inhale committed the scent of pine and dust to memory, and I stepped into the light, holding tight to Signy's hand.

CHAPTER 4

WE WERE SUCKED UPWARD with a deafening *whoosh*. My brain may as well have been smashed in a vise—the pressure between my ears was so intense that I closed my eyes and prayed for the transport to end. Thin air chilled my nostrils as my head began to spin. Either I was oxygen-deprived, or overwhelmed with the centrifugal forces, or just plain freaked out.

Or all three.

After an eternity, the forces shifted. We began a free fall that pulled my neck taut and left me wondering if I was about to suffer death by dismemberment. The pressure increased as we slowed nearly to a standstill. I opened one eye to take in the kaleidoscope of colors tunneling around me and, through a haze, the brilliant green hues of the planet far below. Signy wrapped one arm around me, using the other to pull us toward the green world. We were stuck in some kind of webbing, whether real or imagined I couldn't tell. The next instant we again barreled downward.

When I was positive the rainbow ride of doom would never end, strong hands gripped my shoulders and held me tight. An arm tucked beneath the backs of my knees and I was lifted, cradled securely so I barely felt the jarring bump of impact. When I forced my eyes open, the rainbow was gone. Signy set me on my feet in a wide meadow carpeted in soft grass and violet flowers, and peppered with terrified teenagers.

Our landing spot was a far cry from the bleak landscape I'd imagined Alfheim would be. The velvety grass and vibrant blooms of the meadow were bordered by a ring of lilac-leaved trees. A large, frothy waterfall cascaded down an enormous mountain range to my left, and directly in front of me stood a white-trunked tree, easily four stories in height. Its silvery leaves were wide and glossy, and ivory flowers bloomed in clusters at the edge of its branches. The setting was the epitome of peace.

The mood, however, was flat-out pandemonium. Roughly a half-dozen girls—adults in tow—stood around the meadow, some screaming, some crying, and a few squealing excitedly. Britney had her head against her mother's chest, her shoulders heaving up and down as she wept. She looked up as the Bifrost retracted behind me, the kohl that normally lined her amber eyes marking an uneven path down her cheeks. She was probably mourning her forced relocation on the eve of homecoming. *So tragic.*

Elin moved to my side while her mom fell in line next to Signy. "Do you see those women?" Elin jutted her chin toward the edge of the meadow.

I followed Elin's sightline along the edge of the trees. *Yikes.* "The ones with the perma-frowns holding bows and arrows? Or the ones holding the electric spears?" The presence of the weapon-wielders left me edgier than I already was. "We couldn't escape if we wanted to."

"She could." Elin tilted her head at a girl hovering a few feet above the ground. Pale blue wings emitted shimmering, powdery particles that reflected light as they fell softly to the ground. Signy had told me stories about the *älva*, the winged species of light elves humans called faeries, or maybe fairies—I'd never been sure. Either way, they were very rare, and very strong. Apparently, the "fairy tales" Signy had drilled into to me were more fact-based than I'd realized.

"Ladies!" A melodic voice carried across the meadow, drawing our attention upward. "Calm yourselves."

A lithe, impossibly beautiful woman leapt from the top of the white-trunked tree to float into the center of the meadow, where she touched down in the grass in one fluid movement. Her silver-streaked, chestnut waves were pinned behind her ears with pearl clips, and her lavender-colored wings glittered in the sunlight. With the absolute authority emanating from her wrinkle-lined eyes, she reminded me of a stern ballet mistress.

"Who's that?" I whispered out of the corner of my mouth.

"The queen," Signy whispered back.

"*Skit.*"

"Aura! Language!" Signy chastened.

"*Crêpes,*" I corrected myself. I pushed my anxiety down and studied the winged woman more closely. Stress lined her pale blue eyes, and two frown lines nestled deeply between her brows. The tendons in her thin neck protruded and her jaw twitched, as if she bore down on her distaste. Nothing about her screamed "warmth" or "love" or any of the qualities I associated with the fictional grandmothers from my storybooks. But she didn't look like the monster I knew her to be, either. She looked like, well, like an attractive old lady. Was this woman really responsible for erecting the barrier? And by default, for everything bad that had happened in Alfheim since?

"And that," Signy nudged me, "Is the queen's Minister of State—Fyrs Narrik. He's responsible for stripping regions of resources and tearing families apart in the name of protecting the barrier. Do *not* get on his bad side."

I followed Signy's gaze to the serious, grey haired man standing at attention near the base of the white tree. His shoulders were taut, his hands folded behind his back, and his crisp black coat bore some kind of military insignia. He frowned at the gathering, his disapproval etched firmly across his weathered face.

"Jerk," I muttered.

"Agreed."

The queen's focus shifted at Signy's whispered word. Her eyes rested briefly on my aunt before landing on me. She studied me in silence, her impassive expression softening as her eyes moved from my blond hair down to my scuffed black boots. The next minute she raised her chin, drew her shoulders back, and clasped her hands at her waist. Her white dress billowed as her wings lifted her several feet off the ground.

"*Protektors*," she ordered. "Still your charges."

Ivy took a step forward. She wrapped her arms around the still-weeping Britney until agonized wretches became pathetic sniffles. The rest of the adults followed suit until the only sounds in the meadow were a handful of giggles and muted sniffles.

"*Velkommen*," the queen began. "On behalf of the brethren of Alfheim. I am Queen Constance, ruler of the Light Realm. Lest there be any doubt, you are here because Svartalfheim ordered a Key Strike—the first in sixteen years."

An anxious murmur ripped through the meadow.

"I am pleased to see that all of our female Keys have arrived safely. We await the extraction of our sole male Key and intend good energy for his safety." Queen Constance bowed her head, and the adults in the meadow followed suit. Minister Narrik kept his head raised, his fierce eyes likely scanning the crowd for dissenters. Gods only knew what he'd do if he found any.

"That's right, there's only one guy coming," Elin whispered. "I call dibs."

I snorted.

"The Key Strike was one wave of this attempted siege. A subsequent attack occurred while we were occupied with arranging transport. The dark elves managed to breach our security, and the *Sterkvart* crystal was stolen from the Alfheim Tree." Queen Constance gestured to the white-trunked tree behind her.

The adults broke into frantic conversations. Signy had shown me drawings of the *Sterkvart*—it was a pale, green gem, about the size of a golf ball. As the heart of the tree, it transferred energy to the other realms, fulfilling our cosmic purpose of instilling light to all. Without it, the tree wouldn't last long . . . and the realms would be cloaked in darkness.

"With the crystal gone, the branches of the tree will die until Alfheim is linked only to its energetic opposite, granting Svartalfheim direct access to our realm. Recovering the *Sterkvart* crystal is now our realm's top priority. Every citizen, including yourselves, is hereby ordered to do their part to recover the piece so vital to our survival."

"How are we supposed to do that?" Elin blurted.

"Shh," I hissed.

Had she not gotten the same speeches I had about the evil queen and her elf-offing flunkies?

Elin waved me away. "Look, we *just* got here. We're going to need more direction than 'find a crystal.'"

Queen Constance raised an angular brow, and my stomach clenched. I would *so* cut her if she laid a single bony finger on my best friend.

Nearby, Narrik cleared his throat and glared at Elin.

I would cut him too.

After an eternity, the queen turned her attention to Larkin. "How fitting that the only daughter ever born to a *Protektor* speaks out of turn."

Larkin bristled, but in typical Elin fashion, the queen's dig rolled right off her back. She stood firm as Queen Constance lifted her chin. "Each of you will use your gifts to identify potential locations—and theoretical abductors—of the crystal. As Keys you must act as leaders in spearheading the hunt to retrieve this vital piece of our—"

The crackle of burning wood interrupted the Queen as smoke began to mist one of the upper branches. A few garbled cries rang out as the branch shriveled and turned dark. My stomach felt the burn the second the limb blackened. My hands flew to my belly button, and I clutched my torso, pressing against the stabbing sensation in a pointless effort to stop the pain. Whatever was happening to that tree was happening inside of me, too.

And it hurt like no other.

I dropped to my knees and breathed into the pain,

waiting for it to pass. By the time I looked up, the remains of the branch lay smoldering on the ground. All that was left on the tree was a blackened nub of a limb.

What the Helheim just happened?

Signy knelt at my side, running her hand along my lower back. Calming pulses filled my body, but nothing could stop the panic rooting in my head.

None of the other girls standing in the meadow had been taken down by a dying tree branch. Why was I the only one affected that strongly? Was it because I was a princess, or was I just a doubly massive freak?

Elin stared down at me, fear blazing in her eyes. "Let's burn down the entire tree," she blurted. Minister Narrik glared at Elin, his eyes surging with even more disapproval than before.

"Please, stop talking," I begged.

But if Elin heard my words, or noticed Narrik's refocused ire, she didn't show it. "If we burn the tree, we won't be able to use it to bring light to . . . wherever. But I'm sure we can figure out another way."

The queen pressed her lips together in a thin line. "The limbs may die, but the tree itself cannot be destroyed. The Norns who crafted it took pains to ensure that could not happen. To destroy the tree would eliminate our very purpose."

Queen Constance turned her attention to me. I shifted uncomfortably under her stare.

"It is of vital importance that every citizen of Alfheim take up the charge to retrieve the *Sterkvart* crystal. Your *Protektors* and professors will offer guidance as to how you may best use your individual gifts to aid the search." Queen Constance clasped her hands at her waist. Minister Narrik approached to whisper something into her ear before snapping back to military attention. The queen glanced around the meadow, then raised her voice again. "I must attend to a Council matter. In the meantime, you shall commence your formal training. You may now report to your residence, where a course of study has been established with your destined discipline in mind."

Elin shot me a worried look. "Destined discipline? What if I'm *destined* to be something boring on this planet, like a lawyer?"

"I think you're good. I'm sure they need artists here, too." Alfheim sure as hell needed *someone* to give it hope.

"They'd better," she muttered.

The queen raised one bejeweled hand. "*Protektors,* escort your charges to their new home. And do not forget your primary task. Many worlds are counting on you." With that she turned to Minister Narrik. They spoke quietly for a moment before the queen unfurled her wings and flew high above the field. Narrik stalked from the gathering as the queen soared into the distance.

Signy and Larkin turned to Elin and me. "Are you ready?" Larkin asked.

"Not in the slightest." I frowned. "Where is this new home, anyway?"

Signy wrapped an arm around my shoulders and followed the crowd toward the edge of the meadow. "Our new home is within our realm's most revered learning institution. Ladies, allow me to introduce you to Alfheim Academy."

CHAPTER 5

"**T**HIS PLACE IS *INSANE*." Elin's words bounced off of high, stone walls, her voice reverberating in my head as our tour group followed a fourth-year student named Evensong through the halls of Alfheim Academy. With its high ceilings, lavender scented air, and cream-on-white décor, the school was an oasis of calm in a realm wracked by fear. Its exterior was reminiscent of a medieval Midgardian castle, while its inside was opulent elegance. Glossy wood floors covered the central curved staircase, stretched across the main entryway, and ran the length of the hall that I presumed led to the classrooms. Floor-to-ceiling windows formed the inside walls of the academy, providing a see-through partition that allowed beams of sunlight to dapple the space.

Insane didn't begin to cover it. This place was a masterpiece.

"Keep walking, ladies," Evensong trilled.

Elin and I hastened to catch up as she rounded a corner and stepped through a glass door onto a stone path. Outside, flowering vines snaked along the low rock walls, their sweet fragrance enveloping the handful of blazer-clad girls and boys resting their forearms on the ledges while surreptitiously pointing at us. Mid-term transfers at Alfheim Academy must have been a rarity. And a still-sniffling tour group must have been rarest of all.

Evensong's long black waves brushed against her deeply tanned arm as she turned to face us. "Alfheim Academy is laid out in a classic *U* design, with each of the four dormitories housed in one of the anchor towers. Our educational divisions are scattered throughout the main structure, with the exception of the *Våxa, Dyr* and *Verge* programs."

"The what programs, now?" Elin whispered.

I shrugged. We hadn't covered the academy during our Alfheim lessons, on account of our expecting to graduate from Granite High. We hadn't planned on moving realms until we turned eighteen either, but here we were.

Is this seriously my life now?

Evensong pointed with two fingers. "Out here you'll find the horticultural quadrant. It's maintained by students in our *Våxa* department, and open twenty-four hours a day to faculty. Students, of course, are welcome to visit between sunrise and an hour past sunset. Curfew is strictly enforced, so unless you want to face the disciplinary council, be sure to be inside your dormitories before the final bell stroke."

Evensong stepped under a rose-laced arch, leading us through an elaborately designed garden filled with lavender blooms I'd never seen in Granite Ridge. At the edge of the horticultural quadrant stood two greenhouses, which appeared to hold larger, even more exotic plants.

Whoa.

"The castle itself dates back a thousand years, but it did not function as a school until a few hundred years ago, when King Leon and Queen Helena mandated a formalized education. At that time, they gifted this addition to the facility." Evensong made a sharp right behind the greenhouses. A newer-looking structure rested just behind the castle wall. Cream-colored walls bordered high windows, and the rear of the building opened up to a neatly manicured field.

"Is this a meditation center?" One of the girls tentatively raised her hand.

"Quite the opposite. This is the *Verge* training facility," Evensong explained. "Elves with a propensity for combat are enrolled in our *Verge* discipline, where they undergo rigorous physical training. Those with the highest marks pursue careers as peacekeeping elves, warriors, and even *Protektors*."

Elin nudged my shoulder. "If Signy has her way, we can all just stay here, then."

"Gods, I hope not." On Midgard, my aunt had been

in charge of our physical conditioning and meditation practice—the latter of which I'd been wretched at. While Larkin had overseen Alfheim lessons, Signy made sure Elin, Britney and I meditated three times a week and worked out every single day—twice, on weekends. Now that I knew the horrors of fire-breathing deer, I was grateful for what I'd privately called Torture Trainings . . . but I still didn't want it to be my major.

"Back inside the castle now." Evensong led us past the field and pulled back the curtain of ivy cascading down the castle wall. Behind the green was a door-sized hole in the stones. We passed through the opening in the wall, walked across a courtyard, and re-entered the castle.

Evensong pointed to the tower on her right. "Up there you'll find the Astronomy wing, where *Astrals* learn to chart the courses of planets, stars, and of course, dreams. Also in that wing, the *Styra* gather data and channel energy to influence the course of major events for the greater good of the cosmos."

Up ahead of me, Britney blinked longingly at the tower. I disguised my snort with a cough. Event manipulator was *definitely* Bitch-Face's calling.

"Our scientifically inclined students enroll in our *Elementär* discipline, where they study everything from biology to physics in that tower." Evensong raised a manicured hand to her left. Her fingernails bore a translucent sparkle, and it took me a minute to realize the glow came from the glitter itself.

"Look." I nudged Elin, whose own nails were done in a rainbow of colors. Her eyes widened.

"That is *so cool!*" she squealed.

"In the north tower," Evensong continued, "you'll find our *Musa* working to perfect their art, music, dance and craftsmanship. Also in the north, *Kurera* study ancient, modern, and holistic medicinal practices from across the realms, to heal our sick and injured. Our *Dyr* study animal husbandry in a facility behind the south wall, adjacent to the forest for obvious reasons. And most of the other classrooms are housed on the first two floors of the west wing."

Evensong clapped her hands together and turned to our group with a smile. "If you don't have any questions, I'll take you to your common room, where your resident advisors are waiting to introduce you to your roomma—"

A sudden stab in my upper abdomen brought me to my knees. My hands flew to my stomach and I pressed hard, willing whatever was clawing its way out to stay put. The stabbing intensified, forcing me into the fetal position. The pain was so intense that the courtyard ebbed in and out of focus.

"Aura!" Signy's cry filled my ears, and Elin's tropical shampoo wafted past my nose, but I couldn't open my eyes to look at either of them. I was frozen in agony.

"Oh, my goodness." Evensong's voice came closer. "I can call for a *Kurera*, or—"

"Give us room," Signy commanded. Footsteps

retreated until a small buffer of calm surrounded me. Signy was working her magic. Again.

"Can you tell me what you're feeling?" Signy kept her tone calm.

"My stomach," I gasped. "It feels like . . . when I was in the meadow. Like it's . . . it's being ripped open."

"It's the Alfheim Tree." Signy raised her voice. "Alert the faculty another limb is lost."

Warm fingers pried my hands away from my body, lifted my shirt above my belly button and gently probed my midsection. "Your stomach appears to be fine, Aura. This is an energetic wound." Signy's words were barely more than a whisper. "Whatever you feel intruding on your space, push it out."

"I don't think I can." The words came on a squeak as I succumbed to another wave of pain.

"Try," Signy urged. "The energy will follow your intention. I'll help you."

I drew a deep breath and imagined pushing away whatever was causing the mind-numbing pain. After a slow eternity the stabbing had lessened, and I opened my eyes and gripped Signy's arm. "What was that?"

"You're shaking." Signy's brow furrowed.

"You'd be shaking too if something clawed its way out of your stomach and . . ." I tugged at my shirt to examine my unruptured skin. How was that even possible? "What's happening to me?"

Signy wrapped her arms around me and held tight. "I don't know."

An amplified voice filled the courtyard, halting our group's worried whispers.

"Attention, students. The Vanaheim Branch of the Alfheim Tree has fallen. Please return to your dormitories until the Council completes its scan for portals. *Empati* who experienced a physical reaction to this disconnect must see an advisor for a healing."

Signy's emerald eyes darkened with concern. "The *Empati* were affected. It wasn't just you."

"And the *Empati* are who, again?"

"Our empaths." Signy pressed her lips together. "They feel things more strongly than the rest of us."

If this was a typical *Empati* day, I sure as Helheim hoped I one of those warrior students, instead.

Evensong cleared her throat. Her porcelain face was several shades paler than it had been at the beginning of our tour. "Aura, would you like me to summon a *Kurera*? We can take you to the healing wing instead of your dorm."

"I'll be okay." I let Signy wrap an arm around my waist and guide me to my feet. As we moved, Elin placed a gentle hand atop my shoulder.

"Tell me if you change your mind." Evensong waved us forward. "Inside, everyone. Go straight through this entry and make a left at the end of the hall. Hurry, now! If a portal has opened, we don't want to be exposed."

We followed Evensong down a long stone corridor. Signy and Elin took turns shooting me concerned looks, but I didn't know what to tell them. If Signy couldn't explain what was happening to me, and if dark portals could be opened every time one of those branches fell . . .

This was officially the worst birthday on record.

"Right this way." Evensong opened a thick, wooden door and ushered our group through. When we were safely inside, she closed the door behind her, fastened its absurd number of locks, and pressed her fingertips to a pad on the wall. "The Keys are secure," she murmured into the speaker. Then she turned to our group with a tight smile. "That was an eventful welcome tour."

Elin wrung her hands together. "Are there a lot of lockdowns?"

"They're very rare." A new voice spoke up from behind. We turned to the wall by the staircase, where a tall, willowy redhead stood in front of a paper-laden table. "I'm Renwyn, one of your resident advisors. In the four years that I've been at Alfheim Academy, we've only had three lockdowns, two of which have been this week."

Evensong shook her head. "The attacks on the realm have caused substantial security concerns. But Headmistress Herliefer is one of the most formidable *Verge* graduates in the history of the academy, and we have every reason to believe she'll keep us safe."

"In the meantime, I have your room assignments and your course schedules." Renwyn turned to her table and picked up a stack of golden envelopes. "Now is as good a time as any to go upstairs, meet your roommates, and get settled. If the scouts don't find any portals, the lockdown should be lifted in time for dinner. *Protektors* who are not residing on campus may say goodbye to your charges. Batni Johanssen, please come forward to receive your welcome packet."

As Renwyn raised a golden envelope, Signy pulled me in for a light hug.

"Are you feeling okay?" she asked.

"It hurts a little less now, I just . . . I hope the branches stop dying."

I truly did. Both for the sake of the realm, and the sake of my stomach.

Signy pulled back. "Me too."

"Do you have to go?"

"Oh, sweet girl." Signy stroked my hair. "First of all, we're in a lockdown. I can't leave this room."

Oh. Right.

"And second, when I go I'll only be a tower away. Larkin and I have adjacent suites in the Faculty wing."

"Oh, thank gods." I threw my arms around Signy and squeezed.

"You two take care of each other." Larkin nodded at Elin. "Don't let her get into too much trouble."

"Like I could stop her." I rolled my eyes.

Larkin laughed. "True."

"Elin Eklund." Renwyn's clear voice cut through the low murmur of voices. "I have your room assignment."

"Here goes nothing." Elin shot me a nervous grin as she strode across the room.

"Aura Nilssen." Renwyn smiled as I claimed my own envelope. "Welcome to Alfheim Academy."

"Thanks," I murmured.

Elin and I hurriedly moved to occupy the two empty chairs by the couch, where Signy and Larkin had struck up a conversation with some other *Protektors*.

"Are you ready?" I poised my fingers to tear open the envelope.

"Yup. One. Two. Three."

We ripped our packets open at the same time.

"Oh, thank gods we're roommates." I exhaled in relief. "We're taking third year classes—that must be what they call juniors here?"

"I guess," Elin shrugged.

"And we have another roommate named . . . Finna?"

"I'm in the *Musa* program." Elin ran her rainbow fingernails through her ombré blue-blond hair. "Good. Law school would have sucked."

I peeked at her assignment. "An artist, huh? Shocking."

"What's your specialty?" Elin leaned over to look at my paper.

"I can't tell." I shook my head. "They have me down for combat, meditation, and inter-realm relations. But there's no specialty listed."

"Maybe they want you to be well rounded?" Elin guessed.

"Maybe."

Larkin leaned toward us from the couch, a sparkle in her eye. "What did you get?"

"I'm a *Musa* and Aura's undeclared. And we're roommates," Elin summarized.

"Undeclared." Signy winked, and I suddenly understood. She'd done this. I didn't have a specialty because I was a princess, and it was my job to know as much as possible about every discipline.

Great.

Twinkling chimes interrupted us. "Attention students," trilled an amplified announcement. "The threat has been neutralized, and you may now leave you dormitories."

A relieved buzz flowed through the room as unfamiliar faces poured out of the main door, while the girls from our tour group filtered up the staircase.

"Well?" Elin gestured toward the stairs.

"Let's go." I pocketed my envelope. We said goodbye to Signy and Larkin, and walked up the narrow staircase. At the top we turned right, and headed down a corridor with large, open windows until we reached the fourth doorway.

Elin placed her hand on the knob and took a deep breath. "I guess we live here now."

"I guess we do." For better or worse, I was now sixteen, a princess, and an official resident of Alfheim Academy. I took a small amount of comfort in knowing that tomorrow would probably be excruciatingly boring when compared with today.

I hoped.

Elin turned the knob with a nod. "After you."

Here we go.

CHAPTER 6

"**M**OTHER OF FRIGGA." ELIN gawked as she pushed the door open. "Get a load of this place."

My jaw dropped as I stepped through the door. A small entry gave way to a massive room, with one side comprised of an oversized mirror, and a door leading to a marble-floored bathroom. Three mahogany sleigh beds were spaced between eight-foot-high windows, each draped in thick, cream-colored fabric and offering views of the forest below. A dresser and wardrobe bordered each bed, and clear crystals dangled from an opulent chandelier, reflecting beams of sunlight around the space. Wall sconces shone softly, illuminating the bedroom in warm, soothing candlelight.

"This is our room?" I squeaked.

"Not too shabby, *ja?*" A girl with warm, brown skin scooted off the edge of one of the beds. Her jet-black curls were tinted with ruby highlights, and her movements were so seamless, she appeared to float to where Elin and I stood, mouths still agape at the opulent decor. She held out one hand, and the glowing sparkles in her nail polish caught my eye. I was definitely buying Elin a bottle. "You must be the new Keys. I'm Finna Skylark. I'm a third year *Elementär*, and I'm glad to *finally* have some company in here."

I shook Finna's hand. "I'm Aura Nilssen. And this is Elin Eklund. Our paperwork says we're taking third year classes, too."

"This place is *way* cooler than our school on Midgard," Elin gushed. I blinked at her, and she shrugged. "Well, it is."

"You are not nearly freaked out enough by all of this."

Elin shrugged again. "Freaking out's not going to change anything."

Point, Elin.

"You grew up on Midgard? I've heard it's a beautiful realm. I've always wanted to visit but the restriction on inter-realm travel prohibited—oh, good!" Finna interrupted herself. "Your cases arrived."

"I didn't pack a case," I said. "Signy magicked everything in our house into one suitcase, then shrunk it down and put it in her pocket. She didn't sort anything."

"She must have. Look." Elin pointed to our beds, where two containers stood.

The tip of my ponytail hit my cheek as I whipped

my head around. "Those weren't there a minute ago. How did the—"

"Portal," Finna said simply. "The telepaths handle transport. I have no idea how they do it—they don't teach the rest of us how to move things. Especially not the rock nerds." At my tilted head she clarified, "Crystals are my specialty."

"Really?" I raked my bottom lip between my teeth. "So, I guess the queen has you all over this missing *Sterkvart?*"

"Yes." Finna pointed at the data pad on her bed. "Our department just got a message. We have a brainstorming meeting tomorrow."

"Where do you think it is?" Elin asked.

"I have no idea." Finna frowned. "A crystal that powerful carries a strong energy signature. Even those of us who weren't *Empati* could feel it every time we walked by the tree. Whoever's taken it has either figured out a way to conceal one of the highest resonances in our realm, or they've taken it so far away that we can't sense it anymore."

"What did it feel like?" I asked.

Finna glanced up at the chandelier. "It was warm. A slow vibration that felt like hope."

Whoa.

Elin turned to me. "Think you can feel anything?"

"I was hardly Signy's best meditation student," I pointed out.

"You were way better than me and Bitch-Face," Elin countered.

"Who?" Finna asked.

"Britney Blomgren—the third Midgard Key," Elin explained.

"She's *really* awful," I added.

"Ah." Finna nodded. "So, *can* you feel anything, Aura?"

I closed my eyes and waited. Nothing happened. *Typical.*

"Nope." I opened my eyes. "But I do want to help, so let me know what happens with your meeting and tell me what I can do."

"Me too," Elin added.

Finna nodded. "The more help we have, the faster things can get back to normal."

Whatever normal was, here.

"What department were you assigned to?" Finna asked me.

"So far, I'm undeclared." I shifted my attention to my trunk and commenced moving t-shirts to drawers.

"What about you, Elin?"

"I'm a *Musa*. I can't wait to see the art facilities." Elin tucked a flannel shirt into her top drawer.

"They're beautiful." Finna grinned. "And you're going to love the stained glass outside our Great Hall. When you're finished unpacking, get changed and I can take you down there for dinner."

"Get changed?" Elin flipped the latch on her trunk closed. She slid the case underneath her bed and pulled the hem of her favorite plaid shirt. "Is there a dress code for dinner?"

"There's a dress code for everything. And an audience with the disciplinary council for failure to comply." Finna pointed to the mahogany wardrobe next to Elin's bed. My friend opened it to reveal a tidy row of pleated skirts in khaki or navy, starched white blouses, and blazers.

I bit down on my bottom lip before Elin caught my snicker. She'd never worn khaki *anything* in her life. Her world was always vibrant with color, as evidenced by her ever-changing nail polish and the blue tips of her white-blonde hair.

"We're supposed to wear . . . *these*?" Elin plucked a silk scarf from a hanger. "How am I supposed to create artistic masterpieces wearing . . . gingham?"

"The checks are a little bit Picasso-y," I tried. "In a, um, geometric kind of way?"

"They pick out our shoes for us, too?" Elin pushed her head into the wardrobe. "Are these *nude pumps?*"

"The school provides a selection of heeled footwear for those who prefer consistency, but you do get to choose your shoes. The headmistress encourages individuality in moderation. She just doesn't want 'outward appearance to interfere with inner transformation.'" Finna used her fingers to make quotes around the last words.

"Is that from the mission statement?" I joked.

"Verbatim," Finna confirmed. *Oh.* "But you do get to change for certain classes. The *Verge* obviously have athletic clothing for combat classes, and the *Musa* get to wear work clothes so they don't get their uniforms dirty. Look in the back, Elin. You probably have painting clothes in there too."

"I'd better," Elin muttered.

"Before I forget, your communication devices are on your desks. Every student gets a wrist com and a data pad."

I picked up the watch-like device that resembled Signy's and pressed the button on its side. The screen lit up, revealing a keypad not unlike those on smart-watches.

"Come on, get changed. I'll get ready and we can walk down together." Finna headed into the large bath-room and stood in front of one of two sinks. She picked up a makeup brush and dusted it over her cheeks.

"Do we have to wear makeup to dinner, too?" Unlike my artsy best friend, I'd never had any interest in the stuff.

"It's not required." Finna looked over her shoulder. "But I heard there was a boy enrolling with your Key group, so some of the girls are going to be pretty done up."

I crossed to my wardrobe, selected a blazer, and slipped into the requisite dining attire. The letters *A.A.* scrolled in swirling script were stitched to the left side of my jacket, beneath an emblem I assumed was the schools crest. Gods, this was preppy.

"Why are girls getting made up for the boy Key?" I asked. "I saw plenty of guys on our tour."

"Female enrollment at the academy is higher than

male enrollment . . . which mirrors Alfheim's population breakdown. Since we're a matriarchal realm, we need more females than males to fill our governing roles." Finna slicked gloss over her lips. "It works out numbers wise, since the elves going into peacekeeping professions—warriors, diplomats, and *Protektors*—aren't supposed to take partners anyway."

"Right." We'd learned that much in Alfheim lessons. "But what's the big deal about a boy Key?"

"There have only been a handful of male Keys in the entire history of Alfheim." Finna's voice rose in excitement. "And every single one of them has gone on to do great things for the realm. Whoever this guy is, he's destined to be really powerful. Who knows, he might even be our future king consort!"

A lump lodged in my throat and I coughed hard until I'd freed it. I'd been through enough for one day; I was *not* meeting my future husband at dinner.

"Aura?" Elin stopped buttoning her blouse to shoot me a worried look.

"Are you all right?" Finna lowered her lip gloss.

"I'm fine." I waved a hand. "Let's just go."

"I'm dressed." Elin glared at her blazer, khaki skirt . . . and hand-painted canvas shoes. At my bemused grin, she lifted her chin in defiance. "Finna said we could wear our own shoes."

"That I did." Finna went back to perfecting her makeup, and I walked over to the window. Just beyond the quad stood a massive forest—a boundless, green sentinel protecting the school from the darkness facing the rest of the realm. The tree tops stretched for miles, before climbing a massive white-capped mountain range. It was breathtakingly beautiful . . . and completely and totally unfamiliar.

How long would it take until this place felt like home?

"What's that?" I pointed to a plume of black smoke rising from the base of the mountain.

"What's what?" Finna emerged from the bathroom. Her gaze followed my pointed finger. "Oh."

The syllable was laced with desolation.

"There was a fire in the town of Meina," Finna said. "Their monument was torched."

"What happened?" I asked.

"Minister Narrik burned it down."

"What?" Elin and I squawked in unison.

"Meina is a . . . progressive colony," Finna explained. "Lots of artists and philosophers and activists live there —individuals who believe Alfheim should return to the inclusive realm it once was. Their protests are peaceful, and within the bounds of the law, but they make no secret of their displeasure with the current regime. And Minister Narrik, well . . . he doesn't welcome opposition."

"I gather," I muttered.

"A rally was scheduled for yesterday. Narrik said that if it went forward there would be consequences." Finna lifted her hand to the window. "He kept his word."

"Was anyone hurt?" I asked.

Finna only nodded.

"That's terrible," Elin whispered.

I blinked at the thick, black plume. Its tendrils snaked all the way to the clouds.

"This school is a sanctuary." Finna turned away from the window. She crossed to her wardrobe and removed a blazer. "But the darkness will reach us eventually. Today's Alfheim is filled with intolerance, bigotry, and hatred. We can't hide forever."

Elin met my anxious gaze. "What's going to happen?"

"I don't honestly know. Unless someone stops the queen and her cabinet, the *Kongelig* will continue to gain power." Finna smiled sadly. "For now, just be thankful that you're here—and not on the outside, where things are, well . . ."

My stomach churned as I stared at the plume of smoke. As crown princess, I could push for the change Alfheim desperately needed. But I was underage, untrained, and unprepared. How could I possibly stand up to a government that would hurt its own citizens?

"We should go." Finna's soft voice rang from the entry. "We don't want to be late. Are you ready?"

No. I'm not ready for any of this.

But instead of voicing my fear, I reached out to grasp Elin's hand. I plastered a smile on my face, I tried to project a confidence I didn't feel—and might not ever feel again.

"Ready as we'll ever be." I exhaled. "Let's go."

CHAPTER 7

W**E FOLLOWED FINNA AS** she sashayed through the well-lit, neutrally decorated hallways. Ivory walls and cream-colored draperies were offset by narrow tables bearing vases of pastel blooms. Finna called out to an indigo-haired girl as she scurried back toward the dorms. "Study session in the library after the strategy meeting, Parys! Remind Elowyn!" The girl spun around with a friendly smile but didn't break her stride—nor did she trip while practically sprinting backwards.

They'd been wrong about the pointy ears, but the humans were spot on about elves and grace.

"*Hei hei*, Jande!" Finna raised a ring-laden hand. The large crystals on her fingers glinted in the light, the perfect complement to her sparkling nails.

"Finna." A tall boy with sun-kissed skin held out his arms in welcome. "These must be your new roommates. I told you Renwyn wouldn't let you keep that single."

Finna hugged Jande lightly before pulling away with a smile. "Aura, Elin, I'd like you to meet one of my oldest friends. Jande and I grew up together in Skang—a farming region south of Alfheim's tallest waterfall."

"And this one's been trailing me across the realm ever since." Jande pointed one finger at Finna, his own crystal rings glinting in the light of the sconces. "Primary school, summer excursions, now here at the academy. I don't know how many times I have to tell you to stop following me, love. You are *not* my type."

"Jande!" Finna's laughter had the same tinkling tone as Evensong's. It echoed down the hallway with a joyful peal.

"Anyway, I hear there's a new *bo-oy*—" Jande managed to stretch the word over two syllables, "—showing up soon. As I am currently under-accessorized, I'll catch you in a few."

Finna grabbed Jande's hand and studied his rings. "Rose quartz, malachite, that's good. But you're looking for a *harmonious* match, Jande. Where's your green jade?"

"Back in the dorm." Jande snatched his hand back. "Which is why I'm walking *away* from where my soulmate will be."

"The new guy might not be into guys." Finna's eyes filled with warmth.

"Everyone's into this." Jande swept his hand from his

broad shoulders to the muscular legs that strained against his regulation khakis. "And I've catalogued *all* my marks, so I'll tell you the minute I confirm Key Boy's my mate."

"Your marks?" I asked curiously. "What do you mean?"

"My marks." Jande shrugged. "Freckles, beauty spots, the whole nine."

Elin angled her head to Finna and muttered out of the corner of her mouth. "What's he talking about?"

"What's he . . . what am I . . . do you not know about marks?" Jande blinked at us. "What is wrong with you?"

"They're new," Finna reminded Jande. She turned to me and Elin. "Mate marks are an old wives' tale—a silly myth for romantics."

"Oh, like you don't believe." Jande raised a brow.

"I *kind of* believe," Finna admitted. "The myth is that mates have a mirrored mark hidden somewhere on their bodies, placed there by the Norns to identify them as *perfekt* matches."

"The Norns, as in the prophets?" Elin balked. "So, what, you just know if somebody's for you if they have the same mole? That's weird."

"It's efficient," Finna countered. "And it's just a myth, anyway."

"You keep telling yourself that." Jande crossed his arms.

"What if you don't like your mate?" Elin ventured.

"You'll like your mate." Finna smiled. "The Norns don't make mistakes."

"What if you don't want a mate?" I blurted.

Jande crossed his arms, so his taut shoulders strained against his blazer. He looked really strong—he must have been a *Verge.* "Who doesn't want a mate? Especially a hot Key?"

"You don't know if he's hot," Finna reminded Jande. "You've never seen him."

"I don't have to. He's a boy Key." Jande spoke as if we were all slightly slow. "Now if you'll excuse me, I have a lucky ring to find."

He spun around and sauntered toward the dorm.

"Nice to meet you!" I called.

"Ditto!" he yelled over his shoulder.

Finna smiled fondly as she led us to the dining room. "Jande's the best. We were so excited when we got into the *Elementär* program together."

There went my *Verge* theory. "That buff guy is a science geek?"

"Bigtime." Finna's smile faltered. "But his little sister's not entering secondary school until next year. And since their mom was born off-world, and the full-blood admissions policy will be in effect then . . . she'll have to go to one of the lower rated schools. Those have a significantly smaller placement rate in top government jobs."

Fear for the future fluttered in my stomach. Darkness clawed at the academy doors . . . a darkness that was directly traceable to my grandmother. Once everyone figured out I was related to *her,* they'd expect me to fix things. But I didn't know the first thing about challenging a corrupt government. I didn't even know how to navigate my own school. If I was going to make any kind of a difference, I had a *lot* of catching up to do.

I drew back my shoulders and smoothed the front of my blazer. "Teach me everything there is to know about this place. If we're going to fix what's broken, we'll need to know where to start. Right?"

Elin held out her fist and rapped my knuckles. "I'm in."

The fear fluttered again, but I pushed it back down. There was no time for nerves. If we were going to stand up to a legion of bigoted politicians, we'd need every possible advantage.

It was time to study up.

Minutes later, the three of us sat at a white-linen-clad table in the Great Hall. Finna chose one of the four-tops nestled between their long, rectangular counterparts, and she'd sat with her back to the enormous windows that made up the western-facing wall. This gave me and Elin a prime view of the majestic forest sitting a hundred yards behind the castle. Though the sun was now low, I easily made out the enormous, ancient-looking trees providing the rich green and plum backdrop outside. As the sun dipped below the horizon, the needles of the trees emitted a dim glow— one that illuminated the forest in a silvery purple luminescence. Pulses of color ebbed from one tree to the next, in a natural light show unlike anything I'd ever seen . . . or even imagined.

Inside the Hall, whites, creams, and silver dominated the color scheme that glinted in the light of dimmed chandeliers and softly glowing taper candles. The silverware sparkled as if it had been freshly polished, and ornate plates of varying sizes were nestled three high at each seat. The academy cafeteria was the fanciest restaurant I'd ever been in.

Too bad I was too stressed to appreciate it.

"Okay, fill us in." I scanned the students sitting around the dining hall. "How do we stay above water here?"

"First thing to know—steer clear of the *Styra*." Finna smoothed her napkin over her lap, and Elin and I did the same. "They're predisposed to control, and they see the *Kongelig* as a means to an end—a regime they can manipulate to shape the realm to their advantage."

I frowned. "So, the *Styra* are bad?"

"Not all of them. Alfheim needs *Styra*—their ability to influence outcomes helps us resolve dangerous conflicts." Finna ran her fingers along the edge of her plate. "But many of them use their gift for selfish purposes, in which case they open themselves up to darkness and risk becoming Huldra."

"What?" Elin asked.

"Master manipulators—beautiful women who lure men into the woods and steal their souls to extend their own lives." Finna's glossed lips pressed together in a line.

I shuddered.

"Oh, no." Finna frowned. "There's another one."

"Another what?" I swiveled in my chair, following Finna's sightline until I caught Britney standing with a leggy brunette. She'd rolled her skirt so it ended a solid six inches above her knees, and she'd caked on a thick coat of makeup. She smiled beatifically at a platinum blond who sat at the head of one of the rectangular tables. She held out a hand, and Britney and her guide sat at the table of overly made-up girls. The seat in the center of their table remained empty.

"You know Bitch-Face?" Elin stuck out her tongue.

"Is that who that is?" Finna asked.

"Yup." I pulled a face. "We've spent the last sixteen years living with her, going to school with her, being tortured by her . . ."

"Well, she's off to an unfortunate start. She's sitting with the *Styra* prefects." A deep *V* formed between Finna's brows.

"You don't like them," I surmised.

"Not at—"

"What the Helheim?" Elin's eyebrows shot to her hairline as a heaping bowl of lettuce, cucumber and croutons suddenly appeared in the center of our table. "Where'd that come from?"

"The telepaths transport the food, too." Finna picked up tongs and doled out salad.

Of course they do.

I wrenched my eyes away from Britney's table to

focus on Finna. "Okay, so the *Styra* suck. Who else should we know?"

Finna took a bite of lettuce and chewed before tilting her head toward the front of the room. "Up there you have the *Verge.* Most of them are training to be warriors, which means they're not allowed to date and therefore not going to fight the *Styra* for the new boy."

"Ooh, is Key Boy here yet?" Jande arrived and dropped into the fourth chair.

Finna laughed. "I was just telling Aura and Elin about the *Verge*, and how easygoing they are."

Sure enough, the *Verge* table was filled with a handful of reasonable-looking girls and two boys, all of whom laughed, passed food, and seemingly had a drama-free time.

"Easygoing and *hot*. They make the best gym part-ners." Jande beamed at one of the *Verge* boys, who looked up from his plate to shoot Jande a wink. *Sweet.*

Finna handed Jande a lettuce-filled plate before resuming her tour.

"Over there are the *Empati.*" Finna nodded at the back of the room, where a comparatively calm table hosted a quiet group. "Some of them can see into the future, so they tend to stress less than, say, the *Musa.* Some of our artists are a bit on the temperamental side." Finna tilted her head to a long table by the window. The artsy-looking girls had accessorized their boring blazers with hand-made brooches and what looked like freshly woven flower crowns, while the guys had tied painted bandanas around their heads.

"Me and Jande's classmates are by the entrance. *Elementär* are pretty easy to get along with, so long as you don't mess up our lab or break our Bunsen burners," Finna joked.

I tilted my fork toward a table of raven-haired elves, all of whom wore a thick layer of eyeliner—even the guys. "What about them?"

Finna frowned. "Those are the *Bridgers*. They can communicate with spirits—bridge the worlds between the living and the dead."

Say what, now?

"There are students who talk to the dead?" Elin squeaked.

Finna nodded. "I'm not sure how they learn, but I prefer to keep my distance."

One of the *Bridgers* lifted her head and met my eyes. Behind her heavily lined lids and solemn expression was a look that bordered on sympathy. I shivered, before turning my attention back to Finna.

"And in the center, you'll see—"

Jande rapped the back of his fork against Finna's shoulder. "Key Boy's here!"

"What? Where?" Finna dabbed at the corners of her mouth with her napkin before drawing her shoulders back. A quick glance around the room revealed girls fluffing their hair, pinching their cheeks, and slicking on lip gloss. Even Elin sat up a little straighter, her salad long forgotten.

They had to be kidding. All of this for some guy?

I followed Jande's rapt stare to the front of the Great Hall, where a tall boy with broad shoulders and wavy black hair stood framed in the doorway. He smoothed the front of his cream-colored blazer and sauntered into the room with unbridled arrogance.

I narrowed my eyes. "Are we sure that's him? He looks pretty normal to me."

"If by normal you mean drop-dead gorgeous, then I am right there with you." Jande leaned forward to rest his jaw on his fingertips.

Oh, come on.

But Jande held the popular opinion—apparently, the presence of a male Key turned the student body into groupies. Key Boy strutted through the dining room, offering winks and waves as he moved. As he neared the *Styra,* their leader pulled out the empty chair—an action that yielded giggles and a fury of batted eyelashes. The boy shook his head and kept walking, intent on a course that was leading him straight to . . . us?

Wait. What? *Is he staring at me?*

By the time the boy was three tables away, my stomach churned with nerves. If he sat with us, my goal of staying under the radar would vanish faster than a plate of Signy's Norsk waffles. Unless . . . maybe he was coming over because he had eyes for Jande. *Yes!* Key Boy was way too good looking to be straight, with his chiseled cheeks and strong jawline and emerald green eyes . . . not that I was into him. Because obviously, he played for the other team. *Thank gods.* Drama averted.

By the time the boy reached our four-top, I'd convinced myself that Jande's green jade had worked its magic. Key Boy was his *perfekt* match just like Jande predicted, and they'd be off to their happily ever after in the time it could take me to—

"Mind if I squeeze in?" Key Boy pulled an extra chair from the empty table beside ours. He angled it between Jande's seat and mine.

See? Totally right!

"You can squeeze anywhere you want." Jande batted impossibly long eyelashes before moving his chair a few inches to the right.

"Thanks." Key Boy slid the chair into place and dropped into it before unbuttoning his blazer. But instead of introducing himself or maybe offering an explanation as to why he'd chosen to sit with us instead of the table of now stewing *Styra,* he pinned me with an intense stare. My body went on lockdown as a light fluttering set off in my stomach, followed by a stronger fluttering at my back.

Oh, hell no. I did not have butterflies. Not because of Key Boy. And most definitely not in my *back,* of all places.

"So." Jande angled himself toward the newcomer. "What's your name?"

Finna's waves fell over her shoulder as she leaned forward, and even Elin studied our guest with rapt curiosity. There *was* something interesting about him.

Maybe it was the way his inky black hair formed pristine waves atop a perfectly sculpted face. Or the way his eyes twinkled in barely contained amusement. Or the—wait. What was I doing? *Knock it off, Aura.*

"Your name?" Jande prompted Key Boy again. "I'm Jande and this is Finna, Elin, and Aura." He pointed to each of us in turn. "And *you* are . . ."

"I'm Viggo. Viggo Sorenssön." Key Boy answered without breaking our eye contact. He leaned back in his chair, crossed his arms behind his head, and unleashed the full force of his smile directly on me. "*Hei* there, *Glitre*. I've been looking for you."

CHAPTER 8

"WHAT DID YOU CALL me?" I folded my hands atop my lap.

"*Glitre.*" Viggo shrugged. "You sparkle."

Shock unhinged my jaw, and I gaped at Elin. My best friend's hand clamped tight against her mouth, possibly to quell waves of impending laughter. Did that kind of line actually work on whatever realm Viggo'd come from?

My lips pulled together in a tight line. "I do not sparkle, thank you very much."

"You do." Viggo winked. The dimple that popped with his smile was unnerving.

"You must be the last evacuee," Elin *finally* chimed in. "What realm did they hide you on?"

"Svartalfheim." Viggo fired the word at me.

It was rude, really. He should talk to everyone at the table.

"Svartalfheim?" Finna squeaked. "How long were you there?"

Viggo *still* didn't break our eye contact. "Most of my life."

"That's impossible," Finna argued. "The Council wouldn't hide a light elf in a dark realm. It doesn't matter who you are—that level of evil would turn even the purest heart dark."

Viggo arched a brow. "Who said it didn't?"

Jande shook his head. "Nope. You are *wa-aay* too good looking to be evil."

"Thank you." Viggo finally dragged his eyes from mine to study Jande. "Nice rings," he offered, without a trace of irony.

Jande's eyes lit up like the sky during a meteor shower. He clasped his hands over his heart. "Bless."

"Back at you." Viggo grinned before returning his attention to me. "I have to go, but I'll definitely be seeing you again."

Arrogant much?

I crossed my arms. "You didn't say why you were looking for me."

"That's right. I didn't." Viggo put two fingers to his brow and gave a little salute. "See you around."

With that he stood and sauntered out of the Great Hall. He paused at the exit to grab an aluminum-wrapped carton from the table labeled, "Takeaway Meals." The *Styra's* energetic daggers pierced my back for an endless beat, ebbing as excited chatter filled the vast space.

"What a jerk." I turned back to Elin, Finna and Jande. "Why are you smiling?"

"Because." Elin wore a grin that would have put a canary-eating cat to shame. "He's totally into you."

"He's totally full of himself," I countered.

"He said he liked *my* rings," Jande pointed out.

"Jande, he's into Aura. Not you. You'll get the next one." Finna patted her friend's arm.

"The next one? This is the first Key Boy in two hundred *years!*" Jande dropped his head to his hands.

Wait. What?

"He has beautiful eyes." Finna beamed. "And beautiful hair. Well done, Aura."

I rolled my eyes. "Key Boys may be few and far between, but I guarantee that is *not* the guy for me."

Elin raised one eyebrow. "You sure about that?"

"Absolutely." I balled up my napkin and flung it on the table. My appetite vanished the minute Key Boy made his self-righteous retreat. "I'll meet you guys back in the dorm."

Jande looked me up and down with a long-suffering sigh. "Oh, fine. If he *must* be straight, I suppose you are an acceptable choice. Your legs are to die for."

"I don't want him!"

"Do you want us to leave with you?" Finna offered.

"No." I shook my head. "But thanks. I'll see you later."

I hurried toward the exit. As I passed the *Styra* table a sharp voice pierced my focus. "I cannot fathom *why* he wanted to talk to a loser like Aura. Gods, she's so pathetic."

Skit.

I could have walked right by; pretended I hadn't heard Britney. Signy would have advised doing exactly that. But Signy hadn't spent every year of her life being tormented by someone who clearly had a rock where her heart should have been. The only way to shut Britney up was to fight back. Again.

I met Britney's cold stare with equal parts ice and venom. "What did you say?"

A serpentine smile stretched across Britney's crimson lips. "You heard me. Loser."

The blonde at Britney's table studied her with an appraising look. She was either impressed, or wondering when Bitch-Face would make a play for her rung on the social ladder.

"What's the matter, Britney?" I crossed my arms. "Worried you'll flunk out of here like you did Freshman math? *And* science?"

"Go away." Britney flicked her fingers at me, as if shooing away a bug. "Run to the library, or your aunt, or whatever it is losers do on Friday nights."

I shrugged. "At least Signy cares about me. Your mom took off straight from the meadow—where's she at, right now? Shacked up with *another* guy?"

Britney's eyes bored into me with a hatred so intense, I wondered for the hundredth time what I'd done to earn her ire.

"You can move realms all you want, but nothing will

change how pathetic you are." Britney leaned back in her chair. "Go to Helheim, Aura."

"Anywhere to get away from you." I turned on one heel and stormed from the Great Hall, ignoring the glares stabbing my back. I'd hoped that being on another realm would mean Britney and I could stick to our own corners. But Viggo had shoved me right into the fire by taking away the one thing Britney prized above all else: attention.

I stomped the rest of the way to my room, wishing all the way that Alfheim would spit Britney straight back to Earth . . . and that I'd never see Viggo Sorensön again.

Back in the dorm, three cupcakes rested on my night-stand in a white box. The corners of my mouth tugged up as I opened the envelope beside the chocolaty treat. *Signy.* She'd written that the offering was only a modicum of the pastry-palooza she'd planned for my not-so-sweet sixteen, but things being what they'd were she'd had to improvise. And she promised to make it up to me.

I left the treats to share with my roommates tomor-row, changed into flannel pajamas, and buried myself in thick, downy layers of bedding. All I wanted was to slip into a dreamless oblivion. But my overwrought mind refused to slow, and instead of falling asleep I lay on my back, staring at the moonlight streaming through the eight-foot windows. It glinted off the crystals of the chandelier, forming an intricate pattern along the ceiling. Since I was too exhausted to get up and close the drapes, I stared at the light reflected on the fact that everything I'd ever known had disappeared in one explosively awful day.

Back home I'd known exactly how to spend my weekends, which hiking trails were poison oak-free, and which television channels ran Sunday superhero movie-marathons. But here, I knew *nothing* beyond the fact that my grandmother had stripped Alfheim of hope, her cabinet torched towns of dissenters, and there was a potentially evil faction of Britney clones running around my new school. I had no idea who I could trust; who would be an ally in standing up to the queen versus who would turn me in for dissention or out me as a princess.

Out me as a princess . . .

My fingertips worried the edge of my duvet, and I turned to my side and tucked my knees to my chest. I needed to stay under the radar long enough to prove I was nothing like the queen. But then what was I supposed to do? Challenge my grandmother to a duel? Debate her for the throne? If there was a way to remove her, surely someone would have done it by now. A blood heir must have been the only one who could. And since all of Alfheim believed no such heir existed . . .

But I don't want to be Queen. I just want to be sixteen.

An incessant, rhythmic chirping pulled my attention to the window. Did Alfheim have crickets? Or cicadas? Or some weird alien insect I'd never heard of? Even with all the lessons back home, there was still so much I didn't know about this place. What kinds of animals lived here? Were there birds, or butterflies, or bobcats like Bob . . .

Gods, I hoped Bob was okay. We'd Bifrosted out of Midgard so fast, I hadn't even gotten to say goodbye. What if . . .

I squeezed my eyes shut. Bob was fine. I was fine. Everything was fine. Or it would be. Right after I fell asleep.

I squeezed my eyes shut and counted imaginary sheep. At some point, Elin and Finna tiptoed in, climbed into their beds, and fell into deep, rhythmic breathing. After an eternity, my own breath slowed. My fists unclenched as I slipped slowly away. But instead of blissful peace, my dreams were filled with the nightmarish acts of a faceless figure. The black-cloaked creature torched an unsuspecting town; herded protesters into a cell; and finally, scaled a mountain of smoldering carcasses to claim dominion over each of the nine realms. When the creature had destroyed every bit of light in the cosmos, bony figures pulled back its hood, and I woke with a gasp, cold sweat pouring down my back.

The creature beneath the hood was me.

CHAPTER 9

INNA WALKED ME TO the *Verge* facility after breakfast. Her first class of the day, Elemental Formations, involved fieldwork in the forest behind the training center. Her department would meet afterward to brainstorm recovering the *Sterkvart* crystal, and she, Elin and I would hold a strategy session of our own after dinner. But first, I had a full day of classes —*Verge* in the morning, followed by *Empati* in the afternoon. My stomach was a knot of anticipation and it wasn't even eight a.m.

Trial by fire wasn't my forte.

Finna left me at the locker room door with a cheery wave before gliding down the corridor, her pleated skirt swishing softly around her legs with each step. The gong of the clock tower reminded me I was cutting it close, so I darted into the empty locker room to change. I tossed my duffel bag on a bench, and hurriedly traded my regulation prepster garb for the

77

all-black combat ensemble of the *Verge* discipline—tight workout pants, a clingy tank top with A.A. embroidered on the chest in gold, and running shoes. After shoving my uniform into a locker, I pushed through the door labeled *Training Room*.

What I saw nearly made me turn right back around.

Signy had put us through the paces on Midgard, but this facility was next-level intimidating. Weapons of every imaginable shape lined one wall of the *Verge* room—thick swords, tiny daggers, spiked balls on long sticks, mid-sized sticks on long chains, and an axe. *An axe!* The opposite wall played host to a series of climbing apparatus, with rock-holds, rings, and angled sticks. A portion of the floor housed weight machines, parallel bars, and something that looked suspiciously like a pommel horse. Did we have to learn gymnastics here, too?

In the center of the room lay a thick training mat. At the edge stood a half-dozen girls and two boys in a line, their feet shoulder-width apart and their hands folded at the smalls of their backs. The girls wore their hair in tight ponytails and boasted the kinds of muscles I'd never seen on a teenager. At five-foot, nine-inches, I'd been considered pretty tall in Granite Ridge. But each of these girls stood at least a full six feet, with a confident air that made them seem like giants. And the guys . . . *holy crêpes.* The one thing I'd been confident about had been my physical training. But one look around this room, and it was clear I was totally out of my league.

Again.

"Fall in, Aura," a familiar voice whispered in my ear. I whipped my head to the right, where my aunt stood with a clipboard.

"Signy!" I exclaimed. "You're my teacher?"

"I'm one of them." Amusement sparkled in her eyes. "And I'm Professor Bergen here. You'd better fall in— Headmistress Herliefer is a stickler for punctuality. She's the head of the *Verge* program, and she's running today's training, so look sharp."

Signy gestured to the line, and I scooted into place beside a raven-haired girl who stood a whole head taller than me. She looked down her pointed nose and gave a slight nod. I nodded back and mirrored her posture, willing my muscles to grow. I didn't want to be the weakling Earth girl among the Amazonian women of Alfheim.

"You must be Viggo." Signy spoke behind me. "You're cutting it close. Fall in."

"Sorry. I'll just take my place right . . . here."

Oh no. No, no, no. Just no.

I closed my eyes and prayed for a miracle that didn't come. A cloud of cedar and pride filled the space next to me as the deep voice I'd hoped I'd never hear again murmured softly in my ear. "Good morning, *Glitre*."

I ground my teeth together, ignoring the pop in my jaw. Misguided butterflies nudged at my back, and I willed them to go away.

"What's the matter, *Glitre*? Helbeast got your tongue?" Viggo chuckled.

My ponytail swung in an arc as I whipped my head around. "For your information, I'm—"

"*God morgen,* class. *Velkommen* to our new students, Aura and Viggo. My name is Headmistress Herliefer, and I am charged with instructing you in combat arts." A tall, thin woman with the grace of a ballet mistress glided across the mat. The whistle at her neck and clipboard in her hands reminded me of my old gym teacher—a matronly woman who insisted we refer to her class as physical education, because, "my name's not Jim, ladies!" But if the hardware on the west wall was any indication, the games I was in for here would be much more strenuous than noodle tag and dodge ball.

"You may have noticed we have a new teacher with us. Professor Bergen was one of my finest *Verge* students during her tenure at the academy, and I was most pleased when she agreed to help mold our current class. Today, we will continue our agility regimen with your training partners. Prefects, take positions on the climbing wall. Agni and Miral, commence weight work with emphasis on power bursts. Svor and Vans, work in with them. Wren and Djenga, sprints on the field. Aura and Viggo, Professor Bergen will evaluate your respective combative abilities on the mat." Headmistress Herliefer blew her whistle, and my classmates jogged to their assigned stations. I ignored the smirking male beside me as I followed Signy to the mat.

"The new guy is a jerk," I whispered to her.

"I heard that." Viggo sounded amused.

"Viggo." Signy faced him when she reached the mat. "It's nice to finally meet you. Erik and I were good friends when we were at the academy together. I was sorry to hear of his passing."

"Thanks. That means a lot." Viggo gave a nod.

I shot Signy a curious glance. Who was Erik?

"Surviving in Svartalfheim without your *Protektor* must have been difficult—and so soon after you'd lost your parents." Signy frowned. *Wait. What?* "We tried to extract you last year, but we couldn't locate you."

"I had to go dark for a while. We were being tracked pretty hard." Viggo shrugged as if being parent-and-*Protektor*-less in Svartalfheim was no big deal. Maybe to him, it wasn't.

"We're lucky you were able to find your way when we sent the evacuation code."

"Erik passed his communicator to me before he was killed. By then it was pretty badly damaged." Viggo tapped the device on his wrist. It was considerably more worn than my day-old version. "It took me a while to figure out what your code meant."

"I'm just glad you made it." Signy placed a hand on Viggo's arm. "Your parents and *Protektor* were champions of the light. If I can help you in any way, don't hesitate to ask."

"Thanks. But I'm here now, so let's get to work." He shot me a wink that sent the butterflies pinging between my back and my belly.

I exhaled forcibly. "What do you want us to do, Signy—eh, Professor?"

"Square off and execute a basic attack sequence," Signy instructed. "Omicron formation, with Aura taking offensive. Do you both know that choreography?"

"Yes," I confirmed, at the same time Viggo smirked and said, "Of course."

"Excellent. In three." Signy counted down. "Two. One."

I threw myself at Viggo. He ducked to his right, and I fell flat on my face. The smattering of laughter from behind let me know the other *Verge* were watching.

Awesome.

I scrambled to my feet and walked in a slow arc. Viggo mirrored my movements, apparently waiting for me to strike. I pulled my left arm back to distract him and swung my right foot in a low circle. It connected with his ankle and swept his feet out from beneath him in one, quick movement. Score one, Aura.

Viggo lay on the ground, amusement in his clear green eyes. He arched his back and leapt to his feet, then charged at me with a series of punches. I blocked the first three, and on the fourth, grabbed his fist and used his weight to launch him over my shoulder. He landed hard, his back slapping loudly against the firm mat. There was a smattering of applause from the rest of the *Verge. They're rooting for me over Key Boy? Thank you, sisterhood! And brotherhood?* I peeked over my shoulder, and sure enough the two guys were clapping for me too. *Yes!*

Viggo jumped back on his feet, his eyes crinkled in a smile.

"Oh, this is going to be fun." He pointed a finger at the shiny threads of the A.A. on my shirt. "*Glitre,* you're extra sparkly today."

"If you think getting your butt handed to you by a girl is fun, then bring it."

Viggo raised an eyebrow. "Oh, I will."

I ground my teeth again and aimed a right hook at Viggo's face. He threw up his forearm and wrenched my arm to my waist, then spun me around. With one arm, he pinned my back against his chest. With the other, he pressed hard against my neck. One of the watching *Verge* let out a groan at my apparent defeat.

"Professor Bergen," Viggo called. "I believe this is a check."

I stomped hard on my captor's instep and threw an elbow behind me. The jab landed just below Viggo's sternum, and the whoosh of air left his chest as he leaned forward. I took advantage of the slack in his arms and turned, ducking out of Viggo's grip. While he was still doubled over I unleashed a front kick that knocked him onto the ground, then straddled him and pressed his neck with my forearm. The nearby *Verge* cheered loudly.

"I believe that is a check*mate.*" I grinned. "I win."

Viggo gripped my knees with large hands and lifted me easily off his chest. I wrenched my body to the side, but he quickly rolled so he was on top of me. Despite my ardent struggle, he pinned me easily.

"No, *Glitre. That's* a checkmate." He winked. I glared. The rest of the *Verge* applauded our match.

"Two out of three," I offered.

"That won't be necessary." Signy made a mark on her clipboard.

"Students, back to work. All of you," Headmistress Herliefer ordered. The *Verge* called out to each other as they returned to their workouts.

Signy turned to me and Viggo. "Nicely done. Headmistress Herliefer wanted to see how disparate your skills were, to evaluate how to shuffle training partners. But seeing as you're equally matched in hand to hand. . ."

Oh, no. NO.

"We'll evaluate you on additional apparatus, but barring any unforeseen imbalance, it looks like the two of you will be well matched training partners." Signy beamed at me.

"Aren't you the lucky one." Viggo reached down to tuck an errant strand of hair behind my ear.

"Get off of me," I grumbled.

Viggo raised an eyebrow. As he rose, a rush of air escaped my chest. He held out a hand, and I grudgingly allowed him to help me stand. I ignored the fluttering in my stomach and the nudge at my back as he wrapped his large hand around my smaller one.

What is wrong with me?

A blast of Herliefer's whistle signaled it was time to

switch stations. Despite my very best efforts, Viggo and I possessed equal skill on the climbing apparatus, bars, horse, and in weapons. At the end of the three-hour class my palms had blisters, my clothes were soaked with sweat, and every muscle in my body throbbed. But I'd held my own against Viggo; proven myself the equal of the first male Key in centuries, and a few times bested the guy who'd apparently grown up fending for himself in the dark realm. Plus, my classmates had cheered for me—something that had never once happened at Granite High.

If it wasn't for the fact that I'd been bequeathed the world's most irritating training partner, with whom I was to work out incessantly until graduation, it would have been a glorious day.

"Settle into your sacred inner space and root your energy to the center of the realm. Imagine the Alfheim Tree enveloping you in its timeless, mystical branches, then anchoring you down, down, down to the core of Alfheim. Good. Does everyone feel well and truly grounded?"

I was ninety minutes into my afternoon meditation lab, where Professor Asling wove her way through the dozen students meditating atop thick velvet pillows. Although my eyes were squeezed firmly shut as per her instructions, the multitude of jingling bangles kept me apprised of the professor's whereabouts. I bit down on my bottom lip and tried to picture tree roots snaking through the layers of soil, rock, and sediment, knowing fully well that no amount of imagining would put me on par with the other students. My classmates were light years ahead of me. And despite Signy's valiant efforts to Zen me out, mindfulness had never been my forte.

This class was going to be my undoing.

"Aura, dear." Professor Asling's cool hand rested lightly on my shoulder. "You've hardly got any grounding cord at all. Try envisioning a copper tube enveloping your body and tunneling all the way to the center of the realm. Ah, there it is. Oops. There it went."

I ground my teeth together and willed tube envelopment. I'd been a decent student at Granite High, and things had been going so well in my *Verge* class this morning. It seriously sucked to be the class idiot here.

"Once your grounding is well established, I want you to focus on each of the seven centers that run from the base of your spine to your head. Clear out all energies that no longer serve you." Professor Asling's bejeweled fingernails clicked together, possibly flicking away unseen energy. Though for all I knew, she was texting her lunch order to the dining staff. It was hard to tell what was happening with my eyes squeezed shut and my consciousness focused on an invisible room somewhere inside of my head.

I *so* hated meditating.

"Begin with the first center, your grounding center,"

Professor Asling purred. "Now move up to your second, and just *observe* the duality within before visiting your third—own your personal power in this class, this school, this realm. Very good. Now move to your fourth—oh, your hearts shine so beautifully, girls." Professor Asling clucked her tongue approvingly. "Now your fifth—your throat center is your voice in the world. Fully embody it at all times. Now your sixth—your third, inner eye. And finally, your seventh—your spirit's portal to your body.

Because that made sense.

"Now, with your centers clear, I want you to sense the boundary at the edge of your space—the protective bubble that surrounds you. Your aura." Professor Asling's nails flicked again. "Do you feel it, Imogen?"

"I do, Professor!" The sprightly student to my right sounded incredibly pleased with herself. I scrunched my face up and tried harder. The pressure building behind my eyes wasn't helping.

"Who else can feel their aura? That slightly buoyant energy all around you that weeds out unwanted energies and protects against assault from the outside world? Sora, what does yours feel like? Go ahead, hold up your hands and touch it."

The security of our entire realm was at risk, and we were supposed to pat an invisible energy bubble?

"It feels . . ." The girl in front of me paused. "Like a porous cloud."

"Mine feels like a warm river," offered a girl to my

left. "One with luminescent particles that ping against my touch."

I felt a big fat zip. It was ironic, really.

"Well done, ladies," Professor Asling approved. "Today I'm going to teach you how to expand and contract that aura. To enlarge it, simply strengthen your grounding cord and retreat to your sacred inner space. Draw energy from the realm through your feet, and intend that your aura expand. Some students find it useful to bring their hands into their navel, drawing power into their center, before turning their palms away and pushing their energy outward. Go ahead and try this now."

Here goes nothing.

I followed the directions to the best of my ability, but given that I barely felt my grounding cord, and I most definitely did not feel my inner space, it was a futile exercise.

Professor Asling whispered in my ear. "May I assist you?"

"Please," I muttered.

"I will hold your grounding for you. You just have to focus on expansion. Can you do that?"

Probably not. But I nodded, with my eyes still squeezed shut.

"Go ahead, Aura."

With Professor Asling's fingernails once again flicking, I imagined myself sitting inside a big balloon. I exhaled slowly, willing the balloon to grow.

"Aura! Very good work. You have a propensity for

protection. The thickening in your aura is so tangible, its expansion very nearly overtakes—ah, how fleeting. It has gone." With a delicate pat on my shoulder, my teacher leaned down to whisper again. "That was progress. Continue in that vein, and you may catch up to your classmates."

Professor Asling moved on to the next student and I pressed the heels of my hands to my eyes, stopping the dull throb from overtaking my senses. When I opened my lids, Professor Asling stood beside the student to my right. Her expression was considerably more joyful than the one she'd probably had while teaching me.

"Very good, Svarri." Professor Asling clapped her hands together. "Imogen, did you feel her press against your space? Had she encased you, her aura would have served as a double protection—guarding both herself *and* you against unwanted intrusions. This is a time-honored practice of our energetic warriors, who fight not with swords and arrows, but with energetic blows. Those with the gift of protecting not only themselves, but also their sisters and brothers in arms, are commended with the highest of honors."

Alfheim had energetic warriors? Like, wizards? Was that what my hands had done to that deer back home? Why had they gone completely dormant since I'd arrived on Alfheim?

How was I this behind on my first day?

"I do hope you will continue your practice, Svarri. Shielding another is a tremendous skill to master," Professor Asling praised.

"Oh, I will, Professor," Svarri chirped. *Showoff.*

"Through proper management of energy, each of you can become invincible."

Signy had been preaching that one for years. Maybe she'd had Professor Asling when she was at the academy, too.

"Your homework is to work on your protections. Your aura is your buffer against the world. Strengthen it, and you strengthen yourself. Make it impenetrable, and no energetic harm can come to you."

Professor Asling's bracelets tinkled as she held her hands out to her sides, pushing up and down against some invisible barrier. With her long robes, flowered headdress, and peculiar hand motions, she could have been the love child of a hippie and a mime. I quickly closed my eyes as she moved toward the front of the room.

"And now," Professor Asling continued. "We will bring this meditation to a close and move on to discussion. Intend that your aura protect you throughout the sun cycle. Intend that you remain grounded as we discuss the trying era that has dawned on our realm. And give yourselves a loving hug, thanking your spirit for participating so fully in today's lab."

All around me I heard the murmurs of students thanking their spirits. I opened my eyes to their sanguine expressions and wondered if I would ever get any better at this *Empati* thing. Asling made Signy's seemingly impossible meditation classes look like a walk in the park.

I tentatively raised my hand.

"Yes, my butterfly?" Professor Asling turned to me.

"What we're doing . . . this whole energy thing. Is this what the Midgardians call magic?"

"In a way," Professor Asling mused. "Magic—true magic—is simply a manipulation of energy. Today you're learning to block—to create a shield around you. As you advance through your practice, you'll learn to debilitate. A strike to the base will destabilize power, one to the mind can block mental awareness, or visual acuity."

"My aunt can do that," I remembered. "She told me during our lessons back home. Is that a *Protektor* skill?"

"Only in a handful of cases," Professor Asling said. "Most *Protektors* come from the *Verge* discipline, while energy manipulation is usually limited to our *Empati*. It is the rare warrior who can do both."

Go, Signy!

"I understand that you are also learning both disciplines," Professor Asling offered.

"Yeah, but . . . I'm a lot better at one than the other."

"You will learn," Professor Asling said gently. "And you may just find that you are in a unique position to better our realm."

The way my grandmother was running things, I'd better be.

CHAPTER 10

"**N**OW, MOVE YOUR PILLOWS into a circle. Leave no gaps. For this exercise, it is imperative that we create a sacred ring of healing." Professor Asling waved her hands, and my classmates calmly shifted positions. Once we sat in the round, she gave an approving nod before crossing the room. She glanced into the hall, toward the long, spiral staircase that led to the base of the tower, before gently closing the door. The soft click echoed through the classroom.

"I wish to impart that no matter what else is happening in our realm, *this* is a safe space for each of you." Professor Asling dropped onto an empty pillow and joined us in our circle. "I know that some of you have seen alarming actions from our government. I am saddened to know that more will come, given the anxiety the theft of the *Sterkvart* has created amongst our fear-guided leaders. It is cause for concern in all of us," she conceded. "The crystal is of vital importance to our realm. But so are each of you. And I know many of your families are suffering." Our teacher turned to me. "Until recently, our citizens have lived in tight-knit communities—some metropolitan and diverse, others rural and sorted according to the calling of their residents—meadow elves, water elves, resource gatherers."

I nodded. That much I knew.

"But as the *Kongelig* rose in power, the government seized control and forced citizens to perform work with no pay, in the name of service to the realm. The resource gathering communities, for example, have been forced to harvest so extensively that entire ecosystems have died. Alfheim itself is a living organism, and as portions of the realm expire, the realm itself suffers irreparable harm. This, coupled with the fear that has overtaken our world, undermines the very purpose of the realm—to spread light and love through the cosmos."

All around, students wrung their hands together. *What have they seen?*

Professor Asling's kind eyes scanned our group. "Would anyone care to unburden their experiences?"

Svarri raised a tentative hand.

"Yes, butterfly?"

"I got a letter from my sister yesterday—our grandparents were taken to the mining camp." Svarri drew a ragged breath. "Sirra heard Minister Narrik's men enter our home during the night, but our grandmother told her to hide—if they took her too, nobody would be left to look after my brothers."

A lead ball hardened in my gut.

"Oh, Svarri." A blond girl reached over to place a hand on Svarri's knee. "Can they come stay at the school with us?"

"The board says they're too young. When they're old enough for enrollment, if they're deemed useful enough to earn a spot, then maybe." Svarri's lower lip quivered.

"What's the mining camp?" I asked. Every head in the room turned to look at me. "Sorry. There's still a lot I don't know."

"It's all right, dear. Let me show you." Professor Asling tapped the device on her wrist, activating the hologram. It hovered over her hand as she drew it out with her fingertips, expanding its scope until it formed a screen that stretched the length of the smartboard. She tapped the screen, and workers appeared in the image. Some dragged loads that looked much too large for their weary frames, while others drove axes into unyielding stone walls. Every single one of them looked exhausted. Haggard. Completely devoid of hope.

Behind the workers stood uniformed guards, each with a weapon in hand. My stomach churned at the sight of an old woman, her hands on her knees as she gave in to a violent coughing fit. She covered her mouth as one of the guards approached, electric prod raised. The woman rose unsteadily, her back hunched from age or exhaustion—or both—and resumed funneling a beam of light from her palm to the rock, until a large chunk splintered to the ground. A piece landed on her foot and though she dropped to a knee, she quickly resumed her task.

Was this really the realm I was born to rule? Where was the light? The love?

The hope?

Professor Asling folded her hands together, the movement closing down the screen. "In the years before you girls were born, we enjoyed a period of peace. At the time of your births, Svartalfheim had not attacked our realm in nearly twenty years. But after the barrier's erection and the first Key Strike, the attacks resumed, and the queen ordered continual fortification in the barrier's security. But the crystals powering the barrier possess a finite charge, and a constant source of replacements was required. Minister Narrik ordered all abled bodied beings in the mineral-rich regions to work in mines from dawn to dusk. This practice continues today."

"My grandparents aren't able-bodied!" Svarri cried. "Grandpa can't even stand without his cane. Working that hard will kill him!"

"The government doesn't care." A curly haired girl sniffled. "They care only about what *they* think is the good of the entire realm."

"I know, Andya." Svarri groaned.

"But without good for the individual, there can be no good for the realm." My hands balled into fists. "Surely they understand that."

Andya shook her head. "It's been that way all my life

—and it's not getting any better. My family used to be really close—we lived in one of the communal towns in the northern farming region."

"We're from there too," a short girl with crimson hair chimed in. "Or, we were before Minister Narrik stripped the materials from our region and sent them to the barrier. Our families worked that land for five hundred years . . . but it only took them two days to shut down our community."

"That's horrible, Lyria." Andya sniffled again. "It took them a month to shut down ours—at least we saw it coming. Not that it made it any easier."

"Wait, how does the government shut down an entire community?" I asked.

"The queen's cabinet found out about our town meetings." Andya sighed. "A *lot* of members of our community were drafted and killed defending the barrier. We wanted to stand up to the queen—let her know we refused to lose anyone else for a cause we didn't believe in."

All around the room, students nodded in agreement.

"But . . ." I waited.

"But the cabinet caught wind of our plan and stopped us," Andya said. "Poisoned the community's crops, razed the fields, and published a Notice of Evacuation. They pulled our town's charter, claiming a transference of minerals through the soil made the atmosphere too dangerous for dwellings. They imposed a military presence 'for our own safety' until we left."

How was this happening? "Where did you go?"

"I was already enrolled here, so I came back to school. But my twin sisters were denied admission to next year's class. They live with my parents on our new farm—a much smaller plot, and one that's failed to turn a profit now that we don't have any community support."

"Didn't everybody from your neighborhood move together?" I asked.

"Minister Narrik wouldn't allow it. He declared our community subversive, and mandated all citizens live no closer than thirty miles from one another, or face incarceration."

Our government could do that?

"I'm . . . I'm so sorry." These girls deserved better. Their families deserved better. The *realm* deserved better. "Can't anyone stand up to these monsters?"

"Those who do tend to disappear," Professor Asling offered gently. "Before they were marginalized, the *Opprør* were able to improve the living situation for the more remote regions. But as you may know, their leaders were recently taken, so we're left with just the queen and the *Kongelig* to govern us. And so long as the queen is in power, there's little anyone can do to effect long-term change. The succession laws of Alfheim mandate that only a blood heir can challenge the current ruler for the throne. Without one, the queen must die before a new ruler cannot be nominated and confirmed."

Was *that* why the queen hadn't acknowledged me? Because I could actually threaten her rule? Icicles traipsed along my spine. How would I even do that? The *Opprør's* leaders were missing. And if I challenged the queen without any support . . . and if I failed . . .

What would happen to me?

Andya and Svarri exchanged glances while I tried not to openly panic.

"Ladies." Professor Asling shook her head. "You don't mean that."

The girls' cheeks flushed in shame. "Sorry, Professor."

Had she just read their minds? Oh gods, did that mean she could read mine, too?

"The queen will pass when it is her time," our teacher chastened. "And when that day comes, we must be prepared to present a candidate who will honor *all* of the realm—not just those who line its purse or manipulate its leaders. But in the meantime, we have another pressing matter."

"The missing crystal," the curly haired girl whispered.

"Precisely." Professor Asling rose seamlessly. She moved to the smartboard and scrawled loopy letters across the blank canvas. "Your homework for the week is to meditate on the crystal's whereabouts. Recall the warmth it emitted and seek out that energy in your meditations. If you come across anything you believe may be useful—no matter how small—come to me immediately. We must all work together to salvage what we can of our realm. As *Empati* it is our duty to preserve the light of Alfheim . . . and to spread that light in any way we are able." She used one finger to tap the *Auric Adventures* textbook that stood on the smartboard's tray, and it floated neatly into the hand-woven bag hung from her desk chair. "Class is dismissed."

Muted chatter filled the tower as the students packed up their tablets. They filed from the classroom, pleated skirts swishing at their knees, until only Professor Asling and I remained. The teacher's back was to me, but being all knowing and such, she must have sensed my presence—she addressed me without turning around.

"Yes, my butterfly?" Bangle-lined wrists jingled as Professor Asling waved her hand at the eraser. It scrubbed the board clean.

"Oh. Um. I'm just wondering if you know . . . I mean . . ." I paused before blurting, "Why do the dying tree branches hurt me more than the *Empati* students?"

"You are an *Empati* student too, Sister Aura." Professor Asling smiled kindly over her shoulder.

"Not a full time one." I fidgeted with the strap of my book bag. "The administration doesn't seem to know what to make of me."

"Perhaps that is because you do not yet know what to make of yourself." Professor Asling guided the eraser to its holder. She turned around and crossed to her desk. "You have tremendous strength, both energetically and physically, but you do not seem to recognize it. What is it that you fear?"

At the moment, I feared the queen, her council, that Narrik creep, the *Kongelig* at large, and the imminent destruction of my new home due to a missing crystal. But I doubted any of those were the answer she was looking for.

"Do you know what I believe you fear, Sister Aura?" Professor Asling held her tunic-clad arms at her side.

"What?" I rubbed one of the buttons on my blazer.

"I believe you fear your power. I sense you know you have a significant purpose to serve, and you fear the cost of fulfilling that purpose." Professor Asling raised one eyebrow. "Am I correct?"

"I don't know," I answered honestly.

"Mmm." Professor Asling closed her eyes. "Meditate on that. But to answer your question, I sense you are more affected than your peers because you have a deeper connection to the Alfheim Tree than they do."

"If I'm more connected to the tree, does that mean I have a chance at figuring out where the crystal is?" Being the one to bring it home would definitely earn me points if I wanted to move in on my grandmother's job.

"Possibly." Professor Asling opened her eyes. "If you are as tied to the tree as I know you to be, you may have tools others do not. And those tools may enable you to sense the *Sterkvart*."

"How do I find those tools?"

"That is an answer I cannot give you. I can tell you

to focus on your grounding so that when the answer comes to you, you are present and prepared to receive it."

Right. "I'll try."

"As often as possible, retreat to your quiet, inner space, and know that your spirit will reveal what is needed at the proper time."

"Well, thanks. I appreciate your help."

"Love and light to you, Aura." Professor Asling raised her hand in farewell. With a nod, I shifted my bag and exited the classroom. My feet moved quickly along the stones of the tower staircase, and in no time, I'd passed through the glass doors that led to the courtyard.

"Aura." I jumped at the sound of my aunt's voice. Where had she come from?

"I didn't hear you. You're sneaky!" I accused.

"And you're distracted. What's going on?" Signy fell into step beside me. She steered me gently away from the throng of students who streamed from the castle, and navigated us back into the school, toward the area I remembered from yesterday's tour as the faculty wing.

"It's been a *really* long first day." I followed Signy down a wide hallway, and paused outside what I assumed was her door. "Professor Asling showed my *Empati* class what's happening in the mining camps. One of the girls' grandparents were sent there last night. How long has it been this bad?"

Signy frowned. "The queen didn't used to rule this

way. She's always been a colder ruler than her parents were, but she used to see the big picture. Things changed when Lily died."

Signy unlocked the door and gestured for me to go inside. I stepped into the foyer and set my bag on the hardwood floor while my aunt closed the door behind her. She crossed to the kitchenette just off the entry and set to task preparing tea. I explored the apartment, lightly trailing my fingertips along the back of the plush, tan couch, the blue and white blanket I recognized from home, and the framed photos she'd taken of the two of us over the years. Her new home was small but pretty, with the same ornate draperies and dark-wood furniture I had in my dorm.

"Mom's death must have been hard for her," I said. "But to do what she's done to an entire realm . . . to break apart communities and destroy families . . ."

"I don't understand it. And I don't excuse it." Signy emerged from the kitchen to set a plate of cookies on the small dining table. She strode into the other room, returning a moment later with three sets of plates, saucers and teacups. When she'd made a third trip and placed a steaming kettle on a trivet, she stood back to admire her handiwork. "That will do."

"It's perfect. Wait, why are there three cups? Is Larkin coming over?"

"No." Signy bit down on her bottom lip. "Aura, I don't know how to tell you this, but . . ."

What now?

A curt rap at the door sent my heartrate skyrocketing. Signy's nostrils flared as she looked over her shoulder. "She's here."

"Who's here?" I asked. "Signy, what is going on?"

"Listen." Signy took both of my hands in hers, a gesture I associated with an imminent *serious talk*. Anxiety trickled through me. "I just want you to know that whatever happens, I love you with all of my heart. You are my family, and nothing is ever going to change that."

"Why would anything change that? Why are you acting weird?"

"Just remember my words." Signy released her hands. She threw her arms around me and squeezed tight. Whatever was going on was most definitely not good.

Signy released me and darted to the door. She opened it, and ushered its knocker in with a hurried, "Welcome, Your Majesty."

Welcome, your *who*, now?

My jaw unhinged as Queen Constance floated into the room, butterfly wings fluttering in all their glory. Her white gown swayed until she came to a stop in front of the table. My aunt bowed, and not knowing what else to do, I copied her.

"Be seated, Aura." Queen Constance held out her hand. She lowered herself into one of the chairs, and Signy and I did the same. The three of us stared at each other uncomfortably. With everything I'd learned about my grandmother, I wasn't sure if I should try to talk sense into her or club her over the head and hide the body.

Maybe I should have a go at both.

My aunt poured each of us a cup of tea.

"You may leave us, Signy," the queen declared.

What? Why?

"With due respect, Your Majesty, Aura is under my care, and I have reason to believe it is not in her best interest to be left alone with you." Signy kept her voice steady, though she now pushed back her cuticles—something she only did under *extreme* stress.

"I beg your pardon?" the queen trilled.

"I have been at Aura's side since her mother's death, and I don't intend to leave her now. She has experienced tremendous upheaval in the past few days, and meeting you marks a major life transition for her. I am staying." Signy reached over to squeeze my hand.

"I will allow it." The queen raised her chin. "Aura."

"Yes?" My voice bore the enthusiasm of a sedated turtle.

"How was your first day of classes?" The queen smoothed the front of her long skirt.

"Um . . . fine?"

"I suppose there's no point beating around the bush. I requested this meeting because . . ." The lines around Queen Constance's mouth softened slightly. "You have her eyes. Her hair."

"She is the splitting image of Lily," Signy said fondly. "Both inside and out."

Queen Constance bristled. "In that case, you will be

wise to remember no good comes from venturing below your station."

Signy's eyes narrowed. "I raised Aura to espouse the values Lily prized. An open heart. The honoring of *all* life. Tolerance."

The last word hovered between the two women like a loaded gun.

"Then you have done her a great disservice." The queen's voice carried an icy edge. "Aura's prophecy does not allow for such luxuries."

"My what?" I asked.

"Your prophecy." The queen drummed pink fingernails on the wooden table. "Surely you know what the Norns foresaw for you?"

"Aura will forge her own destiny," Signy said fiercely.

"That is not how things work—especially not for royalty." The queen shifted to look down her nose at me. "After your birth, the Norns decreed that one of two futures awaited you. You shall guide the realms to a century of peace . . . or you shall destroy them in war."

My jaw unhinged. "I'm going to . . . to . . . destroy the realms?"

"I would prefer that you guide them to peace. Of course, that depends on whether you are willing to fall in line." The queen resumed her fingernail drumming.

Skit.

"Aura, it doesn't matter what the Norns said," Signy

urged. "Your choices determine your future—nothing else."

"It is her *choices* that concern me." Queen Constance's eyes blazed. "I will not have my grand-daughter destroy the realm I've sacrificed everything to protect."

"Your so-called 'protection' has brought the realm to its knees," Signy countered. "We've lost countless lives, given up our freedoms, abandoned any concept of hope. Our heartbreak prevents us from fulfilling our purpose. How can we share light when our own citizens live under a cloak of darkness?"

"What choice did I have? When our enemies robbed me of my daughter and attacked the realm, came after our infant Keys . . . I vowed that Svartalfheim would never again breach our defenses."

"Yes, but . . ." I drew a shaky breath. "In doing so, you've robbed *other* parents of their children. So many of your citizens died defending the barrier. Don't you think it's time for a new strategy?"

Queen Constance blinked. "How dare you question your queen?"

"I just think all the pain could—"

"Don't think," she said coolly. "Fall in line, and gods willing, you'll stay alive long enough to carry out my legacy."

My nostrils flared. "I don't want anything to do with your legacy."

"I have held our realm together through some of the worst attacks in our history. And while many question my methods, nobody can deny my effectiveness." The queen leaned forward, a new ferocity burning in her eyes. "I am aware some in Alfheim wish to replace me. But the Norns chose me to lead, and that calling is a duty I will honor until my dying day—no matter what it costs me."

The chill that hadn't quite left my spine swept along my vertebrae anew. I didn't want anything to do with this woman. Not now, not *ever*.

Queen Constance leaned back in her chair, the fire dimming from her eyes. "Now that that's settled, I'll take my leave. With the crystal missing, there are countless security issues to which I must attend."

"About that." I bit back my distaste. I just wanted this meeting to be *over*, but if I had to sit down with the queen, I might as well get something out of it. "Is the crystal tethered to the realm? Does it have some kind of tracking device? Anything that can help us with the search will—"

"If it had a tracking device, I wouldn't be asking *students* to assist in finding it." The queen raised her teacup to her lips. "And yes, it is tethered to the realm—though it was also tethered to the tree, for all the good that did us."

"*Crêpes,*" I whispered.

Signy reached over to rest her hand on mine.

"I just sent your associate, Larkin, on a fact-finding expedition on Midgard." The queen took another sip of tea. "Her knowledge of the humans' realm is impressive, so I assigned her a team of warriors to interrogate anyone who may have information leading to the crystal's whereabouts."

Signy stilled. "We weren't informed of Larkin's departure. Did she get to say goodbye to her daughter?"

"How should I know?" The queen arched one eyebrow. "It is a straightforward mission, she will return in due time. And if she doesn't, well . . . dying in service to Alfheim is the highest honor to which a *Protektor* can aspire."

I sucked air through my teeth. The queen spoke of my best friend's mom as if she were disposable. She really was a monster.

Constance set down her teacup and appraised me with a calculated stare. "I must go, but know one thing. Preserving the safety of one's realm is the single most important thing a ruler can do. If my cabinet hears whisperings of *anyone* attempting to undermine the safety I have fought my entire life to secure, that subversive will be put firmly in their place. *Anyone,*" she reiterated, "no matter their relation to me or their ability to one day accede to my throne." The queen leaned back in her chair. "It is not difficult to remove an heir. Especially one the realm does not yet know exists."

With that, Constance pushed back her chair and stood. With a flap, she floated seamlessly to Signy's door, letting herself out in a wave of white, and wings, and hate. Only when the door clicked closed behind her did I allow myself to exhale.

"I'm going to destroy the realms?" I whispered.

"No." Signy leaned across the table to clasp my hands in hers. "If any part of that prophecy is true, it's that you'll guide the realms to peace. Please don't put any stock in a silly prediction. You're far too strong to let somebody else's words guide your life."

"What if it's true?" I whispered.

"It's not. I know that with absolute certainty." Signy squeezed my hands lightly. I met her eyes, gratitude spilling from mine.

"Thank you. For always being there for me. For everything."

"I love you," Signy said fiercely. "Don't you ever forget that."

"I love you too," I whispered.

We sat in silence for a long time, just holding hands. Eventually I had to leave to meet my roommates for dinner. Signy promised to check on me after she gathered more information about Larkin's mission—she wanted to be able to give Elin her mom's exact whereabouts when she broke the bad news. When I finally left the faculty wing, my mind was slightly less stressed. But my nerves returned the minute I stepped into the dining hall and locked eyes with Britney. A haughty smirk illuminated my nemesis' face as she stepped onto a chair at the *Styra* table.

She had something on me. And she was about to share it with the entire school.

"EVERYBODY SHUT UP!" BRITNEY clapped her hands together. "I have an announcement!"

Oh, gods. It was Granite High, all over again. How was she planning to humiliate me today?

"I know a lot of us were excited to meet Viggo Sorenssön, Alfheim's first male Key in, what is it, two hundred years?" Britney pointed to the table where Viggo sat with his gaggle of admirers. He frowned at the smattering of applause, and went back to shoving forkfuls of what looked like chicken into his mouth. "But did you know you're also in the presence of *royalty?*"

Oh, gods. Oh, gods, no. *No.*

"One of our new students has been keeping a very big secret. She just had a one-on-one meeting with the queen, and it sounds like they'll be working together *very* closely in the future. Aura Nilssen." Britney pinned me with her evil smile. "Would you like to share something with the rest of us?"

A lead ball lodged in my throat. *Skit.*

"Leave her alone, Britney." The angry words came from the table by the window where Elin sat, glaring. Beside her, Jande blinked in surprise, while Finna had paused mid-bite, her hand still halfway to her mouth. "Don't you have anything better to do than make everyone miserable?"

"Aura?" Britney's smirk widened. "We're waiting."

I closed my eyes, trying to forget the confusion that flickered across Elin's eyes. I should have told her. She was going to feel so betrayed.

"*Au-rah?*" Britney sing-songed. Her grating voice snapped me out of my head.

"Get down," I hissed. A lot depended on my lineage staying secret, not the least of which was my own safety. If the queen's thinly veiled threat was true, her attack dogs wouldn't hesitate to eliminate the girl with a legitimate claim to the throne . . . as soon as they figured out I existed.

Double skit.

"Come on, Aura. Don't be shy. Tell everyone how you're not some random orphan like you wanted us all to believe. You're really the granddaughter of the queen —the daughter of the crown princess who ran away and whored it up with Frigga only knows who. You're the only living heir to the throne of Alfheim. And, I suppose, next to follow in Queen Constance's footsteps." Malice sparked in Bitch-Face's eyes as she raised her goblet. "Long live Princess Aura."

How had she found out?

An excited murmur whipped through the Great Hall. Heads turned in my direction, with some students grinning excitedly while others furrowed their brows in disapproval. Slowly, goblets lifted, and as the room clouded then began to turn, I registered the rumble of voices. "Princess Aura."

My knees trembled, the spinning overwhelming me. As I stepped back toward the door, firm hands gripped my arms.

"Ignore her. Ignore them all." Signy must have just come in.

"What are you doing here?"

"I came to give Elin an update on her mom, but now . . ." Signy exhaled sharply.

"How did Britney find out about me?" I whispered.

"I don't know. Either she bugged the faculty wing, or somebody's feeding her information. The question is, who?"

"I can't do this." I tried to back away, but Signy's iron grip made movement impossible.

"Yes, you can." Elin had cut through the throng of students to stand with me. Her shoulders were back and her jaw set, though the corners of her eyes tugged slightly downward. There was no way she wasn't feeling all kinds of lied to.

"I'm so sorry, Elin," I whispered. "I couldn't tell you. You would have been a target, too."

Elin's bottom lip quivered, but the hurt in her eyes dimmed. "How can I help?"

Gods, she was a good friend. The best I'd ever had.

"I don't know."

"Keep your head high and act like everything's normal," Signy advised. "It will be hard at first, but the attention will die down."

"Okay."

Elin linked an arm through mine. "You need to eat. Do you want to grab takeaway bags?"

What I wanted was to run to the nearest Bifrost stop and get the hell away from the sea of staring eyeballs.

"It will be worse if you make a big deal of it," Signy advised. "Let's go in—I'll eat with you."

"You will?" So far, I hadn't seen any faculty members in the dining hall—I hoped she didn't get in trouble.

"Absolutely. Elin, where is your table?"

"By the window." Elin took a step into the Great Hall. Since our arms were still linked, I lurched unsteadily after her.

"All hail the princess. May her reign be *exactly* like her grandmother's," Britney trilled. My gut clenched, and it took everything in me to not haul off and slug her. Did she have any idea what she'd done?

"Elin, take Aura to your table. I need to have a word with Britney." Signy broke away and marched determinedly toward the *Styra* table. She gripped Britney's arm, wrenching her down from the chair to whisper heated words I'd have given my eyeteeth to hear. Britney's face paled considerably and a flicker of fear sparked in her eyes. I had no doubt she'd think twice before messing with Signy again.

But what else could she do to me? As I trod through a sea of stares, some admiring, some judging, I knew without question there was no going back. Any friends I made would know me as their princess first; I'd never know if they liked me for who I was or for what I would one day become. From here on out, I could never be just Aura—nobody would see me that way. Not my teachers, not my classmates, not my training partner . . .

My steps slowed as I neared Viggo's table. He appeared totally unaffected—shoveling chicken into his mouth and shooting the occasional half-grin at one of the adoring girls at his side. But he looked up as I walked past, and that second of eye contact held nothing but judgment. He probably blamed my grandmother for his parents' deaths—since they'd been her warriors, he had every right. And now he probably hated me, too.

Well, there wasn't anything I could do about that. Viggo didn't get to judge me for the sins of my grandmother—a woman I'd never even spoken to until today. I pulled my shoulders back and blew right past him, staring at the wall until Elin and I reached our table. Once there, I dropped into the only chair without food in front of it—which thankfully placed my back to the chatter-filled room—and stared resolutely at the twilight-grey forest outside the window.

"So." Elin slid into place at my side. "Do you want to start with chicken or salad?"

"I'm really not hungry," I muttered, refusing to look at Finna or Jande. Their slack jawed faces were barely visible in my peripheral vision.

"She'll have chicken." Signy pulled an empty chair up to sit beside me. "And so will I. Another plate please," she said to nobody. A fifth place setting appeared at our table.

Because, telepaths.

"You must be Finna." Signy turned to my roommate as Elin dished food onto our plates. "I'm Professor Bergen, Aura's aunt. It's lovely to meet you."

"Thanks," Finna choked out.

"And you are?" Signy faced Jande with her easy smile.

"Ja-uh-Jande. I'm in Finna's *Elementär* class." His voice trembled. When I looked over, he stared back at me with saucer eyes.

"Please act normal," I blurted. "Just treat me like you did yesterday."

"But you're a *puh-rin-cess*." Jande managed to squeeze an extra syllable out of the word. "That is *amazing*."

"It's really not." I stared at my chicken-laden plate.

"Uh, yes, it is." A bevy of crystal-lined bangles clicked as Jande rested his hand on my wrist. "We have a legitimate challenger for the crown, now. And you're not a raging nut job! Do you realize what this means?"

"It means there's a great big target on my back and I'm going to have to look over my shoulder every minute," I offered. "Signy, you'll make sure I'm safe, right?"

"No!" Jande squeezed my arm so tight, I winced. I glanced up to see fire burning in his golden-brown eyes. "It means we have someone on our side to fight for us. I was lucky to get a spot here—the *Kongelig* doesn't want anyone like me in a leadership position. I don't fit their mold, and I sure as Helheim don't endorse their intolerance. There aren't going to be *any* gay students in next year's incoming class, and there never will be again if those bigots get their way. But *you*." Jande's eyes flashed, molten orbs blazing infinite passion. "You can change all that. You *have to* change all that."

"I don't know if I can," I whispered. "I don't know how to do any of this."

"You'll learn," Signy asserted. She handed me the pepper, and I dusted my chicken with it. "We'll get through all of this together. Yes, it's a storm right now, and yes, I will ensure that you're protected. But the gossip will fade. And when it does, the safety of the realm will be of even more importance. I understand you four were supposed to be brainstorming ways to recover the *Sterkvart* crystal?"

"We will, after dinner, but . . ." I raised my shoulders

hopelessly. "Kind of hard to think about that right now."

"It's more important than ever that you think about exactly that," Signy said fiercely. "Aura, the day will come when you'll take the throne—it may be years from now, or it may be sooner, but it *will* happen. And when it does, your constituents will respect you all the more if you contribute to their security in a time of crisis. If they see you acting as a leader now, it will give them hope when they have none."

"Maybe, but—"

"But nothing. Eat your chicken," Signy ordered, every bit the proxy parent she'd always been. "Finna, Jande, I understand your discipline had a meeting this morning. What did you determine?"

"Well, um, we . . ." Finna trailed off. She stared at me with a mixture of awe and fear.

"Please act normal," I begged again. "I swear, I'm not like her."

"I know," Finna said too quickly. But then she reached over to squeeze my hand. "I know," she said again. And her sympathetic gaze let me know she understood.

"Thanks," I whispered.

Finna nodded. She raised her chin, now all business. "Well, Professor Bergen. We confirmed the *Sterkvart* originates from a crystal that has a strong, organic link to the core of Alfheim. This means it's extremely unlikely the *Sterkvart* itself has been taken off-realm. We can focus our efforts on tracking it here."

"That's great!" Relief coursed through me, my personal paranoia momentarily forgotten. "So, we . . . what? Comb the realm region by region until it turns up?"

"That's the thing." Jande frowned. "The *Elementär* faculty already did that, and they can't get a trace on it *anywhere*. Its pulse should make it easily detectible, but nobody picked up on anything. *Anything.*"

"How is that possible?" Elin asked.

"We don't know." Finna leaned forward, her chicken seemingly forgotten. "We're going to have to partner with the other disciplines—maybe the *Astrals* will be able to pick up on something we missed, or the *Empati?*"

"*Empati* are supposed to be scanning the realm," I offered. "I'll talk to some of the other students, see if they'd want to work with us."

"I'm sure they will," Signy confirmed. "It's in everyone's best interest that the crystal be found. We can't afford to lose another limb now that the queen has sent hunting parties off realm."

"Why would she do that knowing the connections are being severed?" Elin put her fork down.

Oh, gods. Elin didn't know. The queen must not have let Larkin tell her.

"Elin," Signy said slowly. "Have you talked to your mom today?"

"I was going to check in with her after dinner. Why?"

"The queen sent a tracking party to Midgard this afternoon. Your mother captained the mission."

"What?" Elin sucked in a breath.

"Apparently, a handful of *Protektors* were called into a meeting and immediately Bifrosted out so their plan couldn't leak," Signy said. "From what I understand, your mother was furious she wasn't able to say goodbye to you. But she's a seasoned warrior, and I know she'll be home quickly, and safely."

Elin's breathing hastened.

"I'm sure she's going to be fine," I blurted, convincing myself every bit as much as my friend.

"Sorry, Elin," Finna clucked.

Jande nodded in agreement. "That sucks."

Elin's jaw twitched.

"Okay." I folded my hands together. "Obviously, we *really* need to prevent the tree from losing its Midgard limb. We're forming a task force. I'll talk to the *Empati* tomorrow and see who's willing to help us. Finna, Jande, any tools you have that will help us track an untraceable crystal, bring 'em on. Signy, do you think you can reach out to any other disciplines for us? Ask the faculty members you trust to send us any students who want to help?"

"Absolutely," Signy vowed.

"Thanks." Curious stares nipped like daggers at my back, but I ignored the room and focused solely on my friend. "We'll make sure your mom gets home safe, Elin. Now everybody eat up. We have work to do."

The week that followed my outing as Princess of Alfheim passed with unfathomable slowness. I distracted myself from the unwanted attention by diving into the *Sterkvart* hunt. With Signy's help, we'd rounded up ten students across five disciplines, who'd agreed to meet twice a week in our dorm and dedicate much of their free time to tracking the crystal. Per the queen's command, the whole school was in on the hunt. But our task force was uniquely poised to pursue results. We'd pulled in some of the brightest, and more importantly most trustworthy, students in the *Musa, Elementär, Empati, Astral and Dyr* disciplines. We'd had two meetings and managed to eliminate the desert region from our potential locations list. Apparently if the *Sterkvart* was taken out of a moderate climate, it would weaken, dissipate, and emit a compulsory energy trace signifying its death. This meant it wasn't in the glacial mountains, either.

Two down, infinity to go.

"Where are we with the *Empati?*" Elin asked quietly. She, Finna and I sat in the wood-paneled academy library, where filtered sunlight streamed through the stained-glass windows, and clusters of students studied quietly at long tables. A few shot me curious glances, but things had calmed a little since the initial excitement.

"They send me updates every morning after their

sunrise mediations, but so far nobody's picked up on anything." I made a note on my tablet. "We're going to scan the meadowlands tomorrow morning, so wish us luck."

"Good luck," Finna said sincerely. "Any word from your mom, Elin?"

"Still nothing." Elin gritted her teeth. "I can't believe that monster sent her away without letting her say goodbye."

"I can't believe she hasn't brought Larkin's team back yet," I seconded. "We know the crystal's tethered to Alfheim. Right, Finna?"

"Right," Finna confirmed. "But I suppose there could still be intel on Midgard. Someone who knows something. I'm guessing that's what your mom's team is looking for?"

"I guess," Elin bit out. "Let's talk about something else. Aura, how's it going with your hot training partner?"

"He's not hot. And it's fine, I guess. When he's not being a jerk." Like that morning, when he'd literally run circles around me on the training field. Then laughed.

"Maybe arrogance is his mask," Finna offered. "I'm no *Empati*, but I'd wager that behind the snark and dimples is a guy who could use a friend."

"I seriously doubt Viggo needs anyth—arugh!" I clutched my stomach and rolled out of my chair. My shoulder hit the ground with a dull crack. Books, students, and furniture blurred together in a dizzying whirl before the light streaming through the library windows narrowed my world to a singular, pain-centered focus. I zeroed in on the too-bright beam, breathing into the agony long enough to croak out, "It's happening again."

"What's happening again?" Finna jumped to her feet.

"The ripping. Like last week," I moaned.

"We'll take you to the *Kurera* ward and—"

"Don't touch me!" I cried. "It hurts!"

Elin's chair skidded against the floor. "Finna, have the librarian call Signy Bergen and tell her Aura's having another episode. Aura, stay still. We'll get help."

Elin knelt at my side as Finna raced away. "I'm going to try to make you more comfortable," she said in a calm voice. She gently lifted my head so it rested in her lap, then placed her hands over mine. I stopped clawing at my stomach long enough to meet her eyes.

"It really hurts," I whispered.

"I know. Whatever's happening is hitting that table, too." I struggled to follow Elin's sight line. Through my haze of pain, I saw a table of *Empati* in varying states of discomfort. One clutched her head, one squeezed her eyes closed, and another, like me, had her hands on her stomach. What was going on?

"Attention students." The now-familiar, lyrical voice rang through the speakers. "Please return to your common rooms immediately. Another branch has died on the Alfheim Tree, and the Council of *Protektors* has ordered a lockdown while the realm is searched for portals. *Empati,* please report to the Great Hall for your healings. Thank you."

Chaos broke out as a library full of light elves raced for the door. When the room emptied, Elin looked at me with concern. "Can you move?"

"Do I have a choice?" I asked. Elin held my hand as I struggled to my feet. As soon as I pushed myself up, a wave of dizziness overwhelmed me. I swayed, my palms slapping the table to stop my fall.

"Professor Bergen says she's sending someone to retrieve you." Finna's breath came in gasps as she raced back toward us. "She'll meet you at her living quarters."

"That someone is me. I'll carry her." The deep male voice behind me was heavy with concern. "You all right, *Glitre?*"

Dread coursed through me, an endless waterfall of horror. "Please go away."

"Not on your life." Viggo took my arm from Elin and wrapped it around his shoulders. There was a light pressure at the back of my knees, and the next thing I knew I was cradled in strong arms that weren't altogether uncomfortable. *Stop it, Aura. Yes, they are. So very uncomfortable.*

Finna wrung her hands together. "I'm sorry, but I have to go back to the residence hall—Renwyn assigned me to help with the first years. Aura, will you be all right with Elin and Viggo?"

"I'll be all right with Elin. Viggo, you can go back to the dorm." I tried.

"Nope. See you later, Finna. Elin, follow me." Viggo

broke into a jog while Finna hurried in the opposite direction. Viggo made long strides down the noisy corridors, parting the sea of frenzied girls with apparent ease.

"That hurts," I moaned as Viggo ran. "Why would Signy send *you*? Is she trying to torture me?"

"Real nice, Aura," Viggo chastened. "We were in a private training session when we saw the branch fall. Then Finna called, so Professor Bergen asked me to get you to her apartment straight away, and to bring Elin with us if I could find her." Viggo continued running, but his movements were slightly less jerky.

"I could have gotten there myself," I protested. "Besides, if this is a lockdown, shouldn't Signy want me in my common room with the rest of my house?"

"You need a healing." Elin jogged alongside us. "The *Empati* are being sent to the Great Hall instead of their houses. You guys feel the death of the branches harder than the rest of the school, and you need help more than you need to be in your common rooms right now."

Viggo looked down at me as he ran. "I thought you were a *Verge*."

"I take *Empati* classes, but I take *Verge* classes too. I'm both. Or neither. I don't know. Ouch!"

"Sorry." Viggo slowed down as he entered the faculty residence wing. His emerald eyes appraised Elin. "I don't know which room is Professor Bergen's."

"I do." Elin marched to Signy's door. Before she could knock, Signy charged up the hallway.

"Thank Frigga you're here. Get in, all of you, quick." Signy unlocked her door and waved us inside.

"I can walk now," I protested. But Viggo carried me over the threshold, through the entryway, and into Signy's immaculate living area. He stood beside the light tan couch, holding me tight to his chest so I couldn't help but breathe in his light, cedar scent. I sniffed one last time before cutting myself off with a sigh. I was delirious with pain—obviously, I needed to up my oxygen intake.

"You can set Aura down there." Signy pointed to the couch. Viggo frowned slightly as he loosened his grip and lowered me onto the sofa. He grabbed a soft throw from the basket beneath the end table, then tucked it tight around my legs.

"There." He nodded.

Elin sat beside me, biting back a smile.

"Shut up," I hissed.

She held up her hands. "I didn't say anything."

"You didn't have to."

"What's going on?" Elin turned to my aunt. "Did you call us here so you could heal Aura?"

"Yes and no," Signy began. "You're here because what happened to the tree affects you both. A branch died off—"

"We know," Elin interrupted. "Aura almost passed out."

"I'll need to heal Aura straight away. But Elin, you need to hear this, too. The branch we lost was our link to Midgard."

My stomach tugged, the hole expanding to accommodate the bottomless loss. We weren't returning to our former home any time soon. But worse than that—

"Mom," Elin whispered.

"Larkin," Signy confirmed. She knelt in front of the couch and took Elin's hand in hers. "Her party hadn't gathered any intel, so they were due to return tomorrow. But with the branch down, our connection is lost. I'm so sorry, Elin. She's trapped for now."

Elin's already-pale skin turned white as snow. A wave of sorrow hit me in the gut as I absorbed the heartbreak streaming from my friend. I leaned over to wrap an arm around her, ignoring the piercing pangs brought on by the movement.

"Mom," Elin whispered. Tears welled, pooling against the blue backdrop of her eyes. They paused briefly before toppling over to trickle down her face.

"I'm sure she's fine. Your mother is one of the most formidable *Protektors* I know, and she'll keep her team safe until they can come home," Signy assured. She rubbed Elin's hands softly. "Will you be okay, sweetheart?

"No." Elin's normally joyful eyes shot venom. "When we figure out who stole the *Sterkvart* crystal, I'm going to make them pay."

Viggo's breathing hitched.

"We both are," I chimed in. And we were. Right after the mind-numbing pain in my gut stopped making me want to claw my stomach out.

"It's normal to want justice for a wrongdoing," Signy said. "But the Council of *Protektors* is doing everything within their power to ensure the safety of the Keys, the realm, and the greater good of Alfheim. We will make this right. We will bring Larkin back. And we will punish those who wish to harm our realm to the fullest extent of Alfheimian law. You have my word."

Elin pulled her hands away from Signy's to wipe her eyes. "Good."

"I'm sorry, Elin," I whispered.

"Don't be sorry for me," Elin said. "Be sorry for the idiot that thought they could mess with my family. When I'm through with whoever did this, they'll wish they'd never been born."

"Aura, I need to assess the damage the loss of the Midgard branch has done to your energy centers. Lean back for me." Signy took my hand in hers and closed her eyes. "Ouch, that's a sharp wound to your first center."

"Everything hurts." I cringed. It was true. My entire body, from head to toe, was wracked with pain. I willed everything to shut down and imagined myself inside a thick cocoon, like Signy had taught me back home. Just before the quiet overtook me, I was struck by the disparate vibes in the room. Coming from Signy was a deep sorrow—the resonance of the loss, even one we hoped was only temporary, of a friend. While Viggo was giving off something different—concern, no doubt. But his worry was tempered by something else. Something heavier.

Viggo put out an almost paralyzing level of fear. What could possibly make my arrogant, over-confident training partner afraid?

CHAPTER 12

BY THE NEXT DAY, my physical pain had diminished, but my emotional anguish had intensified. My best friend had cried herself to sleep. With each congested inhale, Elin's delicate sniffles elicited a fresh crack in my heart. We had to find that crystal, like, *yesterday*. Everything depended on it.

By the time I'd finished my assigned morning meditation, attended my *Empati* lab, and chowed my way through an open-faced sandwich in the Great Hall, I was exhausted. I said goodbye to Finna, Elin, and Jande and headed outside, hoping to clear my brain with a walk. As I made my way onto the grass, a grating voice set my teeth on edge.

"Princess Aura."

I turned to find Bitch-Face on the courtyard steps, surrounded by her minions.

"Britney." I continued walking forward, but fingernails on my arm stopped me.

"I'm *talking* to you." Malice sparked from Britney's eyes.

"And I'm ignoring you." I ripped my arm from her grasp. Two students I recognized as *Astrals* and another three I remembered from the *Styra* table circled around. Anger percolated in my gut, but I snuffed it out. These girls weren't worth my energy. "What do you want?"

Britney leaned forward so her shoulder bumped against my chest. Anger bubbled again, this time more violently than before. "She's going to discredit you, you know."

"Who?" I gritted.

"The queen." Britney sneered.

"How the hell could you possibly know what the queen's going to do? Are you a spy, on top of being a bitch?"

Britney ignored my words. "She knows you're not loyal to her, and she's going to prove you're unfit to inherit the crown. Not that it'll take much. Your own mother didn't care about our realm—from what I hear, she ran off with the first guy who looked twice at her and got herself knocked up. It was a blessing, really— she set the bar so low that nobody expects *anything* of you."

To my horror, tears pricked at my eyes. I whirled around before Britney could see me cry. Why did she have to be so awful? Our realm was on the verge of collapse, our ruler was terrorizing families and destroying ecosystems, and the security of Alfheim—

not to mention the safety of Elin's mom and the rest of the *Protektors* trapped on Midgard—was at stake. Couldn't Britney stop being a cow for one single minute?

"You know, Britney, I'm sad for you." I spoke over my shoulder, not bothering to turn around. "My mom may not have been perfect, and I may not have gotten to know her the way I wish I had, but at least she made sure I grew up with someone who taught me kindness, and priorities. Alfheim needs every bit of light it can get right now. If you cared about anyone but yourself, you'd help us make things right."

I hurried toward the forest without giving Britney a chance to answer. As I moved, a solitary girl caught my eye. She sat on the library steps on the far end of the quad, staring at me with unnerving intensity. She wore the regulation blazer and pleated skirt, but her hair was coal-colored, and she sported black nail polish and thick eyeliner. This was the girl from the dining hall, the one I'd seen looking at me with that same level of interest on my first day. What was her deal?

With tears threatening to spill over my own un-lined lids, I didn't get to give the girl a further thought. Instead, I hurried for the forest. I stopped just long enough to take off my heels and stuff them in my book bag, before breaking into a run. I hurtled through the trees, passing purple-tufted evergreens and smooth-barked alders as I went. I didn't stop running until I reached the edge of a small lake. There I dropped to my knees, dug my hands in the earth, and cried.

The deep baritone of a nearby voice jarred me from my cry-fest. I used the back of my hand to swipe the excess moisture away before grabbing my bag and diving behind a nearby tree. My back nestled tight against the thick trunk while I held myself as still as possible. The voice definitely belonged to Viggo, but I couldn't see who he was talking to. Not that it mattered—being outed for crying in the middle of the forest by my tougher-than-thou training partner was the last thing I needed.

"It's too risky to open a portal. This place is crawling with warriors." Viggo stalked into view. With his back to me, I could barely make out the pale blue light coming off his communicator.

What was Viggo up to?

Though I strained my eyes, I couldn't see the figure moving inside the blue light. I only made out the fitted lines of Viggo's black training pants and the toned muscles peeking out from beneath his sleeveless shirt. I craned my neck for a better view.

No. Do not check out his arms. Priorities, Aura.

"Uh-uh, that won't work. The *Protektors* will see right through it." Viggo shook his head. I scanned the forest but saw nobody else. Viggo's only company was that faint blue light. Who was he talking to inside that communicator?

"I thought of that." Viggo ran a hand through his

inky hair. "The barrier would throw up a red flag and alert the guards. The blockade barely let me in—it dropped for the first Bifrost, but since I was late I had to override the hold."

The hairs on the back of my neck prickled. Viggo had *forced* his way into Alfheim? Why? If he was a Key, he was a native-born light elf, and by right allowed to enter the realm. The barrier may have slowed him down to run a second check on him because he'd come from Svartalfheim, but it would have let him in eventually . . . right?

"Listen, I understand what you're saying. But I can't bring you in yet." There was a long pause. "You know why. I have to win their trust first."

The blue light flickered. "Hold on." Viggo raised his arm. "I'm losing you. Let me see if the reception is better over here."

He spun around, and the blue light came into focus. I pressed myself tighter against the tree and clamped down on my bottom lip. Viggo's face was visible at this distance, but the figure in the hologram still wasn't. The blue light was nothing more than a flickering, hooded cloak atop what seemed to be a muscular frame.

Who is he helping?

I carefully peeked around the other side of the tree to try for a better view.

"It's clear. Now what did you say?" Viggo's brow furrowed as he studied the hologram. The figure inside made a fist and waved his arms, but the audio was too low to make out any words. *If Viggo would just come a little closer, I could hear both sides of the conversation. Ugh!*

"I know." Viggo sighed. "I'm doing everything I can. The *Protektors* are making it impossible. I promise, I'll find a way to get you in. What you do after that is up to you."

I leaned forward, trying to get a better look at the hologram, but my balance shifted unexpectedly. As I sidestepped to avoid a fall, a branch cracked loudly beneath my bare feet. *Ouch. Also, crêpes.* I quickly scooted behind the tree.

Viggo's voice dropped to a whisper. "Someone's here. I'll contact you when I've got news. Later."

I pressed myself closer to the tree and closed my eyes, channeling invisibility. I'd ridden on a magic rainbow bridge, so maybe disappearing into thin air wasn't totally impossible.

Seriously, Aura?

I held very still as Viggo called out in a threatening voice, "Show yourself."

I could take him if it came to it. I'd pinned him in five out of nine sparring matches that week. Or was it three? I couldn't remember.

"I know you're behind that tree." Leaves crunched as Viggo stormed closer.

Please go away, please go away. I inched around the tree trunk as my training partner's footsteps grew louder.

"Last chance," Viggo growled. He was unnervingly close. My eyes locked in on the thickest part of the tree line, and I rose onto the balls of my feet, preparing for escape.

Before I could make my move, a thick hand whipped around the tree to clutch my neck. Viggo yanked me from my hiding spot, wrenching my body into view. He held his arm perpendicular to his six-plus-foot frame, so I dangled in his grasp. In his other hand, he gripped a thick dagger. *Crêpes.* My hands flew to Viggo's wrist and I dug in my fingernails, intending to break his hold before my air supply ran out. But as I clawed against his hold our eyes locked, and Viggo opened his palm. I fell to the ground in a heap, then leapt to my feet, brushing broken branches off my pants as I stood.

"You." Viggo's normally charming tone had an edge. "What did you hear?"

"I heard enough." I widened my stance in case I needed to deliver a roundhouse. Or worse. "You broke into Alfheim? What are you doing here?"

"You don't know what you heard." Viggo took a step to his right. I mirrored him.

"Is that so?" We continued our dance, two animals squaring off for a fight. "Then why don't you tell me what I heard? Because it sounded an awful lot like you broke into Alfheim and you're planning something stupid."

"Stupid?" Amusement danced across Viggo's eyes as anger percolated beneath my skin. I took deep breaths until the emotion stilled.

"What would you call what you're doing?" I pressed.

Viggo's features hardened as he took another step. "How was your meeting with the queen the other day? Lots to catch up on, I'm sure."

My eyes narrowed. "What do you care?"

"I care when someone strips my realm of its freedoms. Not that you'd understand anything about that."

The anger bubbled again, fiercer. Hotter. "I'll ask you one more time. What were you doing just now?"

"If I thought you'd understand, I'd tell you. Just know that I'm acting for the *real* Alfheim." Viggo's hand flexed, and his dagger glinted under the filtered light of the forest. My hands balled into fists and I took a step forward. I didn't have a weapon, but if that jerk thought he could silence me, he had another thing coming.

Viggo stepped into my space, his chest inches from mine. I ignored the piney scent wafting off his training clothes and focused on perfecting my glare.

"Go home, *Glitre*," Viggo spoke softly into my ear. "Keep your *perfekt* little life in order."

Laughter tickled my throat. "*Perfekt*. Right."

Viggo leaned back just enough to meet my eyes. "Someone looked out for you from the minute you were born. From where I'm sitting, that's a pretty good deal."

"You don't know the first thing about me."

Viggo shifted so our foreheads practically touched. Butterflies burst into flight in my stomach and at my shoulder blades. *What the hell is wrong with me?*

"I know you're the heir to the throne," he growled.

"I know you met with the queen last week. And I know you haven't stepped up to challenge her. I can connect the dots as to which side you're on."

A low whistle pierced the forest as I sucked air through my teeth. Viggo Sörensson had *no freaking clue.* "You know I'm going to tell Signy about this."

Viggo shrugged. "Go ahead. But for the record, I'm warning you to stay out of it. If anything happens, it's on you."

"Noted." I took another breath as Viggo leaned forward again. His shoulder brushed against mine as he walked by, and the nudging at my back became so adamant, I was positive something was about to crawl right out of my skin. But the jabbing ebbed as Viggo marched forward. He didn't turn around until he reached the thicker tapestry of trees.

Even at this distance, I caught the pop of his dimple. "Give Professor Bergen my best."

Then he turned and disappeared into the forest, leaving me with a litany of questions.

What was Viggo Sorenssön up to?

SIGNY AGREED TO TALK to Viggo about his *obviously* suspicious behavior. But she remained adamant that it was impossible hack into the realm.

"That barrier is impenetrable. And so long as the last light branch sits on the tree, there is absolutely no way a non-native can enter Alfheim without authorization. Even with the help of a Key." Signy shook her head. "What am I missing? Why don't you like Viggo?"

Because he calls me Glitre. And he's got an ego the size of all of Alfheim. And every time he looks at me I get butterflies in my stomach and my back of all places, which is unbelievably awkward. And also, weird.

But I didn't share my thoughts out loud. Instead I muttered, "I just don't."

Signy eyed me levelly. "I'll speak with Viggo about what happened. In the meantime, it would serve you to be nicer to your training partner. You'll be spending the next two years together—longer, if he takes on a role in your administration."

Ugh.

Viggo and I regarded each other with extreme caution after the encounter in the forest. Our training sessions lived somewhere on the border of mortifying and irritating, as I tried to keep from blushing every time he pinned me, and he attempted to best me without ever actually making eye contact. He promptly disappeared at the end of every *Verge* class, and though I enlisted both Elin and Finna to help me track him, he was untraceable. It was as if he turned invisible as soon as his feet hit the forest floor. Finna assured me even the *Elementär* didn't have that ability, and stressed that if anyone could have mastered using elements to manifest invisibility, it would be Alfheim's resident science geeks. Like Signy, she'd given Viggo the benefit of the doubt, choosing to believe he was overwhelmed by the hormonal horde of *Styra* chasing him across campus, and simply seeking solace with a benevolent friend.

"He could have been talking to a cousin in Vanaheim or something," Finna rationalized. "Lots of students have relatives on other realms. I'm sure it's not as bad as you're thinking."

Yeah, right.

Only Elin believed me, whether out of friendship or her own assessment of Viggo's character, I didn't know. But with the *Sterkvart* still AWOL, we didn't have time to worry about what my training partner was up to. Instead, we kept our heads to the ground, working with our hand-chosen task force to eliminate more regions from the vast list of places the crystal could be hidden. Thanks to the work of the animal friendly *Dyr*, who'd used trained birds to scour the forest regions, we knew it wasn't in the woods near campus, the forest at the base of the mountains, or in the southern fern groves. Our search area was still massive, but every little bit helped, and we were grateful for what amounted to a crumb of progress.

But as the days went on, my heart grew heavy. I'd never have admitted it out loud, but ours was beginning to feel like an endless battle—one we had no chance of winning. One night after dinner, Elin and I retired to the quad. My heart tugged at her sluggish steps across the grass. Not even the orange-tinted sunset could improve her mood—a sight my *Musa* friend would once have studied until twilight, then rushed home to paint. My own mood wasn't much better—everything about this situation sucked.

"I don't know what else to do." I rubbed my temples as I sucked in the crisp, evening air. "We've physically searched the grounds, the forest, and the meadow surrounding the tree. We've energetically searched huge regions of the realm and sent animals to examine still more. We've meditated for hours asking the crystal to reveal itself. We've asked advice from every teacher, read half the books in the library, and interrogated the entire *Elementär* department. I'm running out of ideas."

Elin didn't say a word. She didn't have to—the deep frown lines and heavy circles under her eyes spoke volumes. She'd barely slept during her mom's absence. And if the way her skirt hung low on her hips was any indication, she'd barely eaten, either.

"Come on, let's get you some chocolate. You barely touched your dinner, and you need to get calories from somewh—why are you pulling my arm?"

"Because." Elin's emotionless voice was barely above a whisper. "I think she wants to talk to you."

"She who?" A cursory scan of the quad revealed nobody paying attention to me—for once. In one corner, five *Styra* stood in a tight circle, scowling at a group of first years. In another, four *Verge* kicked around a tiny ball. Up ahead, a small gathering of *Empati* sat on the ground in silent meditation.

"She, *her*." Elin gestured to the column adjacent to the library. A raven-haired girl rested casually against the stone pillar, her kohl-lined eyes focused intently on me. Her slightly crooked nose and deep brown eyes were familiar, and I quickly sorted through the new faces I'd catalogued since my arrival at the academy.

"I've seen her before. She's a *Bridger*." I nodded at the girl, and she ducked behind the column. A moment later she emerged, walking steadily toward the rear wall of the quad. When she reached the ivy-covered door, she looked over her shoulder, nodded back at me, and walked through. I wrapped my hand around Elin's and squeezed. "Are we supposed to follow her?"

"Highly likely," Elin said dryly. "But I don't make a habit of following goth chicks into the forest at dusk."

"*Bridgers* can communicate with energies the rest of

us can't." I reminded my friend. "We've gotten nowhere on the crystal. Don't you want to see if she has a lead?"

"I want the lead," Elin said. "It's the energy communication I'm not so sure about. I don't think it's smart to talk to dead people."

My heart fluttered. While I was inclined to agree, a part of me wondered if the *Bridger* could help me talk to my mom. Actually hear her voice, since I couldn't remember it; find out what she'd liked, what she hadn't; if there was anything she wished we could have done together; anything she wanted to say to me . . .

"I'll follow her. You can stay here." I squeezed Elin's hand again before walking across the grass.

"Aura, wait." I could practically hear Elin's eyes roll as her hand-painted shoes pounded across the grass. "Of course I'm coming with you."

"You don't have to," I argued. "The *Bridger's* been watching me for a while. She probably wants to talk alone."

"No," Elin countered. "Friends don't send friends into potentially hostile territory without backup."

I shot her a sideways glance.

"What?" She shrugged. "There's no rule that says I can't read your *Verge* textbooks. You leave them on your desk."

"Fair enough. Come on." I raced across the quad with Elin on my heels. At the edge of the grass, I pulled the ivy covering the wall to the side and ducked through the hidden door. The *Bridger* stood at the edge of the woods, her straight black hair hanging over her shoulders. When she saw us, she turned on one knee-high boot, and shuffled into the woods. Her regulation pleated skirt barely moved against her black tights as she ploughed ahead. She was either really graceful, or really good at trying to blend in.

"Excuse me," I called after her. Elin shot me another worried look. I wasn't sure I blamed her—following a stranger into the forest while Alfheim was subjected regular portal checks for enemy infiltration, and the *Kongelig* made a habit of torching civic monuments, wasn't the most prudent plan. "Could we talk out here?"

The *Bridger* didn't acknowledge my words. She kept walking until I could barely make out her shadow.

Elin let out a sigh. "We're going after her, aren't we?"

"Guess so," I said.

We began a steady march through the trees, with leaves and branches crunching beneath our feet. Every once in a while, we caught a glimpse of the *Bridger's* khaki skirt, and we picked up our pace so we didn't lose her completely. She moved through the woods, pausing when she came to the far edge of the forest. When she looked over her shoulder again, the fading rays of the sun lined her silhouette as if she glowed. She raised one arm, touched a knot on the base of a white-trunked tree, and stepped into the meadow on the other side of the forest. As her feet made contact with the grass, she disappeared.

What. The. Actual. Helheim?

Elin's nails dug into my forearm. "Did you see that?"

"Maybe we should turn back," I hedged. Yes, I wanted to know where the crystal was so we could save Elin's mom—if the *Bridger* could even tell us that. But I wanted to make it to seventeen, more.

"No way. If that tree grants invisibility powers, I want in." Elin tugged on my arm, and I reluctantly followed. When we reached the white tree, Elin bent to touch the knob.

"Nothing happened," I whispered.

"Maybe the invisibility is tied to the ground. The *Bridger* walked onto the grass before she disappeared, right?" Elin drew a slow breath.

"Right." I nodded. If someone had told me two months ago that I'd be following a spirit-channeling goth elf with invisibility powers on a wild goose chase to *maybe* get some information about a stolen crystal on an alien planet, I'd have called them insane.

Now I just called it Tuesday.

"Hold my hand." Elin clasped my palm. "One. Two. Three."

We stepped together into the meadow.

"Nothing happened," I whispered again. "Maybe the —good gods, what is that?"

The ground beneath me shook with an intensity that matched my immediate surge of panic. I threw my arms around Elin, biting down on my bottom lip to silence my escaping scream. We clung to each other as the ripple passed through our feet, up our legs, along our spines, and through our heads. In an instant the meadow disappeared, replaced by a thick, deciduous forest. We were in a fresh sea of hundred-foot-tall trees, and when I looked back, a seamless line marked the former border of the forest. Trees blended into trees, as if we were simply in an extension of the woods we'd been in moments before. How was Alfheim still finding new ways to surprise me?

"Look." Elin pointed to a faraway figure. The pale skirt of the black-haired girl moved slightly as she pivoted to make sure we were still following her. She turned quickly, continuing on her path.

"Come on." I marched determinedly forward, following the *Bridger* past a decrepit cabin engulfed by an ambitious berry bush, over a log bridging a wide stream, and under a fallen tree. I was fairly positive we'd walked a good mile before the *Bridger* stopped in a clearing. Towering sequoia-like trees with glittery silver needles rose in a circle around her, and the forest floor was coated in ferns, low plants, yellow flowers, and a thick moss that crawled over every stagnant surface. The butterflies in my back nudged at my shoulder blades, and I immediately went into *Verge* mode, scanning the area for threats. But despite the insanity of my situation, nothing in my surroundings struck me as even remotely dangerous. If anything, there was something—or someone—I knew in this space. But what? Or who?

"There's something here . . . it feels familiar," I whispered.

The *Bridger* nodded.

"But I've never been in the . . ." I fumbled for the words. "In the, uh, invisible forest?"

The *Bridger* offered a shy smile. "We call it The Cloak."

"Why did you bring us here?" Elin planted her hands on her hips. "What do you want from Aura?"

The *Bridger* studied Elin's gaunt face, tight fists, and defensive stance. "I don't want anything from Aura," she said in a gentle voice. "But someone on the other side has something to share with her."

My heart pounded beneath my ribcage. "So, you *can* talk to spirits?"

The *Bridger* shook her head. "I don't talk to them. They talk to me."

"Sure." Elin raised her chin bravely. But she rubbed her fingertips together—something she only did when she was nervous.

The *Bridger* frowned. "If you're going to be negative, you might as well leave. He won't talk to me if he doesn't feel safe.

"He?" Elin looked over her shoulder. "Who is talking to you? Is he talking to you right now?"

"He's been talking to me for a while—ever since you showed up in this realm." The *Bridger* dug the toe of her boot into the ground. Her soft voice quivered as she met my eyes. "Your dad is here, Aura. And he really wants to meet you."

CHAPTER 14

"**M**Y *DAD? HERE?*" I whipped around so quickly, the end of my ponytail slapped my face. "Where?"

The *Bridger's* eyes danced with amusement. "He's behind you. Standing in front of that tree."

I spun around. My heart thundered against my ribcage as I stared at the thick trunk of a silver-needled evergreen. Somewhere over there was my dad. *My dad* —a man I'd never met, whose name I didn't know. I'd never even seen a picture of him, though I'd imagined him thousands of times. In my imagination, he was tall; a sandy-haired light elf, with twinkling eyes and a booming laugh that filled an entire room with joy. When I'd grown older, and Signy told me my dad had been an off-worlder, I'd altered his race from light elf to human—because obviously, I was too tall to be half dwarf, and Asgard would have claimed me if I was a demigod. But I never had any way of knowing if my fantasies were close to reality. By the time my mom summoned Signy to take me to Midgard, the dark elves had already murdered my father. And my mother died before she could tell Signy who he was, which meant I'd grown up knowing nothing of my dad.

Until now.

My heart ratcheted in my chest, nerves flooding my body as my head drowned in a sea of questions. What was my dad like? Where was he from? What did he think of me?

"Aura." Elin placed her hand on my arm to steady me. "Are you all right?"

"No," I answered honestly. My fingers shook as I ran them over my blazer to smooth it.

"He's just as nervous to meet you," the *Bridger* said softly. Her eyes met mine in a moment of under-standing.

"What's your name?"

"I'm Wynter." She held out a hand and we shook. "I'd ask yours, but your dad already told me."

"Well, I'm Elin." My best friend raised an arm. "And if you or Aura's dad have any intention of hurting her, then you should know—"

"I told you before that if you continued to act this way, I'd ask you to leave." Wynter kept her voice gentle, but her eyes belied her seriousness. "Negativity renders bridgings ineffective."

"I trust her," I whispered to Elin.

"Why? You don't know her."

"I know, but . . ." My blood beat a frenzied cadence

through my veins as I closed my eyes and tried to read the room. I felt my friend's protective energy, Wynter's compassion, and a third, unfamiliar presence that was a mixture of pride and nerves. Was that my father? *My father!*

Maybe I wasn't as bad at this whole *Empati* thing as I thought.

"We're okay," I assured Elin, as I opened my eyes. "Trust me."

Elin set her jaw. "Fine. But if that girl tries anything funny, I'm going ninja warrior on her butt."

"I'd expect nothing less."

"If you two are done, Kegoth would like a word." Wynter tilted her head toward the tree.

"Kegoth," I whispered. My father's name was Kegoth.

Wynter walked over to the tree and stood in front of a cluster of glittery white flowers that were shaped like lilies. *Lilies.* I studied the ground, noticing for the first time that the clearing was absolutely covered in them. *Of course.* These may have been more sparkly than the Midgard variety, but Alfheim's counterpart bore a striking resemblance to my mom's namesake bloom. My dad must have chosen this spot to honor her.

To honor our family.

My breath hitched as Wynter raised her left hand to the tree. With her right, she moved her fingers in a slow circle, as if she was turning the dial on a stove. A blue luminescence flickered in front of the tree, where a grainy image appeared in the light. It shifted slowly into focus, so that soon I made out the figure of a man. He was definitely tall—easily six and a half feet, if not seven, with dark hair and eyes that sparkled with joy. His lips parted in the same jubilant grin I got whenever Signy baked me a cake, or Elin made me laugh. For the first time in my life, I was looking at my father.

And he smiled back at me.

"Hello, Aura."

"Dad," I whispered. "How are you here?"

"I've wanted to meet you for a long time. Wynter showed up and gave me the chance."

My hands trembled. "I'm . . . I . . ."

The corners of my father's lips turned down. "I know it wasn't easy to grow up without me or your mother. When she passed, we decided that she would ascend to Valhalla and I would remain here, so we could protect you from both sides. We did the best we could, but it wasn't enough. I'm so sorry for the hardships you've endured. I hope you know that I am tremendously proud of what you've become."

I closed my eyes. Tears pricked at the backs of my lids. "You looked out for me?"

"Of course. Since I couldn't physically be with you, I sent a protector to watch over you in the forest. Some kind of Midgardian feline." Dad paused. "I'm not familiar with the species' names on that realm."

My eyes flew open. "Bob? You sent the bobcat to look out for me?"

Dad nodded. "A few years back, there was an influx

of dark energies circling the human's realm. I sensed they were there to track you, so I convinced the cat to follow you whenever you left Signy's protection—to make sure you were all right. The cat even followed you to school. He waited in the woods behind the field while you were in class."

Bob's mysterious appearances and subsequent adhere-to-Aura life plan suddenly made sense.

"If you could talk to Bob, why didn't you just talk to me?" I asked softly. I'd have loved to have known my father was out there.

Wynter shook her head. "That's not how it works. Sprits who remain behind can only contact the living through a *Bridger*. The Norns have very strict rules about interfering with their prophecies, and if Kegoth had reached out to you they would have sent him into the permanent void. Even now, if they discover our communication there will be severe consequences."

I frowned. "So why could he talk to Bob without getting into trouble? Didn't that affect the Norn's prophecies too?"

Dad chuckled. "I found a loophole. One of the prophecies surrounding your existence is that you are to be like the goddess Freya—*protektor* of your realm and guarded by felines."

"Freya? The Goddess of Love?" I snorted. "I'm pretty sure *protektor* isn't in that job description."

Wynter's eyes widened. "You're kidding, right? Destruction stems from anger. Anger stems from fear. And fear is the absence of love. Without Freya, the worlds devolve to chaos. She's one of the most important deities, because her gift ensures peace throughout the realms."

Fair enough.

"So, Dad sent a bobcat to protect me on Midgard." I paused. "Why didn't Bob come here with me? Or is he hiding in the woods somewhere here, too?"

My father shook his head. "I tried to send him, but the cat didn't reappear after the Bifrost transfer. I don't know where to look for him."

"Poor Bob," I whispered.

"What is this place?" Elin asked. "Why can we talk to Aura's dad here?"

"Alfheim's barrier prevents Kegoth from directly entering the realm, so we're in a type of void called The Cloak. The *Bridger* faculty created it. It's completely imperceptible to anyone except the upper level *Bridgers;* even the Norns can't see it. You're only here because I held the portal open long enough for you to follow me through. It wasn't easy, by the way. Your negativity nearly activated a shutdown." Wynter frowned at Elin, who just shrugged.

"Wait." I held up my hand. "The Alfheim barrier blocks off-worlders. How did my dad get through?"

"The void is a neutral zone," Wynter explained. "The entrance bypasses the barrier, so even though your dad's from a dark realm, he was still able to pass through."

My heart stilled. "What did you say?"

Wynter's eyes widened, before crinkling in sadness. "You didn't know."

I drew a shaky breath before shifting my focus to the tree. "Dad?"

"Sweetheart," he said gently. "I need you to know that no matter what I once was, from the moment I fell in love with Lily, and even more from the day we found out she was pregnant with you, I was filled with nothing but love."

"Where are you from?" I asked through gritted teeth. Elin came over and squeezed my hand.

"Aura," Wynter said softly. She met my frustrated gaze, her pale blue eyes brimming over with sadness. "Kegoth is . . . he's . . ."

"What?" Elin pushed. "What is he?"

Dad met my eyes. "I am from Svartalfheim. I'm a dark elf."

My jaw popped as the news socked me in the gut. "If you're a dark elf, then that means I'm . . . I'm . . ."

Dad nodded. "Fifty percent of your genetic makeup is Svartish. You're not just a light elf, Aura. You're a dark elf, too."

ELIN SQUEEZED MY HAND again. "Aura? Are you okay?"

"No," I grunted. The nudging at my shoulder blades had intensified to razor like jabs. Pain wracked my back, and I rued whatever laws of Alfheim had altered my anxiety-induced stomach flutters to the full torso variety. "My back hurts like hell!"

"Should we leave and find Signy or . . ." Elin trailed off.

"Give me a minute." I knelt down, fisting the soft dirt and focusing on the sensation of the grains between my fingertips. I was half dark elf. *Half dark elf.*

Half dark elf?

"Does this mean my genetic programming is set to evil?" Was I going to turn into a monster queen like my grandmother, no matter what kind of ruler I wanted to be?

"Not at all." Wynter sounded *way* calmer than I felt.

"Whatever your genetics, you are good. You are *light*. I've seen it. And Kegoth is the same way. Your dad isn't bad. He was just born into a dark realm. Not all dark elves are evil, just like not all light elves are good."

"That's true—look at Britney. She's here, and obviously the Bifrost should have dropped her in Helheim," Elin chimed in.

My nails dug harder into the earth. "I'm a dark elf."

"Half," Wynter corrected.

"Sweetheart." Dad's deep baritone penetrated my anguish. "If it helps, you take after your mom. The only part of you that's me is your right hook."

I snorted, then coughed as dust flew up my nose. "You're funny. I guess that's a good thing."

"It's not bad," Elin confirmed.

"Do you want to hear about how I met her? Your mother?" Dad offered.

"Yes." I pushed myself to a seated position and tucked my legs against my chest. "Tell me anything. Everything. Please."

My father's eyes crinkled at the corners. "I met your mom when she trekked through the realms after secondary school. We were hiking the same seemingly dormant volcano when it erupted, and we found ourselves fleeing a lava flow. I waved her into an elevated cave to ride out the danger. We ended up trapped in there for the better part of a day, but it only took me an hour to fall in love with the girl with sparkling eyes and an adventurous heart." Dad smiled, seemingly lost in the memory. "We wanted to be together, but didn't know where to go. I couldn't take her home with me—I'd spent the better part of my life looking for a way to break away from my family of origin. And residents of Svartalfheim aren't welcome on other realms, except for Muspelheim. But I didn't want to trade the dark elves I knew for the fire giants I didn't."

"Fair enough."

Elin dropped down to sit beside me. The two of us gripped hands as my father continued.

"Since Lily was the crown princess, she thought her mother might make an exception and let me enter Alfheim. This was when immigration was still permitted between light realms. We wrote to Constance asking her to grant me citizenship. She declined, and within a few weeks Alfheim had not only banned immigration from *any* realm, but also begun construction on the barrier. Constance wrote to Lily, begging her not to compromise the crown for a dark elf. But Lily saw the good in everyone, regardless of their circumstance—it was one of the most beautiful things about her."

Tears pricked at my eyes, but I blinked them back. I didn't want to miss a word.

"Lily asked her mother to admit me as her husband. When Constance refused, we fled to a remote part of Svartalfheim and married in secret. Rather than endure the embarrassment of admitting the crown princess had married a dark elf, Constance told her realm her daughter was away on a diplomatic mission. Lily and I stayed hidden for the short duration of our marriage, while construction on the barrier continued. Then you were born, and your mother and I were absolutely overwhelmed with joy. Our surge of happiness alerted my family to our location." Darkness clouded my father's eyes. "We were ambushed in our sleep. I managed to transport you and Lily to the boundary of Alfheim, but my family killed me before I could get off-world. I never got to tell you or your mother goodbye; never said I love you that last time. But I did love her, and you. More than all the stars in all the cosmos."

I hastily wiped my tears, my dirt-covered palm like sandpaper against my cheek. "I wish I'd known you both."

"I wish that too. More than anything, I regret not being able to be there for you."

My heart tugged. "I'm glad you're here now."

"So am I," he offered. "But my time here is limited, and I need to tell you something important. It will affect whether you join me in the afterlife centuries from now, or in the next few weeks."

"The next few weeks?" My pitch shot up as ice pulsed through my veins. "I'm going to die that soon?"

"We're all going to die that soon if the Alfheim Tree keeps losing branches, and the portal to Svartalfheim opens," Wynter pointed out. "But if we get the crystal back to the tree, the branches regenerate and the portal stays locked. And Kegoth knows who's responsible for the missing crystal."

"Who?" I asked.

My father's lips pushed together. "The dark elf who hired the scouts to track you. He's the reason you grew up without your mother and me—he ordered our deaths, and when you survived, he ordered the assassination of all Alfheim Keys."

My stomach lurched. "Who is it?"

"His name is Dragen, and he's my younger brother—your uncle."

My jaw unhinged. Dad had said his family ambushed him, but I'd figured he'd meant some jerk third cousin or something. "Your *brother* had you and Mom killed?"

Wynter wrung her fingertips together. "There's more."

Of course there was.

"When my family found out I'd married a light elf, they were outraged," Dad explained. "My father, Rankin, was a powerful member of the Svartalfheim senate, and his seat was to pass to me. Rankin had promised my hand to another senator's daughter, and the union of two influential families would have assured a takeover of their political party. Rankin intended to run for chancellor, and having the party's backing would have solidified his victory."

Elin frowned. "I always assumed it was anarchy on Svartalfheim."

"Svartalfheim's political arena has always been corrupt," Dad explained. "The entire senate, with generations of inbred hatred, is destroying their world."

"How so?" I asked.

"Svartalfheim senate seats pass through inheritance. My family had one of the longest held, and most respected seats in the House. But my father's career stalled when I married Lily. A dark elf's word is his most valuable currency, and my marriage to an off-worlder made his word worthless. The only way he could save his career was to disown me, which he promptly did. Then he declared my younger brother his heir. Dragen was meant to inherit our father's seat, and all of the power that once came with it. But then you were born."

"If Rankin disowned you, then my birth shouldn't have mattered. Right?"

"Not quite." Dad sighed. "Under Svartish inheritance laws, I ceased to exist—but as a new life, you became first in line to inherit our family's senate seat."

"I don't want the job. Tell Dragen he can have it." My stomach clenched at my father's frown. "What?"

"You can't turn down a Svartalfheim senate seat. Death or disownment are the only ways out. And Rankin's never going to disown you—not since he learned of your prophecy."

I tried to ignore the nerves that clawed at my stomach. "The one where I become a cat lady like Freya? Or the one . . ."

The queen's words flashed across my mind, sending a fresh wave of dread coursing through me. *Guide the realms to peace . . . or destroy them in war.*

"Oh, gods," I whispered.

Dad nodded. "Because of your duality, being half Svartish and half Alfheimian, and because of your royal lineage, you have the potential to manifest more power than any individual in either realm. If given the right platform, you will guide the realms to peace . . . or destroy them in war."

"Shut up." Elin gawked. She turned to me. "Did you know about this?"

"Kind of," I muttered. *Skit.*

"You have the potential to create for the greater good innate in daughters of Alfheim," Dad explained. "But you also have the physical strength and ability to destroy imbued in children of Svartalfheim."

"Is that why you're taking classes in different programs?" Elin said. "Because your Alfheim side is *Empati,* and your Svartalfheim side is *Verge?*"

A deep shudder wracked my spine. "So, Rankin wants me to come to the dark side and lead the realms to war?"

Dad nodded. "And Dragen wants you dead, so he can inherit your seat. That's why he's after the *Sterkvart* crystal. With Alfheim isolated, the realm will be that much easier to destroy—and you along with it."

"We have got to find that crystal before he does. Wait—does he already have it? Is he the one who took it?"

Wynter's eyes darted nervously to my dad. "We don't have much time left."

"I understand." My father's image flickered. When he

spoke again, his words came out in a torrent. "It's not in Dragen's possession yet. Alfheim's barrier prevents him from entering the realm to collect it from whomever he's working with. But he's definitely getting help from someone inside Alfheim, and it's only a matter of time before they're able to get him in. Either the traitor will find a way to get Dragen past the barrier, or . . ."

"Or?" Elin whispered.

"Or the remaining branches of the tree will die off, and the portal to Svartalfheim will open. If that happens, nothing will prevent my brother from marching in here and claiming the crystal." Dad exhaled. "And claiming you."

Adrenaline coursed through me. "Do you have any idea where the crystal is? Can you see things we can't from . . . the other side?"

"Kegoth," Wynter warned. Dad's image flickered again. "I can't project you much longer."

He nodded. "I haven't seen anything yet, but I'll continue to search, and let Wynter know the minute I find something. She can pass the message along to you."

My eyes narrowed. "What about my training partner? Viggo was acting really weird in the forest. He's definitely got an agenda we don't know about."

"I've wondered that same thing," Wynter agreed.

"Well?" Elin chimed in. We waited while my father pursed his lips.

"I don't know anything about your partner, but I

advise you to trust your instincts. They've never steered you wrong before."

"Thanks," I whispered.

Dad's image flickered again, and Wynter glanced at her com. Her eyebrows shot up as she leapt to her feet. "We need to go. Our time is about to expire, and if the Norns find out your father communicated with you, they'll send him into the permanent void."

My heart tugged as I pushed myself to my feet. I shot an anxious glance at my dad. "Will I get to talk with you again?"

Dad's eyes crinkled in the kind smile I'd imagined so many times. "I am always watching out for you. If I see my brother making a move, or if I see anything that can help you find the missing crystal, I promise I will reach out to Wynter. I only wish I knew where the Bifrost took that bobcat—it's highly unusual for a transport to fail. And the creature was an excellent protector in my proxy. If he were here, I know he'd look after you well."

"Bob was the best," I agreed. Gods, I hoped he was okay—wherever he was.

"You and I will stay in touch, Aura," Wynter promised. "The *Bridgers* come to The Cloak a few mornings a week to monitor communications from banned spirits, or those who are uneasy communicating on the main plane. We ask about the crystal at every session, so I'll let you know what I hear."

"Thank you." I reached over to grasp Wynter's hands. "For everything."

"It's nothing." She met my eyes with a soft smile. "Now go. Head straight for the white tree and touch the trunk on your way past. I'll follow behind so nobody gets suspicious."

"Goodbye, Dad." He'd risked banishment to talk to me. I didn't want to leave him so soon. "I hope we talk again."

"I love you, sweethea—" Dad's image flickered mid-word, and before I could tell him I loved him too, he was gone.

"Hurry!" Wynter urged.

Without another word, I turned and ran for the tree. Elin matched my pace, and we raced out of The Cloak. I threw my arm out as we passed the white-trunked tree, tapping it lightly before pushing forward. The now-expected ripple passed up my body, and Elin and I ran another hundred yards before we finally stopped at the base of an ancient, purple-needled sequoia. I glimpsed the outline of the academy in the distance. We were back on the Alfheim plane . . . but I didn't see Wynter anywhere. Had she made it out before our time expired? I hadn't thought to ask what the consequences were of overstaying our other worldly welcome, and I hoped my new friend wouldn't get in trouble for helping me.

"Come on," I murmured as I stared into the darkest patch of the forest. Night had fallen while we'd been in The Cloak. Through the lightly glowing treetops, a smattering of stars lay visible against the inky backdrop of sky.

"I think I see her," Elin whispered. I scanned the forest until I spotted the dark-haired girl emerging from a dense cluster of trees. She raised a hand in farewell before ducking to her right and hurrying through the woods. She was heading for a different trail, probably so nobody could link our meeting.

"We'd better get back before the curfew bell." I moved toward campus. "Do you have any idea how long we were out there?"

Elin shrugged. "Two hours? Maybe longer? I don't know how time works in that place."

We jogged through the trees in silence. When we reached the back wall of the quad, Elin tugged on my arm.

"Are you okay?" she asked. "That was a lot, meeting your dad—kind of—and hearing about your uncle. And your prophecy. Jeez, Aura. That's heavy."

I ignored the lead lodged in my gut. "The queen told me I'd lead the realms to peace or drive them to war. That was right before she threatened to have me un-princessed if I jeopardized her reign."

Elin blinked. "Why didn't you tell me?"

"I should have," I said. "I just . . . I don't know, it was a lot."

Elin squeezed my elbow. "Don't go through this alone, okay? I'm your friend. I want to help you."

"We *both* have a lot at stake," I said. "And I won't keep anything else from you. I promise."

Elin and I would get through this like we had everything else our entire lives—*together*.

"And speaking of not keeping things a secret"—I pulled the ivy curtain aside and followed Elin into the quad—"I need to talk to my aunt about all of this and it's probably going to take a while. I'll walk back to the dorm with you so I can grab a change of clothes for the queen's stupid speech in the morning. But then I'm going to head over to Signy's."

"Do you want me to go with you?" Elin offered.

"No, thanks. Get some sleep. I still don't understand why the queen is making us get up at dawn on a Saturd—"

"Cutting it awfully close, aren't you?" Britney's nasally voice rang across the quad. "Curfew tolls in three minutes. What are you doing out this late?"

"Soaking in the rays of the full moon to energize our auras. *Empati* assignment." The lie rolled easily off my tongue. I held Britney's gaze long enough to let her know she hadn't intimidated me, before turning the tables. "What are *you* doing out so late?"

"*Styra* patrol the school borders to make sure nobody breaks curfew. You know that," Britney snarked.

Actually, I didn't. With the exception of our crystal meetings, I'd kept pretty much to myself at the academy. Gods, what if my lifelong aversion to group activities was because of my dark DNA? Had I subconsciously tried to protect the world from the monster inside of me all along?

"Aura may have had a class assignment, but you're not an *Empati*." Britney leapt off the low stone wall and sauntered across the grass to stand in front of Elin. "What's your excuse, *Musa?*"

Elin eyed her coolly. "I needed to absorb the creative energies of the full moon. If you had any artistic abilities, you'd know that. *Britney.*"

Ouch.

Britney sneered, and I wrapped my fingers around Elin's wrists. "Let's go. Britney is clearly in another one of her moods." Without another word, I turned on one heel and pulled my friend toward the academy.

"Watch your backs," Britney called after us. "The disciplinary council would *love* to score a one-on-one with their princess."

I ignored her as Elin and I made our way to the dorms. We ducked inside just as the bell tolled its first stroke, and closed the door to our room as the tenth *ping* chimed.

"Shh," I whispered, pointing to Finna asleep in her bed.

"It's okay, I'm not out yet." Finna raised her eye mask and rolled over to prop herself up on one elbow. "Late night?"

"You could say that." I shuffled into the bathroom to grab my toiletries while Elin changed into her pajamas.

"You're sure you don't want me to go with you?" Elin asked.

I grabbed a duffel bag from under my bed and filled it with my toothbrush, pajamas, and a fresh uniform.

"I'm sure. Thanks, though. I'll meet you in the Great Hall at . . . what time does the thing start? At eight?"

"Wait." Finna yawned. "Where are you going?"

"I'm going to stay at Signy's—she and I need to talk. I'll fill you in after the queen's address."

"I wonder what Her Majesty is planning to tell us." Elin rolled her eyes. "Maybe she'll announce what civic monument she's planning to destroy next; give us a chance to stage a protest first."

"More likely, she'll have that monster Narrik interrogate every student about their family's political allegiance and torture the ones who don't answer the way he wants them to." I grimaced.

"Hopefully she'll have some direction for us on the missing crystal," Finna mumbled sleepily. "The Nidavellir branch looks like it could turn black any minute."

The gravity of Finna's words iced my veins. Elin shot me a worried look. If that branch fell, just a handful more stood between us and a direct link to Svartalfheim.

And Frigga only knew what would happen if my uncle got his all-access pass.

CHAPTER 16

SIGNY AND I STAYED up half the night dissecting everything my father told me, and speculating about what it meant for the future. She wasn't upset that the girl she'd raised was half dark elf —she said she would have cherished me if I was Hel herself, so long as I was the kind-hearted girl she knew and loved. She was not, however, so accepting of what she referred to as my "blatant disregard for safety." Given the enormity of the forces conspiring against me, Signy was horrified on learning I'd gone off into the woods with a stranger.

"*Please* be more careful." Signy tucked the blue plaid blanket around my legs before settling back into her corner of the couch and wringing her fingers. "This uncle of yours has another thing coming if he thinks he can hurt you on my watch. But you have to help me keep you safe. Your mother entrusted me with your life. I don't know what I'd do if anything were to happen to you."

"I'm sorry." I truly was. The poor woman looked like she'd been to Helheim and back. "But I had to follow Wynter—I thought she'd have a lead on the crystal's location. Turns out she knew something just as big. Did you have any idea what I was?"

"I wondered," Signy admitted. "I knew Constance was prejudiced against off-worlders, and I knew your mother's 'diplomatic mission' was behind the queen's decision to authorize the barrier. It didn't make sense that Constance would go to that extent to keep out a human or a dwarf. But Lily never told me that when she toured the realms, she toured the dark ones, too. I suppose I should have known that as well—she was determined to be a different kind of ruler than Constance."

Her and me both.

"Mom would have been a good queen?" I genuinely wanted to know.

"She'd have been one of our finest," Signy confirmed. "She was selfless and kind, right up until the moment she . . ."

I tucked my feet underneath me. "I know it's hard for you to remember the . . . the end."

"If Lily had only been able to get through the barrier, she'd still be alive. When I got to her, she was right at the border. Her attackers weren't yet within striking distance. Things could have ended so differently."

"Right." There wasn't much else to say.

"But then, I wouldn't have gotten to raise you." Signy reached over to grasp my hand. "The moment I held you in my arms was the most joyful of my life. In that instant I understood love—true love—in a way I never have before or since. *Please* promise me you won't go chasing any more strangers into the woods. Wynter is trustworthy, thank the gods, but if she had turned out to be someone else; if something had happened to you . . ."

"I'll be more careful, I promise," I vowed. "But I can't sit by anymore. There must be hundreds, if not thousands living on dark realms who want a better life for their families. Our barrier, our ban on off-worlders —it's unconscionable. We have to convince the queen to get rid of it. And to get rid of her horrible cabinet."

"You won't be the first to try," Signy cautioned. "The *Opprør* have worked to achieve that for years, and they've been pushed to the ornamental government posts, and all but run out of many regions. And with their cabinet representatives still missing, they have very little power left."

"True. But the *Opprør* have never had someone on their side with a direct claim to the throne."

Signy raised one eyebrow. "Are you prepared to challenge Constance? Are you ready to rule the citizens of Alfheim as their queen?"

"Of course not! I'm only sixteen! But things can't continue like this. And if my taking over is the only way out . . ."

"It's a process, Aura—challenging a current ruler. You'll need to have cause, which you do, and standing, which as the sole heir, you clearly do. If you're to be successful, you'll need the backing of the people, which means you need to earn their trust, first."

"How do I do that?" I asked. "I'm related to her; won't everyone think I'm just like her?"

"Not if you've taken steps to improve their safety by, say, restoring the *Sterkvart* crystal to the Alfheim Tree. But since we still don't have any leads there . . ." Signy studied the ceiling. "Why don't we make one more attempt at reason? We'll ask Constance for a meeting in your capacity as Princess of Alfheim and make a formal request for removal of the barrier and reinstatement of peacetime governing practices. Set out your logic, I'll serve as witness, and if she still refuses to see sense . . . well, we'll evaluate our next steps."

"Okay." I drew my blanket up around my chin. "I'm not cold," I hastened when Signy reached for another throw. "I'm just freaked out."

"I know, but you'll have my support at every step. You have your mother's sense of fairness—she'd be proud that you have the strength to stand up for what's right." Signy held out her arms, and I scooted into them. She stroked my hair like she'd done when I was a little girl, and I let her soothe my anxiety. In no time, I'd drifted off into a heavy, dreamless sleep.

The next morning, having very nearly overslept, I lumbered into the queen's address with half a minute to spare. My tardiness meant Elin and I couldn't discuss my night with Signy, or our plan to request a meeting with the queen that day. Thankfully, Elin had saved us seats in the back of the hall where I didn't have to feign attentiveness or calm. My friend's presence transformed me from a raging bundle of nerves to a semi-functioning stress case.

Or, it had. Once the queen took her place at the podium, the nerves in my gut churned anew. All around me, students shot anxious glances at their friends, clearly uncomfortable in the presence of the despot whose choices continued to destroy our realm more efficiently than any enemy in Alfheim's history. Only the *Styra* watched with rapt adoration as the queen droned on for what felt like hours. Her address culminated in a renewed plea to locate the missing *Sterkvart* crystal—*without* offering any additional information that might help the hunt. By the time the queen urged us to "bring glory and honor to Alfheim, so She shall bring infinite grace and wisdom to you," I was a keyed up, nerve-wracked mess. I just wanted to deal with my family business, already.

Queen Constance concluded her address with a flourish of her bony hand. Her wings fluttered behind her as she moved to the edge of the temporary stage and floated down the gilded steps. Row after row of blazer-clad students rose begrudgingly to their feet, cheering halfheartedly as their queen floated toward the exit. In the back row, Elin gave a listless golf-clap while I attempted to hide my eye-roll.

"That was pointless," I fumed. "She wants our help in locating the crystal, but gives no additional information. She builds us up as 'beacons of light in a dangerous world,' when she's personally smothering it in darkness. Who does she think she is?"

"Queen of Alfheim," Elin said wryly. "She Who Does No Wrong."

"Apparently." I caught Signy's eye as we exited the address. She moved swiftly to my side. "What's the verdict? Did she agree to the meeting?"

"She'll see you after she debriefs her advisors."

"Good." I planned to let her have it.

Elin looked back and forth between the two of us. "You guys going to clue me in?"

"I'm going to talk to the queen and ask her to remove the barrier." Air streamed from my pursed lips. "I'll fill you in later."

Elin's eyes widened. "You need help?"

"Signy'll be with me. But thanks."

As we moved away from the Great Hall, Minister Narrik appeared outside one of the lounges. Darkness seeped from his military jacket to his shiny boots, the only pop of color the red rank patches at his chest and shoulder. He gave Signy a curt nod before stepping through an open door.

"It's time. Let's go, Aura." Signy linked her arm through mine.

"You have to meet with him, too? Yikes. Good luck," Elin whispered.

"Thanks." I turned on one heel and let Signy lead

me into the lounge. Queen Constance stood by the window, her elongated wings glimmering softly in the recessed lights. Minister Narrik took up a position by the door, feet shoulder width apart and hands folded behind the small of his back. Was he just going to stare at us the whole time?

"You may be seated, Aura." The queen gestured to one of the loveseats. "Signy, you may leave."

"Again, no." Signy squeezed my hand.

I so loved her.

The queen's nostrils flared, but she looked down her nose at me and simply said, "Well?"

"Well, what?" I countered.

"Why have you requested this meeting?" Queen Constance's eyes darted around the room. For the first time, I noticed the armed guards positioned in each corner. Did she think I was going to try to hurt her? Or was she just reminding me that we weren't alone—and that if things went south, I was the one who'd need protecting?

I drew a steady breath and faced the queen head on. "Your barrier has led to countless deaths. It's an outdated, fear-based defense that has caused nothing but heartbreak and loss. As crown princess of Alfheim, I lodge a formal request that you remove the blockade to prevent further loss of life, and to allow entry to those beings who seek a better existence for themselves and for their families."

Narrik's forceful exhale sliced through the tension. The queen silenced him with a pointed look before turning her attention to me. "The crown princess is powerless over the regent. Your demand carries no weight and is dismissed. Will there be anything else?"

Frustration bubbled beneath my skin, but I pushed it down in the name of diplomacy. "You know as well as I do that plenty of off-worlders want to improve their lives. My father wanted that for himself, and for me. Denying immigration on the basis of residence is punitive, and counter to the purpose of our so-called Light Realm."

"How do you know about your father?" the queen barked.

"My mother explained everything to Signy," I lied. No way was I letting my grandmother know I'd communicated with Kegoth. She'd have him sent to the perma-void for sure. "Come on. You have to agree your ban is overly restrictive."

The queen narrowed her eyes. "We cannot discern intentions, Aura, and I am unwilling to place my realm at risk by allowing entry to other-worlders who may or may not be worthy."

"Worthy—do you even hear yourself?" She was using useless parameters. The real test of good vs. evil lay in one's character—something the *Empati* could easily read, if given the chance.

That was it! We didn't need a barrier—we had the tools to protect our realm within the walls of the academy. The queen had just been too blinded by fear or bigotry or *whatever* passed for sense inside her twisted head to see it. I leaned forward, excitement quickening my words. "Hold on—there's a way we can *both* get what we want. You can protect Alfheim *and* let off-worlders in. You can totally discern intentions! You're standing in the middle of a school with an entire curriculum devoted to reading minds, chakras, auras, hidden agendas, all of it. Our *Empati* could easily evaluate the intentions of refugees and—"

"Off-worlders cannot be trusted."

I pushed my frustration back down. "If I approached your council, told them that I am personally willing to oversee an *Empati* led—"

"My council answers to *me*, Aura. Not to a teenage girl, regardless of her lineage." The queen sneered. "So long as I am alive, I will devote myself to the protection of my people. I have always done what I believe to be in their best interest, and I will continue to do so."

"Even when 'their best interest' gets your citizens killed?" I challenged. "Is that really the kind of ruler you are?"

Narrik's low growl made me shiver. But I held my ground.

"You could never understand," the queen dismissed.

I folded my arms across my chest. "Enlighten me."

Constance pulled her shoulders back. Her chest strained against a deep inhalation, and though she bit down on her bottom lip, she kept her head high. "When I was a girl, my best friend was murdered in the castle garden. The arrow was meant for me. It was Svartalfheim's first attempt on my life. Dozens more would follow."

"I'm . . . sorry."

The queen brushed off my sympathy with a flick of her wrist. "When my daughter informed me that she intended to marry a dark elf, I could only fathom the horrors he could inflict on Alfheim from its throne. I forbade the union but Lily did as she had always done; she chose her heart over her duty. The barrier was constructed so that when Svartalfheim attacked, we would be ready. And when the day came, though we weren't without our casualties, the key members of our government were saved."

"But two decades had passed since the last dark elf attack," Signy interjected. "When you authorized construction on the barrier, you had no reason to believe the peace would break. The initial attack—the one that happened shortly after the barrier's completion—was nothing more than a hit on Lily, Aura, and Kegoth. When Aura survived, the siege expanded to include all of Alfheim's Keys, and eventually to the entire realm. But that wasn't until *after* Kegoth transported Lily and Aura to the Alfheim border, and after Aura and I escaped to Midgard. Had the barrier not denied them entry, your daughter and granddaughter would have had time to take refuge in the realm. Lily would still be alive. And Aura . . ." Signy's eyes misted over.

Holy skit.

Queen Constance paled. "My daughter took up with a dark elf from a powerful family. It was only a matter of time before his realm came after mine. I authorized construction on the barrier so that when Svartalfheim struck, Alfheim would be protected. It was only ever meant to be a failsafe—if Svartalfheim never attacked, I never would have had to authorize the barrier's activation. But when our sentries reported assassins approaching from Svartalfheim, I had no choice. I had to protect my realm. I had no idea that activating the barrier would cost me . . ." The queen raised her chin. "I will never apologize for saving Alfheim. Duty to the realm must always take precedence over duty to self."

Ice water doused my veins as I blinked at the queen. "But you knew."

"I knew what?"

"You knew my mother married a dark elf. You knew she'd try to protect him; that if they were ever in danger, she'd bring him to Alfheim. You knew the barrier would never let them both in, and you had to know my mom would never toss someone aside to save herself. You knew the barrier would block his entry . . . that it could get them *both* killed."

The queen snapped. "Do you think I would subject my citizens to all the horrors a dark elf would have the power to inflict as their king?"

My chest clenched, breathing nearly impossible. "You killed them."

Narrik's growl turned feral. "Need I remind you, *child,* I can make life exceedingly miserable for those you care about."

Narrik's threat bounced off the waterfall of rage

that coursed through me. My focus held steady on the queen. "You created your stupid barrier during a time of peace. This wasn't about preventing an attack. It was meant to keep my father out."

"It was meant to do *both*. That barrier is the only thing that kept—"

"Your barrier is responsible for my mother's death." My hands trembled. "And *you* are responsible for my father's—if you'd allowed him and mom to come to Alfheim, his family never could have killed him. You all but signed *both* of my parents' death warrants when you built that blockade. You're the reason I grew up without them. *You.*"

The queen's stoic silence was deafening.

"If you live long enough to become queen, then you will understand," Constance finally said.

"No." I shook my head. "I'll never understand. I would do anything—*anything*—for those I love."

"And I have sacrificed everything for the security of my people." Constance lifted her chin again. "There is no greater love than that."

My grandmother and I stared at each other for a long time. I knew in that moment she'd never lift the barrier; that the only way to stop the cloak of darkness blanketing Alfheim was to take the throne myself. I didn't know when, and I most certainly didn't know how, but I knew in that moment I *wanted* the crown. The Light Realm would collapse under the rule of a woman who had chosen to sacrifice her family rather than open her heart to the possibility of change.

In many ways, it already had.

My hands balled into fists. "I'm done here."

Queen Constance's eyes narrowed to slits, her nostrils practically blazing smoke. But her anger had nothing on mine. I turned on one heel and stalked toward the exit, deliberately bumping Narrik's chest with my elbow on my way out. As I opened the heavy wood door and stormed past the two guards outside, Signy yelled at the queen. Constance shouted back, her shrill voice catching the attention of several students who hurried closer to eavesdrop. I was so focused on shouldering through the bottleneck in the hallway, I didn't realize Narrik had slipped out after me until his fierce grip tightened around my shoulder.

"We aren't finished," he growled.

I wrenched out of his grasp. "Yes. We. Are."

"You have no idea how uncomfortable I can make your life. Or the lives of those you love."

"You already have." Tears pricking at my lids, I stormed through the door and into a throng of oblivious students. I kept my head lowered until I reached the glass doors at the end of the hall and pushed through them to enter the quad. Outside, students were clustered together. A few stared as I stumbled toward the lawn. My fingers shook as my anxiety grew, and I hurried across the grass before the gawkers could notice. I didn't want to cry in front of anyone—and I was on the brink of a full out breakdown.

My to-do list consisted of tracking down an untraceable crystal, the absence of which threatened the very existence of my world; avoiding the uncle who wanted me dead; dethroning the grandmother whose bigotry killed my parents; and figuring out how to rule a realm.

High school was a living nightmare.

Before words could fail me, I leaned over my communicator and typed a message to Signy.

I'm sorry I ran. I'm sorry I failed.

Signy's reply came through seconds later.

Meet me at my suite and we can talk this through.

Gods, I wished.

I need to clear my head. I'll come by later.

Be safe, Aura.

Always looking out for me. *I promise.*

My hands shook as I tapped the communicator. Once it went dark, I moved to the back of the quad. I walked quickly as the trembling moved up my hands to my arms. By the time I pulled back the ivy and raced through the hidden door in the quad's stone wall, the butterflies in my stomach and back vibrated at full force. I barreled across the patch of dirt bordering the wall and the forest, breaking into an all-out sprint when I reached the trees. My feet pounded the dusty earth as I darted between trunks, my shoulders bumping against their rough red bark. Exposed roots nearly took me down, and I silently cursed my footwear. High heels had been mandated for the queenly address, and I wasn't used to walking—much less running—in the death traps. But I pressed forward, running until the familiar red-barked trees gave way to a smattering of white ones, and the leaves beneath my feet were no longer long green and purple needles, but thick yellowing ovals. As I darted through another patch of unfamiliar terrain, a low fern proved my undoing. My toe caught on one of its branches, and I threw my arms out in front of me. My hands took the brunt of my fall as I skidded across the dirt, face first. Small rocks jammed into my palms, the pain of their sharp edges against my skin peaking before I rolled onto my arm. The rip of shredding fabric was followed by a fresh wave of pain along my tricep as another root tore my blazer. I tumbled for what seemed like forever before my shoulder collided with the trunk of a mid-sized tree. It stopped my free-slide, but sent another wave of agony through my body. I rolled onto my back and closed my eyes, letting the pain wash over me. Tears dampened my cheeks, though my frustration far outweighed my physical discomfort.

This was a battle I might not win. My grandmother had created a barrier to keep my father from ever setting foot in Alfheim. In doing so, she'd sentenced both of my parents to death. Her fear and intolerance had destroyed so much, yet she had the backing of the strongest political party in the realm. I was a sixteen-year-old high school girl with no party and no power. How was I supposed to take her crown? And if I failed, how would life on Alfheim ever improve for those whose gifts she deemed less worthy, or whose lifestyles she didn't understand, or whose heritage was less than "pure"? How was I going to fix the mess my grandmother had gotten us into?

And what would happen to our world if I didn't?

When the pain dropped to manageable levels, I sat up and ran a damage scan. My left sleeve was torn and caked in blood, but the wound appeared to be healing. Since blood still seeped from the cut on my face, I ripped off the rest of my sleeve and held it to my cheek. My hands were a hot mess, and my ribs felt bruised at best, so I waited another half minute before picking the rocks out of my palms and climbing unsteadily to my feet. When my ankles wobbled, I yanked off the academy-issued heels that caused this whole debacle and flung them into the forest as hard as I could.

The ensuing yelp of pain was frustratingly familiar. *What is* he *doing in the forest?*

I stormed in the direction I'd thrown my shoes and found my training partner whispering hurriedly into his wrist. The blue light of his communicator flickered to darkness before Viggo straightened up. As he pulled his shoulders back and looked down at me, his expression was a mask of practiced calm. But I saw the muscle over his left jaw flex, as if he was grinding his teeth. Viggo was angry . . . or nervous.

Gotcha.

"What are you doing out here?" I crossed my arms.

"I'd ask you the same thing, but I already know the answer." Viggo bent down and picked up a high-heeled shoe. "Lose something?"

I ignored the offered footwear. "I know you were

talking to someone. Again. Who is it? Is it someone on Svartalfheim? Because so help me, if it's—"

"So what if it is?" Viggo squared his thick shoulders. Since he wore the regulation black tank top and pants issued by the *Verge* program, he must have pulled a quick-change after the queen's address. He'd probably planned to follow his illicit holo-meeting with a Saturday morning workout. *Teacher's pet.*

"You know you're not allowed to communicate with other realms until the crystal is located," I said. "The queen mandated—"

"The queen." Viggo snorted. "My parents died protecting her barrier. And my *Protektor* died stopping Svartalfheim from overriding it."

"I'm sorry, Viggo, but–"

"Of course you think other-worlders are evil. You here to push your grandmother's propaganda on me, Princess?" The words held such venom, I recoiled.

"Is that what you honestly believe?"

"Since you haven't publicly challenged her, I have no reason to think otherwise." Viggo glowered.

"You think because I haven't challenged her, I agree with her?"

"That's generally how things work. My parents led the *Opprør* to resist the queen's fear-based rule and restore our realm to what it was meant to be. All those years, they held out hope another heir was out there somewhere; that that heir would lead us back to peace." Viggo rolled his eyes. "Can you imagine how they'd feel if they'd lived to see what a disappointment you turned out to be?"

"Sorry to let you down." I took a bare-footed step to the side. Viggo mirrored my movement. He still held my shoe in one hand, and any other time I would have laughed at the image of my tougher-than-thou training partner holding a heel. But I was too angry to see the humor in anything. "But believe me, nothing could possibly match the disappointment of finding out your grandmother is the reason your parents are dead."

"What are you talking about?" Viggo took another step. I did the same.

"My dad was a . . . an off-worlder," I fumbled. "So, not that you bothered to actually ask me, but I'm against the barrier, too. I met with the queen to ask her to take it down, *thank you very much.*"

Viggo's eyes widened, but he didn't apologize. "That barrier has done more harm than good. Someone found a way around it anyway, with the Alfheim Tree."

"Was it Svartalfheim who stole the crystal?" We continued our tight circle. "Are you the one who helped them take it?"

"Because I was raised there, I'm automatically evil? You sound like your grandmother."

"Shut up," I spat. "And maybe you are evil. You showed up right when the crystal went missing—"

"So did you," Viggo interjected.

I shot another eyeball dagger and continued as if he hadn't spoken. "And you regularly sneak into the woods and have secret meetings with a hologram. What's that about?"

Viggo raised an eyebrow as he took a step. "What about you? I saw you run off into the woods with a *Bridger*. Care to explain what you were doing with her?"

"I was talking to my dead dad! And figuring out what the Helheim's going on around here!" I threw my hands up in frustration. "Answer my question, Viggo. Who do you talk to on that device?" If it was my uncle I would take Viggo down right here in the forest, shoes or no shoes. *Maybe I could use the shoe to bludgeon him . . .*

"It's none of your business who I talk to. Stay out of my life." Viggo moved forward, breaking our circle. Now he stood directly in front of me, his six-plus-feet towering over me.

"Fine by me. Just get out of my way." I fisted my hands and pushed against his chest, but he didn't move. I shot him a glare that should have burned a hole clear through his thick head, but as he glowered, the green of his eyes lightened from a deep pine to a soft emerald. The muscle clenching across his jaw softened, and one corner of his mouth turned up enough to make his dimple pop.

What is wrong with him? Oh crêpes, what is wrong with me? The familiar flutters at my back sharpened in a stabbing pain, and before I registered what was happening, my blazer pulled taught against my arms. Agony tore through my back from neck to waist. My breath stalled while stabbing pain pierced either side of my spine. Either my shoulder blades were clawing their way out of my body, or I was being ravaged by an invisible animal. *Oh, gods!* A scream ripped from my throat. The sickening sound of tearing flesh was followed by a gurgle as thick, warm liquid oozed slowly down my back. My nostrils were immediately assaulted by an odor that was equal parts metallic tang and cloying fear. I writhed in agony, my body fighting against the unnatural loss of what seemed to be infinite amounts of blood. My vision blurred as the pain overwhelmed me, the forest shifting from vibrant green to faded black. I blinked back tears and pushed myself to my feet, stumbling with the movement.

"Don't move," Viggo ordered. "You'll make it worse."

"What's on my back? Get it off of me!" I squeezed my eyes shut as a fresh wave overtook me, wrapping my arms around my torso, and trying not to writhe in agony. Even the tiniest movement increased my pain by a million. *How can anything hurt this much? Gods, what is happening?*

As quickly as it had come, the mind-numbing pain ebbed to extreme-discomfort levels. I waited another half minute before uncurling my spine. My body still throbbed, but since the worst of the horror seemed to have ended, I tentatively opened one eye to assess the damage. *Yikes.* The scraps of my jacket and blouse lay in bloody tatters by my feet. Thank Frigga I'd worn a racerback tank top under my uniform, instead of the thick strapped tank I usually wore—I would have been topless in front of my training partner. But what had drawn all of that blood? And what had made it stop?

And, most importantly, what were the giant, shimmering *wings* hovering over my shoulder? Had I just been mauled by the world's most vicious butterfly?

I whipped my head to the right, trying to catch a glimpse of whatever creature was attached to the wings, but it ducked out of view. I shifted to my left, but it evaded me again. Too sore to continue, I reached behind me and seized a wing in one hand. When I tried to drag the offending creature in front of me, I felt a painful pull on my back.

Oh, crêpes. I pulled again, harder this time, and a fresh surge of gooey liquid trickled down my spine.

Crêpes, crêpes, crêpes.

I tugged again. And again. And again. With each pull, my back throbbed anew. Which meant . . .

I stared up into the worried green eyes of the boy kneeling in front of me and asked a single question. "Do I have wings?"

"Yes."

Gulp.

"So, I'm not a light elf after all. I'm an *älva.* A . . . a . . ."

"You're a faerie, Aura." Viggo's gentle tone was all it took to push me right over the edge. I plonked down on the soft dirt of the forest, curled into a ball, and cried.

CHAPTER 17

"**H**EY. IT'S GOING TO** be okay." Viggo sat beside me, tossing my shoe onto the ground.

"No, it's not! I am a princess *and* a faerie—I am literally a faerie princess. A winged freak who will forever be associated with the tyrant who's destroying our realm. They're even the same color as hers!"

"Maybe." Viggo tore a less-bloodied piece of fabric from what was left of my blouse and pressed it lightly against my back. "But you're also a winged freak whose bleeding's slowing down. Either this wasn't your first time, or you got really lucky."

"This was lucky?" I croaked. "Wait, why aren't you freaking out? I have . . ." I lowered my voice to a whisper. "I have wings." *Good gods, I have wings.*

"I see you have wings." Viggo's dimple popped again. "Wings don't scare me."

"Yeah, but . . ."

"But what?" Viggo gave my shoulder a light squeeze,

and a warm sensation made its way down to my chest. For reasons I *really* didn't want to think about, it was hard to focus with Viggo touching me.

I ignored the heat building around my heart. No way did I want Viggo to think he had any kind of effect on me. Because he didn't. Right? *Wrong.*

Shut up, brain.

"Hardly anybody around here has wings," I muttered. Besides the queen, I'd only seen that one girl on my first day.

Viggo bent lower so his eyes were level with mine. "Are you sure about that?"

What did *that* mean?

"Stand up, Aura." Viggo released my shoulders, rising in one smooth movement and holding out his hand. I eyed it warily. "Trust me."

I trusted him just fine. It was the inferno in my heart I didn't trust.

Seriously, what was wrong with me?

With a shaky breath, I unwrapped my arms from my knees, tried to forget about the fluttering appendages at my back, and reached up to take Viggo's hand. A fresh wave of heat shot from my palm up my arm, sending a jolt to my heart. *Knock it off, heart.* In typical fashion, my body ignored me.

"Now stand back." Viggo helped me up before releasing my hand. "I don't want to hurt you."

"Then don't hurt me."

Viggo chuckled. "Just watch."

In one swift movement Viggo pulled his shirt over

his head, revealing a lightly tanned chest filled from shoulder to waist with muscles. *Holy. Freaking. Helheim.* Thick pecs gave way to six distinctly defined abdominal muscles, which narrowed to a slim *V* at his waist. His biceps flexed as he tucked his shirt into his back pocket, and the thick muscles along his shoulders popped when he pulled one arm in front of the other in a stretch.

Not that I noticed.

Viggo's biceps flexed again as he made fists at his sides. With a wink, he did something that sent me into such a state of shock, I took a step back.

"Shut up," I whispered. My training partner stood over me, as irritatingly handsome as he'd always been. Only now he was framed by an enormous pair of sheer, silver wings.

Viggo Sörensson was a winged freak, just like me.

"You have them, too?" My chest shuddered with a shaky inhale.

"We're two of a kind, *Glitre*." Viggo offered his hand again. This time when I took it, he pulled me in with enough force to draw me against him. My breath caught as we stood chest to chest. Viggo's eyes lightened to a mint green. He took a slow breath, and his torso expanded against mine. *Oh. My. Gods.* My heart pounded so forcefully, I was sure he could hear it. This was wrong. My jerk-face training partner was sneaking around the forest, sprouting wings, and, worst of all, being *nice* to me. And my stupid heart was acting like a total stereotype.

"I need to deal with this whole wing thing," I declared. *Among other things.*

"Want to take a walk?" Viggo tilted his head toward a thicket of trees.

"I guess."

"Try not to sound too excited." Viggo's dimple popped again. *Stupid dimple.*

Viggo walked away and I followed, only because I'd never been in this part of the forest before. We traveled in silence for a good minute, keeping a careful space between us. My traitorous heart kept pulling me toward Viggo, a ping of electricity shooting through me with each accidental brush of my shimmering wings against his silver ones.

Viggo walked us to a moss-covered wall, then turned the dimple in my direction. "After you," he offered.

"You want me to climb that wall? Or am I supposed to fly up it? Because obviously, I don't know how to use the wings."

"Walk through it, Aura." Viggo pulled the ivy to the side, revealing a small cave. I raised an eyebrow. "Fine." Viggo sighed. "I'll go first."

I followed him into the dark space. "Hey, I hear . . . a river?"

"Not quite. Keep walking." The voice came from somewhere in front of me.

"Oof!" I stumbled on what I hoped was a rock, and my face planted into Viggo's wings. *Double ping.* "Sorry," I mumbled.

"You need me to carry you?"

"No." I quickly straightened up. Thank the gods it was dark in that cave. If the heat on the back of my neck was any indication, I was ten different shades of red.

"We're almost there, anyway. Look." Viggo kept moving toward a sliver of light. It grew as we walked, and by the time we emerged from the cave, I understood what he'd meant.

"It's not a river. It's a waterfall!" I gaped at the thick watery wall cascading in front of me. That thing was *huge*.

"Ever seen the back side of water?"

"Nope."

"Looks like this is a big day for you, then." Viggo's dimple popped again. This time, I couldn't help but smile back. "Hold on to me on the hike down. The path is pretty slick, and you're not wearing any shoes. You know, because you threw them at me."

"Ha. Ha. Ha." Ignoring the protest in my brain, I reached out to grip Viggo's hand. A fresh surge of heat shot straight to my stupid heart, but I ignored it in the name of safety and kept my eyes on the ground. Viggo's boots made sure-footed steps along the moss-covered rocks, and my shoeless feet only slipped once as we scaled down the mountain. I silently cursed myself for chucking my footwear—though I doubted the academy-issued heels would have been much help climbing slippery stones—and sent gratitude to the rocks for only cutting my toes once. When we reached the bottom, I pulled my hand away from Viggo's and looked up.

What I saw took my breath away.

The waterfall was easily a hundred feet tall, cascading down a lush, flower-dusted rock formation. Soft white clouds of mist billowed where the falls hit a pristine blue pond. The pond was moderately sized, maybe two hundred feet in diameter, and it was surrounded by every conceivable kind of tree— towering red-barked giants nestled behind white-trunked behemoths, with silver-leaved weeping willows claiming the spots near the water. Tropical plants bordered the pond, their brightly colored flowers waving in the slight breeze. The whole thing was an ecological anomaly—there was no way species this divergent would live in one climate back on Midgard. And yet here they fit together, a beautifully unexpected scene inside a forest full of surprises.

Alfheim was gorgeous. Unpredictably, heart-stop-pingly, unpretentiously gorgeous. Sure, intolerance was choking the light from vast parts of the realm. But this piece of landscape, and, gods willing, more like it, had survived. An untouched piece of beauty that escaped the fighting, the bigotry, the contention of Alfheim's political upheaval. It was proof that, when left to itself, our realm could not only persevere, but *thrive.*

For the first time since I'd landed here, I felt like things might actually be okay.

"Nice, isn't it?" Viggo looked down at me. "Aura, what's wrong?"

"Nothing." I wiped the moisture under my nose.

Seriously, what is wrong *with me?*

"Let's talk." Viggo crossed to one of the willows. He sat in its shade, patting the ground beside him. I blinked. "I'm not going to bite."

"I know that." I rolled my eyes and stomped bare-footed across the grass. When I reached Viggo, I tilted my torso from side to side, trying to figure out how to sit with three-foot-high anomalies protruding from my back.

"Raise your shoulders," Viggo advised. "The teachers say energy follows intention, right? Your wings are no different. They'll read your intention and lift themselves out of the way. But if you do sit on them, it won't hurt. They're just cartilage and tissue; they're pretty malleable. And when you want to retract them, pull your shoulders forward and intend they disappear. They'll fold right up and settle against your shoulder blades."

"You know an awful lot about wings," I said as I raised my shoulders. Sure enough, my unwanted appendages rose enough to let me sit cross-legged in the flowers.

"I've had mine longer than you." Viggo leaned back on his elbows, and his wings adjusted neatly.

Show-off.

"When did you get them?" I wasn't nearly coordi-nated enough to try the lean-back thing. Instead, I pressed my fingers against the grass and dug into the soft earth.

"About a year before I left Svartalfheim. My parents had already been assassinated when the army took down my *Protektor*. The soldiers deduced he'd have been protecting one of Alfheim's Keys, so they began hunting me. One of them got close to the cave I was hiding in, so I took off. I ran all the way to the top of one of the volcanoes, but one soldier stuck to my trail. He closed in, and my choices were to let him capture me or jump into the crater."

"That's awful."

"It sucked," Viggo agreed. "Jumping was suicide, but I'd have rather died than give myself over to the dark elves. I'd heard rumors about what they did to prisoners, and I figured Valhalla would take me if I died protecting Alfheim's secrets—or what little I knew of them, anyway. So, I jumped."

"But you're not dead."

Viggo shrugged. "My wings popped mid-air and carried me to a cave on the far side of the realm. It took me a while to figure out how to use them, but at that point I had nothing but time. I thought I'd need my *Protektor* to get back into Alfheim, and since he was dead I assumed I'd be stranded on Svartalfheim for life. Then Ondyr found me and things changed."

"Who's that?" I reached out to touch a flower that looked like a glowing, purple daisy. It coated my fingertips in a shimmering plum-hued dust.

"Ondyr is a dark elf who's about our age. We

became friends when he helped me fake my death." Viggo sounded so casual, I thought I'd misheard him.

"He did *what*?"

Viggo tipped his face to the sun. Beams filtered through the palm-sized leaves on the willow, dappling his face in pale yellow light. "He found me when I was scavenging for water. I thought I was as good as dead—at that point, all of Svartalfheim knew there was a light elf hiding in the realm, and there was a pretty hefty reward for anyone who turned me in. But Ondyr didn't tell anyone he'd seen me. He went home and came back with some food. I really appreciated it. All the protein sources had migrated to the northern region for the dry season, and I'd been hungry for a while."

"But how did he help you fake your death?" I pressed.

"When Ondyr caught word of scouts doing a sweep of the caves near mine, he got hold of a bipedal carcass that was about my build, stripped it, and left the bones in the desert so it appeared it had been picked off by pterafugls."

"By what?"

"Pterafugls—Svartish birds. They're scavengers. And before you ask, no, I did not ask where Ondyr got a hold of the carcass."

I shuddered. "Why would he help you? Why didn't he turn you in for the reward?"

Viggo lowered his chin. "Because he wanted out. His life was a nightmare—still is. His mom checked out years ago, and his dad's a tyrant who's obsessed with destroying Alfheim. His grandparents didn't exactly get the nurturing gene, and he doesn't have any siblings. He's a good guy in a lousy situation, and he wants something better." Viggo tilted his head back to the sun and closed his eyes. "Too bad the barrier would shoot him straight back to Svartalfheim, even if he could find a way to get here."

The spark of understanding flared. "That's who you're talking to in the hologram. Ondyr."

"Beautiful *and* smart. You're the whole package, aren't you, *Glitre?*"

I rolled my eyes. "You're trying to help him get into Alfheim?"

"I am." Viggo opened his eyes. He shifted so his weight was on one elbow. "Are you going to stop me?"

"With everything that's going on, looking for a way past the barrier is the *last* thing you should be doing," I said.

"But?" One corner of Viggo's mouth quirked up.

"Signy says we have warriors stationed around the realm who could stop legitimate hostiles from entering. And the *Empati* could discern ill-intentions in potential newcomers if we asked them to. We don't need a stupid blockade to keep out everyone who wasn't born here."

"Why, Princess, I do believe you're smarter than the queen." Viggo chuckled.

"Don't call me that," I warned. "And that's not saying much. That barrier only exists because my mom fell in love with a dark elf. From the little I know about him, he was like Ondyr—a good guy in a bad situation. He loved my mom and wanted to build a life with her *away* from his family, and the darkness of his birth realm. But my grandmother made sure that never happened."

Viggo's wings stilled behind him. "So, your dad's from Svartalfheim."

Oh, crêpes.

I gripped the daisy so hard, my fingertips crushed its petals. *R.I.P., daisy.* Tossing the deceased flower aside, I drew a shaky breath and met Viggo's eyes. "Yeah. Or he was, before his family had him killed. I'm not a full-blooded light elf. I'm half dark elf, too."

My chest hitched with the effort of breath. It was the first time I'd admitted what I was out loud, to anyone but Signy.

Viggo and I locked eyes, each waiting for the other to make the next move. When it became apparent no action was forthcoming from his end, I feigned nonchalance. "If you want a new training partner, that's okay."

Viggo's eyebrows knitted together. "Why would you say that?"

"Because I'm, well . . ." My gaze dropped to the broken daisy in the grass.

Warm fingers pressed gently beneath my chin. "You're you, Aura. Don't ever apologize for being who you are."

My heart thumped violently as I exhaled in relief. Viggo and I weren't besties, or even friends, really. But he was my primary contact in the *Verge* program. I'd spent more one-on-one hours with him in the training center than I had with any other classmate. We might not have been close, but it would have sucked if my family tree had sent him packing.

"I'm not sorry for who I am," I corrected. "I'm just . . . I'm scared."

Viggo's eyes narrowed in concern. "Of what?"

Of everything. I wrapped my arms around my knees. "I'm the granddaughter of a bigot. I recently acquired an unwanted set of wings that I don't know how to use. My best friend's mom—who's one of the few people I consider to be *real* family—is trapped on Midgard with the rest of her *Protektor* team, because of the severed tree branch. My parents are dead, my dad's talking to me from beyond, and my dark elf uncle who tried to kill me once now wants to get his hands on the *Sterkvart* crystal so he can kill me *for good* and take over the realms. Oh, and my training partner's been a real jerk up until today."

"Good gods."

"Yeah." I blew out a breath.

"Well . . ." Viggo paused. "I'll have a word with your training partner about the jerk thing. Sorry about him."

"Thanks."

"Seriously. I'm sorry you've been going through all of this." Viggo released my chin. He slid his fingers along my cheek, using the pad of his thumb to wipe away a tear I hadn't realized was there. A fresh surge of heat hit my heart. Hard.

"It's okay." I ignored the inferno. "Honestly, this is just . . . a lot."

Viggo removed his hand from my face. My heart took its tap-dancing show on the road, morphing into a series of belly flutters.

Seriously, knock it off!

"I can't help much with the family stuff, but I might be able to do something about the crystal . . . and that might help with some of your other, uh, concerns. I've been looking for it, too. In addition to preventing realm-wide destruction, and getting your friend's mom home, returning the crystal to the tree will help me get Ondyr into Alfheim."

"How's that?" I asked.

"Well, the barrier prevents us from opening a portal between Svartalfheim and Alfheim, but we did work out a way to get him to Midgard. So, if we re-connect the crystal, then find a way to isolate and de-activate a spot in the barrier—which is easier with a Midgard transfer than a Svartalfheim one—then we can use the tree to bring Ondyr here. Which solves my Ondyr problem. It also solves your uncle problem, because if we get our hands on the crystal before he does, he won't be able to get into Alfheim to kill you. Right?" Viggo spoke as if he was planning a trip to the market, not the extradition of a dark elf refugee and the subversion of a theft and attempted murder.

No biggie.

"Right."

"Okay." Viggo's biceps popped as he talked through

his plan—not that I noticed. "Obviously Svartalfheim knows all about our tree problem. Ondyr's been keeping me apprised of the rumors through this." He tapped the watch-like device on his wrist.

"Your com," I confirmed.

"Correct. He's heard that the dark elves are attempting to gain access to the crystal by using someone on the inside—someone who convinced one of the tree's caretakers to abandon her post long enough to steal the crystal. The dark elves have a Huldra."

I tried to remember what Finna had said about those on my first day. They were *Styra* who'd chosen the darkness and . . . uh . . .

"What's a Huldra again?"

Viggo let out a low whistle. "They're some scary *skit*. They're forest elves who are hot as Helheim, but twice as manipulative. And they're realm jumpers. They can open portals and go wherever they want. Usually they're only out for themselves, but the rumor going around Svartalfheim is that the Huldra who stole the crystal is a mercenary. And apparently, someone wanted the crystal enough to pay her fee."

The hairs at the back of my neck prickled. "Do you think it was my uncle?"

"I hope not." Viggo ran his fingertips along his jaw, massaging the muscle. I ignored my nonsensical urge to reach out and do it for him. "I hate to be the one to tell you this, especially with what you just told me about the guy. This could be really bad for you."

"You can't make things any worse than they already are."

Viggo moved closer, so his knee brushed against mine. He took both of my hands in his and stared into my eyes. *Breathe, Aura. In through the nose, out through the . . . gods, he smells good.*

No, he doesn't. Stop it.

"Huldras are soul suckers. It's how they keep their immortality. They take whatever they need from their victims, then drain their bodies of energy. Their lifespan extends by the number of years they manage to leech out of their prey."

What. The. Actual. Helheim?

"So, if this Huldra is working for my uncle, that means . . ."

Viggo squeezed my hands. "That means that your uncle doesn't want to kill you himself. He's going to trade you for the crystal . . . and the soul sucker will finish you off."

CHAPTER 18

I WITHDREW ONE HAND from Viggo's and held it up. "That doesn't make sense. If the Huldra already stole the crystal, why hasn't she given it to my uncle yet?"

"Maybe she's waiting until your uncle captures you —or maybe she wants to capture you herself, to make sure she gets paid," Viggo suggested.

"She can't take it off-realm because it's tethered here." I winced. "Finna worked that out with the *Elementär*—it's why we've limited our crystal search to Alfheim. And if the Huldra can't take it to my uncle, then that means—"

"Your uncle's coming here to get it," Viggo finished.

"Awesome." I groaned.

"So, we have to steal the crystal back from the Huldra before your uncle shows up. Then we'll return it to the tree, hope whoever's in charge of guarding it comes up with significantly better security, re-open the channel to Midgard, and bring Ondyr and your friend's mom home." Viggo shook his head. "No big deal, right?"

My head swam. "Right. And if I help retrieve the crystal and save the realm, the *Opprør* will have to back me when I challenge the queen—assuming their leaders get returned soon and can bring their members to my side."

"I think the remaining *Opprør* will back you right now—crystal or no."

Heat flooded my cheeks. "If all of Alfheim can see me as an asset rather than another potential liability, they'll be more likely to stand with me. I can't force the queen off the throne without support."

"Fair enough. How much does Professor Bergen know about all of this?" Viggo asked.

"She knows everything I do. A few of us have been getting together regularly to pool what we know; kind of a task force. I've filled Signy in after every meeting."

"My invite must have gotten lost in the mail."

"You weren't exactly being nice to me." I shot Viggo a pointed look, ignoring the way the sun glinted off his lightly tanned, impressively toned, *still naked* chest. *Yum.*

No, not yum. Stop it.

"Fair enough." Viggo sighed. "But I'm going to work on that."

"I'll believe it when I see it."

Viggo pushed himself to his feet. "Enough talking. Let's go save the world."

I offered a tentative smile as I stood. After weeks of uncomfortable interactions, it was good to have Viggo on my side. Even if . . .

"Hey," I blurted before I could stop myself. "Why did you come up to me in the dining hall that first night? Did you know I was the queen's granddaughter?"

"I did."

"But how? Signy and I never told *anybody*."

"You didn't have to. Svartalfheim knew you'd survived the attack sixteen years ago—or at least, whoever wanted you dead did. My parents heard they were working on a way to track you, but I guess it took a while to develop. Ondyr got a hold of one of the tracking prototypes, gave it to me, and—"

"And you used it to find me in the dining hall. Did you know I was half dark elf all along?"

"I did," Viggo said calmly.

Seriously?

"And it didn't freak you out that your training partner was *half evil?*"

"Not all dark elves are bad, Aura." Viggo shrugged. "Ondyr isn't. And it doesn't sound like your dad was, either, or your mom wouldn't have fallen for him. Right?"

Right.

"Huh. Look at that." Viggo reached out to touch the tip of my wing with a finger. A light shiver radiated down the appendage, zapping me as if I'd been shocked. My eyes immediately went to Viggo's bare abdomen, and it took every ounce of restraint not to drool.

"Look at what?" I squeaked. *Calm, Aura. Take it down a notch.*

"You have one too. See?" Viggo gently pinched my wing between two fingers and pulled it down so it was level with my face. The zapping intensified, shooting just south of my navel. *Double yum.*

"What is that? I have a wing freckle? A wing tattoo? What do you call that thing?" I studied the dark grey mark. It was shaped like a sword, a thick blade ending in an intricate hilt. *Weird. Hold on. Did he just say . . .* My back stiffened, my legs locked, and liquid ice ricocheted through my veins. "Uh, what do you mean, *too?*"

Viggo released my wing and pinched his own. "I have one just like it, in the same spot. See?"

Please, gods, no. My breath stalled as Viggo moved his fingers aside to reveal a dark grey mark. It was an exact replica of my own, down to the thickness of the sword's blade and the intricacies of its hilt.

Holy freaking sugar. Viggo and I had twin marks. If the so-called *myth* Finna had told me on my first day was true, that meant he was . . . that Viggo was . . .

Viggo Sörensson is my mate? I have a freaking mate? What. The. Actual. Helheim?

"When my wings popped and I saw the mark, I figured it was some kind of tribute to my parents— they were both warriors." Viggo's casual tone did not *at all* match the speed at which my world was falling out from under me. Why wasn't he freaking out about being sixteen and mated? *Mated?* Bound together for all eternity and tasked with strengthening the future of the light elf race through *an eternal freaking bond?*

"Uh-huh," I stammered.

My brain spun, trying to rationalize my new reality. Myth marks were just a stupid old wives' tale. There was absolutely no truth to the myth. Zero. Zilch. Because no way could Frigga, Odin, or any deific being with an ounce of compassion expect me to spend the rest of my life with Viggo. He was annoyingly sarcastic—his snide comments had left me fuming more days than I could count. He was overconfident to the point of being cocky—if I had to hear one more time how he went easy on me in the training center, I was going to figure out how to smother him with his ridiculously fitted workout clothes. He was a liar—he'd been sneaking into the woods for weeks trying to smuggle a dark elf into the realm, even if said dark elf was a decent guy. And he was way too into himself. Honestly, how much time could a guy spend arranging his inky black hair into precisely crafted waves? Unless he just rolled out of bed that way. I'd never thought to ask him how he came to look so hot every morning.

Shut up, brain! He is not hot!

My heart thumped. Actually, those overworked waves did frame his face pretty perfectly. His dimple was so irritatingly cute, it occasionally made me forget about his sarcasm. And his snarky remarks *were* kind of funny—especially that one about Britney and her mindless minions. Plus, he modeled the values of the

Verge program to a tee, with his two-a-day workouts, and healthy diet, and impeccable study habits, and *gorgeous* abs, and—

My gods, just stop. Don't talk yourself into liking this guy because of some stupid wing tattoo. Just because you're theoretically mated doesn't mean you have to choose *to be with him. You can still walk away and go live a monastic life with the meadow elves or the tree elves or the cat lady elves . . . can't you?*

I honestly didn't know the answer. I added *Protocol for Mates* to the long list of things I needed to ask Signy.

"That's right. You didn't know your dad." Was Viggo still talking about the wing tattoo? *Oh, jeez.* I'd missed a half-minute of monologue. "Well, maybe the mark has something to do with the *Verge* discipline. Do the other students in the program have these marks too?"

"I—uh . . ." *Oh. Oh! Yes!* My lucky break appeared in a flash of joy. Viggo must not have heard the myth! That blissful piece of ignorance would buy me time to wrap my head around being sixteen *and freaking mated to my freaking training partner.*

If the story was even true.

"Yes. That's it." The lie spilled easily from my lips. "The other *Verge* students must have them too. But I haven't seen them because they're, uh, hidden," I improvised. "We can tuck our wings in, right?"

"Right."

"Well, that's why ours are where they are. So that when we retract our wings, nobody can see our marks.

It lets us go undercover. You know, for warrior-type things."

"That makes sense." Viggo released his wing, and the offending mate mark snapped back. "We wouldn't want to go into hostile situations wearing marks that say *I'm here to kill you.*"

"Exactly." I nodded. "That's it. So it's, you know, probably best if we don't tell anyone about them. You never know who might be listening."

"Smart thinking." Viggo winked, the sparkle in his eye making my heart surge all over again.

This whole thing was seriously going to suck.

"Yep. So. We should probably get back to school. Finna should be out of classes by now, and we can pick her brain about any updates about the crystal from the *Elementär*. Let's go." I took off at a jog.

"Aura?" Viggo called from behind me. "School's that way."

I turned around. "Right. Just up through that, um . . ."

"Through the waterfall." Viggo studied me carefully as I ran toward him. "Are you all right?"

"Never better." I chirped.

"Want me to teach you how to fly?" Viggo leapt into the air and flapped twice, soaring in a graceful arc before landing halfway up the rock formation. "It's a lot easier to get back to campus that way. Especially since you're not wearing shoes. Thanks again for throwing yours at me."

"That's okay," I croaked. "I like climbing."

I'd been through enough today. I'd worry about learning to fly next week. *Or never.*

"Suit yourself." Viggo flapped again so his silver wings brought him back to me. He landed easily in the grass and held up a palm. "Need help getting up to the top? Remember, it's slippery where the mist meets the moss."

"I've got it. Thanks. You can, uh, go second. I might need you to catch me." My cheeks flamed.

"Is that an invitation or a challenge?" Viggo's dimple popped. *Crêpes,* he thought I was flirting. Because I was.

Shut up, no I'm not!

"Just a failsafe." I kept my voice level and focused very hard on not making eye contact. "Training partners have each other's backs, right?"

"Uh-huh." I ignored the amusement in Viggo's voice and began my awkward barefoot climb. When I finally reached the entrance to the cave, my tank top dripped with sweat, my arms trembled, and moss coated my skirt. But I'd avoided flirting with Viggo, and I'd kept our awkward secret to myself. Considering the way my day was going, that was a definite win.

By the time we made it back to school, the queen's entourage had cleared.

"How do I put my wings away, again?" I whispered as we approached campus.

"Shoulders forward, intend they fold up. Why do you want them retracted?" Viggo asked.

"I get stared at enough as it is. I don't need to give anyone a fluttering reason to do it more." *Duh.*

"But being an *älva* is who you are." Viggo's too-intense stare brought heat to my cheeks.

"You've been hiding yours," I countered.

Because *obviously,* the best defense was an offense.

"Of course I have! I'm the first male Key in ages. My parents were leaders of the *Opprør.* And all of Svartalfheim has been hunting me for the past two years. There's a target on my back a mile wide, and my only advantage is that the dark elves don't seem to know what I look like. But they *do* know my parents were *älva,* so you'd better believe they're looking for a guy with a set of wings. Would *you* flaunt your most distinguishing feature?"

Nope.

"So, it's agreed. We hide our wings. Or . . ." I raked my bottom lip between my teeth. Gods, I was so sick of *worrying* all the time. "Or we don't."

Viggo's brows knitted together. "Huh?"

"I'm tired of hiding who I am." I flexed my shoulders, experimentally flapping my wings. "Yes, I'm being hunted by my dark elf-uncle. Yes, I'm related to the monster destroying the realm, and yes, I now have wings too—seriously not cool, by the way—but that doesn't mean I'm anything like her. I'm me. Wings and all. And everyone can just deal with it."

Viggo raised an eyebrow. "You sure about that, *Glitre?*"

"It's all going to come out eventually, isn't it?" I shrugged. "I might as well face the music."

Viggo stared at the sky. "You know what? I'm in. Screw the dark elves. I fly fast—they won't be able to catch me, anyway."

So, he was going to stay shirtless, then? I mean, no way could he fit a shirt over those wings. Right? *Triple yum.*

I ignored the fluttering in my stomach. I hadn't eaten lunch. *Obviously,* the fluttering was a symptom of hunger.

I kept my eyes straight ahead as I entered the courtyard, ignoring the curious stares of the students who gawked at my bare feet, sweaty tank, moss covered skirt, blood-caked *everything*, and fluttering, shimmery appendages. By the time we reached the academy's door, the courtyard was a buzz of whispers and giggles. I didn't turn around. Nothing the student body may have guessed could hold a candle to my reality: a Huldra wanted my soul, my uncle wanted me dead, and Viggo Sörenssen was my mate.

And I wasn't sure which of the three frightened me most.

CHAPTER 19

VIGGO OPENED THE DOOR of my room and held out a hand. "After you."

As I crossed the threshold, Elin's eyes morphed into massive spheres of shock. A glance in the floor-length mirror in the entryway revealed I looked even worse than I'd thought. My clothes were torn and bloodied, my hair was matted, my wings were *glittering*, and I was lacking shoes. Viggo looked, well, perfect. As always.

Plus, he was still shirtless.

"Good gods. What happened to you?" Elin jumped up from her desk. She raced to my side and pulled me in for a gentle hug before leaning back to mouth, *You okay?* When I nodded, she whirled on Viggo, who hadn't quite made it through the doorway. "What did you do to her?"

"Nothing." He held up his hands. "She attacked me with her shoes, and I didn't even defend myself."

"Uh, huh." Elin tapped her foot. For a tiny thing, she did fury like no other.

"He didn't do this to me," I confirmed. "I'm just having a really bad day. You may have noticed I'm a faerie now." I jabbed my thumb over my shoulder.

"Is that where the blood came from?" Elin turned me around to study my wings. "Oh, Aura. It looks so painful!"

"It is. Was. It doesn't hurt anymore. Wait." I whirled around to face Viggo. "It's not going to hurt again, is it? The ripping was a one-time deal?"

"It was a one-time deal," he confirmed, finally stepping into my room. His wings fluttered softly with the movement.

"Thank gods," I muttered.

"You have them too." Elin gaped as Viggo's wings glinted beneath the chandelier.

Viggo shrugged. "We need your help."

"Anything." Elin pulled me toward her bed, appeared to think better of it, then ran to the bathroom. She came back with a plushy towel she placed on the bedspread. "Okay, sit. And talk."

"Where do we begin . . ." Viggo's wings folded neatly around him as he settled into Elin's desk chair. He ran his fingers through his inky hair while I climbed onto the bed and tried not to get dirt and blood on the duvet.

"Hold on. We need to bring Wynter in on this. And Finna. And Signy. Pass me my data pad?" I pointed to the tablet on my nightstand. Viggo reached over to pick it up. Our fingers brushed when he handed it to me, and heat crept steadily up my neck.

Elin smirked.

"Shut up," I hissed.

"I didn't—"

The click of the opening door cut Elin off. Finna backed into the entryway carrying a science project and calling over her shoulder. "Anybody home?"

"Hello?" Jande bellowed from behind Finna.

"In here," Elin said, now snickering at me. I ignored her as I finished typing my first message. I sent it to Wynter, then hurriedly typed a second to Signy. Since Finna was already here, that task was moot.

"Good." Finna set the diorama on the table beneath the key hook and held the door for Jande. "You'll never believe what everyone's talking about. The *Styra* are saying Aura and Viggo came out of the woods with bedhead and either torn or missing clothes, we heard conflicting reports, and with *wings*! Isn't that hysterical. We'd know if Aura had wings. And she would never make out with Viggo in the middle of the—" Finna pivoted on one heel, and her mouth dropped open.

"Well, well, well." Jande looked between Viggo and me, his canary-eating grin stretching from ear to ear as his eyes settled on my training partner's naked chest. "Two winged lovebirds. One sans his shirt. I told you it was true. Finna, you owe me your lapis lazuli."

I held up one hand in a sheepish wave. "The wings part is right, but we didn't make out."

"She just wishes we did," Viggo added. I leaned over to punch him in the shoulder. Hard. "Ouch."

"I'm glad you guys are here—we need your science brains. Tell Viggo about the lock on the *Sterkvart*," I pressed forward. "What exactly keeps it from leaving the realm?"

Finna hung her blazer in her wardrobe and walked to her bed. Her pleated skirt grazed the tops of her knees as she moved. "The senior *Elementär* and *Empati* faculty formulated a charge powered by the crystal's core to act as a gravitational hold. If anyone tries to move the *Sterkvart* crystal beyond the borders of Alfheim, it snaps back to its homing spot—which the faculty coded to be the Alfheim Tree."

"Right." Viggo crossed his arms. I tried not to notice the way his biceps flexed with the movement. "So even if we fail to find it, if we can somehow get whoever's holding it to the edge of the border, it will return to the tree."

"Yes. Why? Do you know who has it?" Jande sat on the edge of Finna's bed.

"Maybe." I hurriedly filled my friends in on the developments with my dad, my uncle, and the Huldra who was out to suck my soul. I left out the parts about Viggo wanting to rescue his friend, and our not-so-mythological mate marks. We could cover those burning topics later . . . or never.

"Wow." Finna exhaled slowly. "No wonder you stayed at your godmother's last night."

"That's where she *told* you she stayed." Jande raised a brow. "Do you believe her?"

"Shut up, Jande!" I hissed.

A quiet chuckle drifted from Viggo's chair. "So, we know the crystal's in the realm. And we know the Huldra's probably here with it. Anybody know where we can find a super-hot, bat-*skit* crazy female?"

"Anybody seen Britney lately?" Elin quipped.

We all froze at the knock on the door.

"Is she a witch?" Elin whispered. "Does she come when you say her name?"

"Anybody there? It's me, Wynter." The tentative voice came from the other side of the door.

Oh. Right. I'd messaged her.

"Thank gods." Elin exhaled. "Though I still think Britney might be a witch."

With a loaded look at Viggo, I pushed myself off the bed. I opened the door and ushered my friend inside.

"Wynter. This is my roommate Finna, our friend Jande, and my *Verge* training partner, Viggo. And you remember Elin." I pointed to my desk chair. "Have a seat. We're talking about the crystal. Also, I'm a faerie now." I quickly brought Wynter up to speed on the day's developments.

"You're an *älva*." Wynter's eyes darted between me and Viggo. "Anything else I should know?"

"Nothing," I answered, my voice too high. I cleared my throat. "Nothing at all."

Wynter pressed her lips together but moved forward without comment. "I was actually on my way here when I got your message. Your dad came to see me while I was on Cloak duty this morning. He saw your uncle planning his move on Alfheim. He's going to make an exchange with a woman in a cottage on the north edge of the Torstein Sea."

My eyes sought out Viggo's. "Either Uncle Crazy has a girlfriend, or he's heading out to retrieve the crystal from the Huldra. We need to go there and get it first."

"*We* can go. *You* can't," Elin said decisively.

"I'm with Elin," Viggo chimed in. "The Huldra may have the crystal your uncle's looking for, but we have the *you* they're *both* looking for. Bringing you to their rendezvous point is the fastest way to get your soul removed. And your soul is kind of growing on me."

It took tremendous effort to keep my cheeks from bursting into flames.

"I'm not sitting here and doing nothing," I argued. "If they're planning to meet in Alfheim, they're coming for me anyway. This way I at least have a shot at getting the crystal into my own hands."

"And then what?" Viggo stared at me. "They come after it again, and off you in the process? I don't think so."

I threw up my hands. "Well then what do you suggest?"

Viggo frowned. After half a minute, he turned to Wynter. "Did Aura's dad say *when* the meet-up is supposed to happen?"

Wynter played with the black gemstone on her

fourth finger. "He said Aura's uncle was planning to leave Svartalfheim tomorrow at dusk."

Viggo typed on his comm. After a moment of scrolling, he looked up. "That gives us plenty of time. The map says the north edge of the Torstein Sea is under an hour away by air, and the royal safe house is on the way there, adjacent to the queen's castle. What if I fly Aura to the safe house, then head over to the Huldra's meet-up spot? I could grab the crystal and be back here before dinner. Easy."

"No. I'm not hiding in a safe house while you risk your life." I held up my hand. "Viggo, thank you for your offer, but the Huldra and my uncle want *my* soul. Not yours. I'm not sending you in to fight my battle for me."

"Well it's *my* mom who's trapped on Midgard because they stole the crystal. I'm going to steal it back with whichever of you two goes." Elin's tone left no room for argument.

My data pad beeped. "Signy's on her way."

"Neither of you are going. It's too dangerous." Viggo turned to face me. "Signy's coming?"

"Yes." I read the incoming message. "She's heading over from the *Verge* center now."

"Good. She and I can steal the crystal while all of you wait here." Viggo leaned back in his chair, his arms crossed. He, Elin, and I stared at each other, the tension shifting between us in waves. Nobody said a word until Wynter cleared her throat.

"Charming as your act of chivalry is, Viggo, Aura is

right," she said. "She's the one they're after, and she's the one the gargoyle will have been coded to animate for. She has to go with you."

Four heads turned to look at her. Jande spoke first. "The gargoyle?"

"Yes," Wynter said. "Aura's dad said the Huldra secured the *Sterkvart* crystal within the heart of a gargoyle. It's on the cottage grounds."

"So, we have to find a statue, crack it open and remove its heart?" Viggo croaked. I didn't blame him. *What the Helheim?*

"Not exactly. Gargoyles aren't statues—they're magical creatures who guard sacred artifacts," Wynter explained. "But they can be animated, and they have the ability to read intentions."

"Meaning?" Elin asked.

"Meaning when someone hides an artifact inside a gargoyle, the gargoyle can read *what* that artifact is to be used for, and *who* it's meant to be used against," Wynter continued. "If the artifact's hidden to cause harm, the gargoyle has the power to animate in the presence of the individual who will be most adversely affected, and warn them. In this case, that would be you, Aura."

"So, you're saying what? The gargoyle will just come to life and hand me the crystal?"

"Not quite." Wynter frowned. "Only the implanter can retrieve the artifact. Unless you break the gargoyle's magic."

"How do you break magic?" I asked.

"With more magic." Jande sat up straight. "We studied this in Mystic Minerals. Remember, Finna?"

"That's right!" Finna's eyes lit up. "There's a stone called diamond aventurine that carries ancient energy strong enough to break a curse. Gargoyles are cursed creatures. They've always protected the sacred, but they didn't used to be cast in stone—they were living, breathing creatures, just like we are. A few hundred years ago, a gargoyle failed to protect an important treasure of Asgard. To punish him, Odin cursed his descendants to an eternity of immobility. But if you animate a gargoyle, then implant diamond aventurine into his heart, the stone's ancient energy breaks that gargoyle's curse so he can act of his own will. Hopefully once he's free, he'll hand the crystal over to us."

"Well said." Wynter smoothed the front of her skirt. "Free a gargoyle, and you have a powerful magical friend for life. But the plan rests on the gargoyle being animated, and because Aura's the one the gargoyle's fail switch is triggered for . . ."

"She has to go." Elin sighed. "I understand."

"Fine. Do we happen to *have* an aventurine crystal on hand?" Viggo rubbed his temples. I didn't blame him. My own head was starting to throb.

"Maybe." Finna glanced at Jande. "We have a rare gems collection in the crystal lab, but I'm not sure if we have that stone. And even if we do, the collection's pretty well guarded. Getting our hands on it will be hard."

"Well, try," Winter advised. "That's the only thing that's going to get us the *Sterkvart*."

"It could take some time . . ." Finna raked her teeth across her bottom lip.

Viggo looked up. "Aura's uncle is meeting the Huldra tomorrow, which means we need to leave as soon as possible. Do you think you could get the aventurine in the next hour?"

"We'll do our best," Finna hedged. "But the better plan is for you guys to set out so we don't lose any time. If we get the stone, we'll send it to you by air."

"Can you fly, too?" Elin asked dryly.

Hold up. Can she?

"No." With one word, Finna dashed my hopes of not being the dorm weirdo. "My friend Evensong is an upper-level *Dyr* and—"

"Hey, I remember her," Elin blurted. "She gave us our first day tour."

"She's the best," Finna said fondly. "Well, she's on aviary duty today. I'm sure she'll let me borrow the Hábrók."

"The what?" I blurted.

"The Hábrók—this really special hawk. The queen keeps her at the school because our *Dyr* program is so good. We're only supposed to fly her for royally sanctioned communications, but . . ." Finna shrugged.

"Great. So, new plan." Viggo rubbed his hands together. "Me, Professor Bergen and the stubborn sisters will head to the cottage on foot while Finna and Jande steal a crystal from the school stash."

"Re-appropriate," Jande corrected, "for the greater good."

It didn't escape my notice that since arriving in my room, all of Jande's words had been spoken directly at Viggo's naked chest.

Viggo shrugged. "Once they get the crystal, they use the Hábrók to send it to us. We'll show Aura to the gargoyle, give him the aventurine, take back the *Sterkvart*, and be home before curfew."

Easy as that. *Snort.*

"What if we can't get a crystal in time?" Finna worried.

"Then we snatch up the gargoyle and bring him back here. Hopefully you'll get one before the Huldra notices he's missing." I stood up, cracking my neck as I angled my head from side to side.

"We're going to need help." Finna moved to her data pad. "I'll let some of the other upper-level *Elementär* know we're going to need assistance with a project that affects the tree."

"And I'll return to The Cloak." Wynter stood and pointed to her communicator. "If I hear anything new from Aura's dad, I'll reach out to you guys through your coms. Just give me your sequences."

Viggo crossed to Wynter and entered a code on her device. "There's mine."

I took Wynter's offered wrist and did the same. She tapped her screen, and Viggo's com lit up, followed by mine. "There. Now you have my sequence too, in case you need me."

"Where's Signy meeting us?" Elin asked. "Here or downstairs?"

"Downstairs. We can take off when she arrives," I confirmed.

"We're settled." Viggo rubbed his hands together. "Wynter heads to The Coat—"

"The Cloak," she corrected.

"Finna and Jande will procure the aventurine." He pulled his tank top out of his back pocket and tucked his wings close to his body before shrugging into the tight garment. "And Aura, Elin, Professor Bergen and I will go find the gargoyle."

I blinked as Viggo stretched his wings free of the arm-holes in his tank. Would I ever be able to control mine like that?

"Did he have to do that?" Jande whispered.

"Do what?" Finna asked quietly.

Jande frowned. "Put his shirt on?"

Oh, honestly.

"So, we're all good?" I moved toward the door.

"Almost." Elin pointed to my bare feet. "You need shoes. And possibly a different traveling outfit. One *not* covered in dirt and blood?" She jumped up and crossed to my dresser, where she pulled out a set of black training clothes. She threw them at me before heading to her own dresser to do the same. "Everybody, out while Aura and I change. We've got some ground to cover—a crystal to bring home, a crown to steal, and a realm to save. So, move it."

Viggo, Finna, and Wynter went outside, while Elin

and I hurriedly changed our clothes. My best friend had to help me wrestle my wings through the arm holes in my own shirt because, *friendship*. Once I was set, she pulled her hair into a bouncy ponytail and we stepped into the hallway. "Let's go kick some Huldra butt."

"Send a message if you hear anything," Viggo said. Wynter nodded.

"Be careful." Finna hugged Elin and me. She gave Viggo a thin smile.

"Don't do anything stupid," Jande ordered.

"We'll be fine," I assured, convincing myself every bit as much as my friends. Given I was a mated teenage faerie princess with a price on my soul, it was hard not to throw my hands in the air and run screaming for the forest.

Though I had to wonder . . . how much worse could things get?

CHAPTER 20

BY THE TIME WE neared our destination, my feet were covered in blisters. "I had no idea it was a four-hour hike *uphill*," I muttered as my boots sought purchase atop a particularly steep knoll. The ocean's salty tang floated along the breeze, assuring me we'd nearly reached our destination. This journey had taken *forever*.

"It would have been a lot faster if you'd let me come alone." Viggo pointed out. "I could have flown in and out and this would all be over with."

"We're a team. We do this together. And two of us can't fly." I kept marching, ignoring the raw skin at the back of my ankles. "Ouch."

Elin shot me a worried look.

"Blisters," I explained.

"Need Viggo to carry you?" She wiggled her eyebrows.

"Ha. Ha." I glared.

"Actually, that's not a bad idea. We can fly the rest of the way from here." Viggo ran his hand through his hair. "I'll take Signy, you take Elin, and we'll—"

"Viggo! I've never flown before! Do you seriously think I could carry someone on my first time out?"

Viggo shrugged. "Never know until you try."

"You don't need to carry us," Signy interjected. "We're nearly there. Just another mile or so."

"Oh!" Elin yelped. "Finna and Jande did it! Look!"

She pointed to the sky, where an enormous winged creature circled. It tucked in its wings and dove for the ground. If it didn't pull up soon, it was going to hit us before we could—

"Arugh!" Elin covered her head, but the creature swerved at the last second, flapping several times before landing easily on Viggo's outstretched wrist.

"Show-off," I muttered.

Viggo just smirked. "The crystal we were waiting on. The diamond . . . whatever." He gently untied a small satchel from the Hábrók's leg, then tossed it to me. He pulled something out of his pocket and offered it to the hawk, who eagerly gripped it in his talons and flew away.

"What did you give him?" I peeked at the shiny stone inside the satchel before shoving it in my pocket, where it sat heavily against my thigh.

"I gave the bird the heart of a troll." Viggo grinned as the blood drained from my face. "I'm kidding. It was reindeer jerky. Do you think I carry troll hearts in my pocket?"

"I don't know what you carry in your pockets," I said. "Or anything about you, really."

"Professor Bergen doesn't allow conversation in the training center." Viggo continued the endless uphill climb. I followed, my heels howling in protest.

"Nope," I agreed. "She doesn't."

"The training room is for *training*," Signy pointed out. "What you do off of my watch is your business."

"Do you *really* mean that?" Elin giggled.

I punched her shoulder. Hard.

"Do you have any objections to our talking *now*, Professor?" Viggo asked. "You said we have another mile to go."

"Then you have a mile's worth of free time," Signy acquiesced. "But once we get to the gargoyle, no more chatter. You're on the clock."

Viggo shot me a grin. "I don't carry troll hearts in my pocket, but I do love being outside. Especially now that I live in a realm that's not cloaked in every conceivable shade of darkness. There, now you know two things about me that aren't related to the angle of my right hook."

Elin nudged me with her elbow. "You guys should go hiking sometime."

"What are you doing?" I hissed.

"Helping. He's obviously into you," she whispered.

"Shut up!"

"So, you like the outdoors," Elin summarized. She smiled sweetly. "What else makes Viggo Sörensson tick?"

Oh, gods. She was the literal worst at this.

But Viggo considered the question. "Well, I don't play mind games, and I don't have patience for anyone who does. That girl Britney is awful."

"Seriously," I agreed at the same time as Elin said, "You're telling me." Even Signy murmured a barely discernable, "Mmm-hmm."

I knew it!

"That's what I like about your other discipline, Aura," Viggo continued. "There's nothing fake about the *Empati*. Being a *Verge* is great—the faculty pretty much beat the physical weaknesses right out of us. But *Empati* learn how to control their feelings, own their own space. That's as real as it gets."

I stepped over a medium sized rock. "Other *Empati* do that. I'm still a work in progress."

Viggo pulled something out of his pocket and tumbled it between his fingers. "You'll get there."

"Maybe." I grimaced. "What's that?"

Viggo followed my gaze to his hand. "This?" He turned his palm upward, revealing a charred, heart shaped rock. "I always carry it. My parents used to take me hiking near the Svartalfheim volcanoes. My mom found this near one of the craters and gave it to me. She said even in a world of darkness, you can find fragments of hope."

Elin sniffled. "That's beautiful."

I voiced my agreement in a quiet, "It is."

"Your parents were brave warriors, Viggo," Signy

said. "Even from Midgard, I knew of their work for the *Opprør*."

"They wanted a better world for me." Viggo tucked the rock back in his pocket.

"And you're helping build a better world for us all," Signy said gently. "Your parents would be proud."

"Thanks," Viggo grunted. He pointed up ahead. "Hey, is that the Huldra's place?"

I squinted at the small structure perched atop the next hill. Since I'd actually been doing Professor Asling's sunrise meditations—and seeing an improvement in my ability to feel both my protective bubble and presences outside of it, *who knew?*—I reached out to see if I could sense anyone inside. My heart leapt as I picked up on something within the cottage. But it quickly plummeted at the darkness that pulsed back. Either some coastal light elf was having a majorly bad day, or we'd found the Huldra's location.

"I think that's what we're looking for," I shared.

Viggo squinted at the tiny house. "Now we just have to find the gargoyle, show you to him, trade the crystals and get out of here before that storm hits."

"Storm?" I questioned. I looked beyond the Huldra's house, where a cluster of thick grey clouds gathered in the distance. *Perfect.*

"Can you see the gargoyle from here?" Elin asked.

"No," Viggo said. "Aura?"

It was time to put my mandated meditating to use.

I closed my eyes and drew in a breath of salty air. With

tremendous focus, I reached out until I sensed the field just outside the cottage. Feeling nothing, I pushed into the yard, where something fuzzy and stagnant pushed back. *The gargoyle?* With another deep breath I pushed even further, this time edging into the cottage itself. That same darkness jabbed back, and I hurriedly retracted. *Yikes.*

"The Huldra's definitely in the house. The gargoyle's in the front garden, closest to the sea."

Elin raised one eyebrow. "Did you just solve a problem by meditating?"

Signy beamed at me, a thousand *told you so's* packed into one proud look.

"Just get the crystal and let's get out of here." Goosebumps broke out across my back as the wind whipped hard off the bluff. "The storm is moving fast."

"Be *very* careful," Signy warned. "I'll hide at the edge of the property so I can debilitate as many threats as possible before I'm spotted. We stand the greatest chance of getting through this alive if you all work quickly."

"Then let's get going." Elin rubbed her hands together. "Aura, keep a read on the Huldra and make sure she stays put. Viggo and Signy, be prepared to do whatever's necessary to keep us alive. I'll introduce Aura to the gargoyle and negotiate the crystal swap."

My friend held up her palm, and I passed over the stone. We hurriedly covered the remaining ground, careful to stay to the right, and away from the cottage window. When we reached the gargoyle, I kept alert while Viggo stood guard.

"Hurry," he urged.

"On it," Elin muttered. She took my hand and approached the small stone figure. With its pointy ears and bulbous nose, it didn't look that different from a lawn ornament. Maybe I'd read this all wrong. Maybe it really was just a statue.

"Elin, I—"

But she cut me off, pushing me directly in front of the gargoyle and announcing in a solemn voice, "Aura Nilssen is here to see you, oh stone one."

Seriously?

All doubt disappeared as the gargoyle shimmered, the dense stone expanding to welcome a wave of light. An endless beat passed before its stone exterior exploded in a shower of fine, powdery glitter.

"Arugh! My eye!" Viggo brought the heel of his hand to his face.

"Seriously?" I whispered. "You're a winged warrior who grew up on a dark realm, and you're upset about glitter in your eye?"

"It burns," Viggo muttered. But he dropped his hand.

"Identify yourself." The gravelly voice pulled my gaze to the ground. *Good gods, was this for real?* What had once been a garden gnome was now a feline with the same grey fur and whiskered cheeks as . . .

"Bob?" I whispered. The bobcat's tail twitched.

"Aura?" He growled. "How did you find me?"

"How are you in Alfheim?" I held out my hand for Bob to nuzzle. "And how are you *talking*?"

"Your father tried to send me after you when you jumped realms." Bob shifted so my hand rested atop his favorite scratching spot. His deep purr vibrated against my fingernails as I scratched behind his ear. "I could not make your transport, so your father arranged for an additional pickup. I was to slip across the Bifrost unnoticed, but when I was detected, the Norns turned me into a gargoyle—their punishment for unsanctioned inter-realm travel. The Huldra picked me up in my stone form, and I have been here ever since."

"Well we're here to un-curse you." Elin raised the diamond aventurine. "We want to offer you a trade—your freedom, in exchange for the gem the Huldra stored in your heart."

Bob wrenched his head from my hand to blink at Elin. His feline features formed a mask of pure awe. "This is for me?"

"It is." I knelt down so I was on Bob's level. "We need the *Sterkvart* to bring Elin's mom home, to challenge the queen, to stop my uncle from killing me and taking over the realms. And you need this aventurine to break your curse. What do you say?"

Bob turned his head back to the cottage. "I will do anything to help you, Aura. But she intends to kill us all."

"If we act fast, she doesn't have to find out," Viggo hissed. His hand flexed over the dagger he'd tucked into his belt.

"Your weapon will not stop her," Bob warned.

"I'll take my chances," Viggo said through gritted teeth.

"Then hurry." Bob looked at the cottage one more time before lying down and exposing his belly. "Hold the aventurine over my heart. Do not let go until it passes through my skin. Once inside, it will eject the Huldra's prize, which I will then be free to give to you. *Quickly*. I sense her moving."

Angry jabs pressed in on my space as thick droplets of water splattered my face. The storm was close. And the Huldra was closer.

"Do it," I ordered.

"Okay." Elin raised the magical stone over Bob's chest. Her hands shook as the crystal jarred violently, as if it were polarized to reject entry. Bob let out an anguished yowl as Elin forced the crystal closer, his agony so intense I nearly begged Elin to find another way. But after an endless moment, the crystal broke through whatever barrier had caused its resistance. The gem slid into Bob's fur with a thick *slurp*.

Air rushed from my lungs on one relieved exhale.

"It's in!" Elin's eyes shone with pride. But they narrowed into worried slits as Bob began to convulse. "This doesn't look good."

"I know." I hovered over my shaking friend. When thick, yellow foam emerged from the corners of his mouth, I turned to Elin. "It isn't working. We need another plan."

"Stay." Bob groaned as his furry face scrunched up in a louder, more intense yowl. His chest quivered, his legs contracting as he hissed. But a second later he was still, and with a *pop* a pale green gem emerged from his chest. He twitched his paw, batting the stone directly into Elin's waiting hands, and my friend hurriedly shoved it deep into her pocket. Was that it? Was the *Sterkvart* crystal really in our possession? Did we actually have the stone with the power to bring Larkin home, and save the tree, and . . .

Warmth flooded my chest, radiating outward until my entire body surged with joy. We'd actually done it. Against every conceivable odd, we'd managed to get the crystal back.

Now we just had to get it to the tree.

Bob's ears twitched a half second before he dropped into a crouch. "She is near. Go."

"I'm not leaving you," I said. "The academy's a few-hour hike that way. Come with us."

"That is not my path." Bob nuzzled my hand before turning to face the house. "Now, go. We will see each other again."

"Time to move, *Glitre*." Viggo's words were clipped. I glanced over my shoulder to find him tapping on his communicator. "Wynter says your uncle's leaving Svartalfheim now. Which means the Huldra's probably going to collect the crystal any—"

Before he could finish the sentence, a woman burst from the front door of the cottage. The quickening wind whipped her white-blond hair across her face, and blew her floor-length black dress so she appeared to float. A fresh gust blew her hair back, revealing high, angular cheekbones, deep red lips, and a delicate nose. The effect was offset by her eyes—their icy blue could once have been beautiful, but now vibrated as bottomless pools of unbridled anger.

"Run," Bob urged. "Get the crystal to safety. Get *yourselves* to safety. I will hold her off."

The Huldra paused at Bob's fierce growl. Her gaze darted between Elin, Viggo, the bobcat, and me. Rage burned in those ice-blue pools, in the seconds before she lowered her head to charge at Elin. My friend leapt to her feet, but the Huldra was fast. In the moment it took me to register what was happening, the Huldra rocketed through the air to tackle my friend.

"Elin!" Signy leapt from behind the boulder where she'd been hiding to send a blinding white beam at the Huldra. The creature tucked and rolled mid-air, avoiding the shot and continuing her trajectory. Any moment now she'd have Elin in her arms. And then . . .

"No!" The universe had taken enough from me. It wasn't taking my best friend, too.

I lifted my shoulders and my wings stretched wide. With a series of flaps that strained muscles I'd never realized I had, I narrowed the distance between the Huldra and me. Powerful strokes from deceptively flimsy-looking appendages carried me through the sky. With a half-second to spare, I wrenched Elin from the ground, leaving the Huldra lying face down on wet grass. A boom of distant thunder clapped and raindrops descended in droves, soaking the Huldra's thin dress and matting her silky hair against her head. She didn't appear to care as she scrambled to her feet and spun to face me.

I adjusted the panicking Elin as I flapped backward, away from the cottage. My friend continued to flail in my grasp, and I shifted her weight so she could wrap her arms around my neck. Thirty feet below, the Huldra's long fingers balled into tight fists. She whirled on Viggo, dug her bare feet into the earth, and charged. He bent his knees and leapt into the air, wings extending as he jumped. As he flew to safety, the Huldra shrieked in frustration.

"Get out of here!" Signy called. She fired another beam at the Huldra, this time grazing the woman's shoulder. The Huldra's grating cry made me cringe.

"Viggo, get Signy!" I screamed. Without a word, my partner dove for the ground, scooped my godmother into his arms, and zoomed back into the sky.

"Go! All of you! I'll keep her here as long as I can." Bob leapt at the Huldra, pinning her to the ground. Although she was thin, she wrestled him off her with a force incongruous to her bone structure. The Huldra was strong. And she was *furious*.

"Come on, Aura. We need to *move*." Viggo flapped directly in front of me. He held out his hands. "Are you okay to carry Elin?"

"I'd better be." I gritted my teeth and pushed forward. "Elin, do you still have the crystal?"

"It's in my pocket. Just get us out of here!" Elin pleaded.

I lowered my head and held tight to Elin, willing

myself to move quickly. Viggo matched my pace, Signy in his arms, and the four of us soared away from the ocean . . . and the homicidal Huldra.

"Are we there yet?" Elin's yell was muffled against my shoulder. Apparently, she wasn't going to look down.

"Are you afraid of heights?" Viggo asked.

"This is not okay. I'm just saying!"

"Know what else is not okay? Waking up one day and sprouting wings." I flapped harder, barely keeping up with my insanely fast training partner. "Just once I'd like to have a day where something extremely weird *does not happen*."

"Today's not the day," Signy called over. "Once the crystal's restored, you'll move to replace their queen with the heir who saved Alfheim; the one who has the leadership and forward thinking to rebuild our broken world."

Right. No pressure at all today.

Beneath me, the pristine forest gave way to a bleak, grey landscape—complete with fallen trees, soot-covered clearings, and the remains of what must have been a fairly sizeable village. "What is that place?"

Signy and Viggo both looked down.

"*Skit*," Viggo swore. "Is that Creyn?"

"It used to be," Signy confirmed.

"What's Creyn?" Elin still spoke into my shoulder.

"One of Alfheim's capital cities," Signy offered. "It sat atop our realm's largest gem mine. Its stones provided energy not only to the city, but to most of the surrounding regions as well. When the *Kongelig* took control of the queen's council they ordered the mines be stripped, and their resources re-appropriated to the barrier expansion."

"What happened to the citizens?" I asked.

"Most of them were relocated to work camps—the stripping of their region went fast, and Minister Narrik was careful not to give them time to think about their next steps or, Frigga forbid, band together to resist his control. Some grew sick from the pollution brought about by the machines. Others suffered mental illnesses from watching their region die. Now Creyn is a shell of a once vibrant town . . . and a warning of what's still to come, if Alfheim continues along its current course." Signy looked down as we passed over the mausoleum of civilization. My chest ached, and in one heartbreaking moment, all residual fear was stripped from my soul.

Sixteen or no, I was taking the queen down. Today.

"We're almost back at school." My steely eyed stare pierced Viggo. "I'm assuming the Huldra's going to follow us."

"Fair assumption," he replied.

Anger burned anew at the thought of my would-be-soul-sucker. "Considering she's an über-dark *Styra*, she sure didn't use her super manipulator powers to keep us from leaving. She didn't even speak."

"She can't. It's the Norns' failsafe." Viggo flew faster and I strained to keep up. "When a *Styra* chooses to use her influence to bring darkness to the worlds—when she crosses over and becomes a Huldra—she loses her power of speech. She can still manipulate, but she can't use verbal language to do it."

"Well, then why didn't she control us silently so we'd stick around?" I asked. "We got away *a lot* easier than I expected."

A line formed between Viggo's brows. "She has a plan, and odds are good we played right into it. But we had to get out of there. We need to get this crystal delivered *now*."

I looked to the ground. "The academy's up ahead. Signy, can you signal Wynter through your communicator? Tell her to let Finna know we've got the *Sterkvart*, but an angry Huldra, and possibly my uncle, aren't far behind. We're going to need warrior backup —and the headmistress should probably put the school on lockdown."

"Of course." Signy spoke hurriedly into her communicator. A moment later, she nodded. "Wynter said she'll have Finna meet us behind the courtyard for retrieval. A team of warriors is on their way to the cottage to detain the Huldra—assuming she's still there —and to intercept your uncle. A second team is coming here, in case . . . well, in case."

"Good." I flapped my wings harder, my breath coming in shallow gasps. Flying was *way* more exhausting than I'd imagined.

"Land down there." Viggo pointed to the clearing at the back wall of the courtyard.

I angled my left shoulder, soaring downward in a

tight circle. The ground came at me faster than I meant it to, and in a horrifying flash I realized a crash was imminent.

"Aura!" Elin shrieked.

"Sorry!" I cried back. I braced myself for the impact, but at the last second my wings flapped. My feet touched down with a grace I didn't anticipate.

"Nice," Viggo praised as he landed beside me, depositing Signy neatly on the ground. Elin scrambled out of my arms and hugged the nearest tree before doubling over to throw up.

"She's not wild about heights," I whispered to Viggo.

"I see that," he whispered back.

"What do we have here?" A familiar, cold voice sent icicles up my spine. Britney stood outside the courtyard wall, a smug smile stretched across blood red lips. "An unsanctioned trip off-campus? What will the headmistress say?"

"She'll tell you to get back inside, young lady." Signy crossed to my nemesis. "If the school isn't already on lockdown, it will be soon."

"You mean because of the Huldra?" Britney tossed her long hair over her shoulder. "She's an academy alumna, you know. If you haven't figured it out already, she's the one who fed me information on Aura—around the time she reached out to the *Styra*, requested we be on the lookout for someone who might try to steal something of hers. I don't suppose the four of you know anything about that?"

Viggo stepped closer, positioning himself slightly in

front of me. The protective thing was cute, but I'd been dealing with Britney for years. I shifted so we stood shoulder to shoulder, our wings fluttering slightly in the breeze.

"You don't understand what you're messing with," I warned. "Warriors have been sent to kill the Huldra and the dark elf she's working with, but we all know missions can fail. And if those monsters make it to the school, they're not going to care that you did what they asked. They'll end you without thinking twice. I know we don't like each other, but for once I need you to trust me and *go inside.* Find your *Protektor* or your mom —they'll shield you from what's coming."

"My mom's not around." Britney snorted. "She dropped me here and shot straight back to Midgard to shack up with that guy."

Britney's eyes darted to Signy, lingering for a beat in a look of . . . gods, was she jealous? *Nope. Not possible. Jealousy requires a heart.* The look disappeared in a flash of malice that shot at me like a white-hot laser. My breath hitched as I struggled to push Britney out of my space. The fury pinging around me was beyond unnerving. But more than that, Britney was . . . I tentatively opened myself up to the craziness that was Britney Blomgren. Envy and disappointment bore down on me with tsunami-level strength. Britney wasn't angry, she was *hurt.* Her eyes flickered back to Signy, and this time I caught the longing in them. In that instant, I understood that Britney's lifelong obsession with torturing me was borne of pain. All this time

I'd envied Britney growing up with her birth mother and her *Protektor*. But the truth was, she was very much alone.

And even in my darkest moments, I'd always known Signy had my back.

My wings fluttered at that thought, the movement catching Britney's attention. "So, the rumors are true. You do have wings." Her gaze zeroed in on the grey sword at the tip, then shifted to the matching one on Viggo's wing. "What are those marks?" she asked.

Crêpes. "Uh, freckles?"

"No, they're not." Britney stepped closer. "Holy Helheim, those are mate marks. You're *mated?* The Norns chose *you* to be with *him . . . forever?*"

Signy's hand flew to her mouth. "Of course."

"Mate marks are myths . . . I mean . . ." My mouth ran dry.

"They're not myths," Signy said softly.

Skit.

Dread washed over me as Viggo's torso stiffened by my side. Without turning my head, I shifted my eyes and caught his ramrod-straight back, taut shoulders, and firmly clenched fists. He'd locked down, his shallow breath and clenched jaw communicating this was *not good news*. Whether he didn't want to be mated to me, or didn't like being the last to know, I couldn't determine. Either way, my brain whirred with tension —if we really were fated to spend a lifetime together, this wasn't a great way to start. But my thoughts couldn't bridge the road to my mouth. Instead, they spun aimlessly inside my head, a racetrack of regret. *I'm sorry I didn't tell you at the waterfall. I'm sorry Bitch-Face had to out me for you to know. I'm sorry you got a mate with zero idea how to do any of this. I'm just . . . sorry.*

Britney's jaw unhinged. Signy's eyes softened as she studied me with compassion. Even Elin looked up from where she was doubled over to shoot me a *sorry, girl,* glance. But through it all Viggo stayed silent.

I wanted to turn and ask him to say something, *anything,* but we had a homicidal Huldra and a deranged uncle to evade. *Priorities.*

"Well then, fine." I exhaled loudly. "If mate marks aren't myths then we're destined to spend eternity together. Whatever. Now *get inside the school or you will die!*"

But Britney stood frozen to the ground, unable—or unwilling—to move. My eyes darted to the tree where Elin still clutched her stomach. Finna hadn't yet arrived, and we needed to get that crystal to its home *now.* We could come back for Britney later. Or better yet, send the warriors for her. The academy-bound unit should be arriving any minute.

"Elin needs to find Finna and deliver the package," I called out. "Signy, take care of Britney. Viggo, help me fly Elin into campus."

I breathed a sigh of relief at Viggo's nod. He was still on my team, in this mission, at least. While Signy attempted to herd an unwilling Britney toward campus, Viggo and I raced to Elin's side. We each lifted an elbow. Our wings flapped, and we rose just high enough to clear the courtyard wall. Poor Elin went limp in our arms, miserable but resigned. We'd nearly cleared the wall when a flash of red light blasted across the sky. It knocked Elin from my grasp, sending her soaring forward into the courtyard. She tumbled across the grass as Viggo and I launched in the opposite direction. My back hit the dirt with a painful thud, and I ignored the crack of my ribs as I struggled to get my bearings. Viggo lay splayed out on his backside a few feet away from me, and Britney no longer stood on the dirt—now she lay motionless in a clearing several yards away. Her face was ghastly pale as her eyes rolled closed. It was impossible to detect any motion in her chest, but her preternatural stillness didn't offer much hope.

Oh, gods.

I exhaled mightily at the sight of Signy unfurling from her defensive ball. She was near enough to Britney that I had no doubt she'd launched herself at the girl in an effort to shield her from the blast. But while my aunt looked merely shaken, Britney was . . .

I couldn't think about it now.

"We all need to get inside!" Signy pushed herself up and hurried to Britney's side, scooping the limp girl in her arms before stumbling toward the school. "You two take care of each other. Move. Now!"

"What was that?" Viggo yelled as the reverberations echoed across the forest.

"I don't know, but I don't think it's our backup," I

cried back. "Elin, get the crystal to the tree. Something's attacking the school!"

As if to prove my point, a second flash burst across the forest, illuminating the feathery tips of the evergreens with its stark, red beam.

"Hurry!" I cried.

"I'm on it." Elin's weak voice contrasted her steady footsteps. The slamming of a door let me know she'd reached the school, and I hoped she found Finna before whatever had caused the flashes descended on Alfheim Academy.

"Move it, Aura. Viggo, help her up. I'll come back for you once I get Britney inside—hopefully she can be revived." Signy's voice filled me with relief. She was beyond the wall, and out of the blast zone. *Thank the gods.*

With tremendous effort, I dug my fingertips into the dirt and rolled onto my stomach. My torso trembled, registering the plummeting temperature as an icy frost settled across the ground. Viggo clamored to his feet, hurrying to help me up while I gawked at the whitening forest floor. Once again, my partner was a step ahead of me. But this time I was grateful.

"Aura," he muttered.

"Huh?" I wiped my frosty fingertips on my pants.

"Look."

I followed his sightline to the edge of the trees, where the air split to reveal a black opening. Large hands settled on either side, pulling it apart from within. A tall, thin man with greasy black hair stepped through the hole. A thick emerald cloak billowed behind his pale form, and once he cleared the opening he held out a hand to help someone else cross the barrier. A manicured hand emerged, followed by the now-bloodied form of a lithe, elegant woman.

The Huldra was back. Which meant the man with her must be . . . *oh, no.*

"Dragen," Viggo's chest rumbled at my back.

"Viggo." My uncle tilted his head. "I thought I'd find you here."

My knees buckled. "You know each other?"

Dragen's eyes moved from my head down to my boots and back up before settling on Viggo's hand, still resting on my waist. His nostrils flared, and a cruel smile stretched across his face. "Viggo and I go way back. Don't we, *son?*"

CHAPTER 21

I **WHIRLED OUT OF** Viggo's grip to gape at him. "My uncle is your dad?" I was mated to my cousin? *Ew!*

"No!" Viggo sounded horrified. "But . . . Dragen is your uncle?"

I nodded.

"He's Ondyr's father. We aren't related. I'm trying to help Ondyr get away from him," Viggo explained.

My brain whirred. Viggo's dark elf best friend was my cousin? That meant I had at least one living blood relative who was neither a despot nor sociopath.

Little victories.

"I'll make this simple, Aura." Dragen held out his hand. "Come with me, and I won't kill Viggo."

"And I'll make it even simpler," I countered. "Go back to Svartalfheim, and our warriors won't kill you."

"Your warriors are dead. I slaughtered the group near the ocean, then picked off another half dozen when I opened that portal." Dragen pointed one long finger at the black orb. "Nobody is coming to save you."

"Then I'll kill you myself," I vowed.

Dragen twisted his wrist and pulled his fingertips to his palms. He wrenched me away from Viggo without ever touching me. My heart constricted, an unseen force clamping down on my chest. But the tension released when Dragen slammed me to the dirt with a painful thud. I scrambled to my feet, intending to run. But with a flick of his hand, Dragen lifted Viggo off the ground. My partner's hands flew to his throat, clawing at the invisible vise as his face pinked. Whatever Dragen had done to my heart was happening to Viggo's neck. His skin shifted from pink to red to crimson. He couldn't breathe!

"If you run, he dies." Dragen made a fist, and twenty feet away, Viggo choked out a garbled gasp.

"You can have Svartalfheim—I don't want your stupid senate seat," I cried. "Just leave this realm alone!"

The Huldra glowered as Dragen tightened his fist. Viggo's face turned a putrid shade of purple. "You *will* guide the realms to peace or war, either as princess of Alfheim or heir of Svartalfheim. And since I can't have you taking my job . . ."

With a twist of his wrist, Dragen flung Viggo to the ground. My heart leapt into my throat as he crumbled into a heap. Stillness crept over his body like a blanket, immobility smothering him until even his wings were unfazed by the light breeze. My pulse quickened, then slowed to a near-standstill as shock sucker-punched me in the gut. A weight settled atop my chest, almost as if *I* was the one struggling to breathe; trying to stay in my body long enough for someone, *anyone*, to jolt me back to consciousness . . . or to life. Agony ripped through me as I bit back a cry. Was Viggo . . . I couldn't bring myself to even think the word. My partner was the toughest *Verge* student I knew. He'd survived being hunted in Svartalfheim. He *would* survive this.

Wouldn't he?

I wanted to run to Viggo; to take him far from that monster; to get him the healing he desperately needed. But my legs refused to comply. Dragen's hold had me on lockdown.

Oh, gods.

There was little left but fear—icy, suffocating fear— as Dragen turned his attention to the Huldra. "Hand over the *Sterkvart*," he commanded. "Then, the girl is yours."

The Huldra let out a high-pitched shriek, jabbing her hands at me.

"You don't have it?" Dragen's eyes went cold. "Where is it?"

The Huldra shrieked again, her wild hair whipping around her head.

"Find the crystal," Dragen ordered. "Or you won't live long enough to regret your failure."

The Huldra whirled in a circle, her icy eyes ablaze as she looked from the forest to the school. When she zeroed in on the ivy-covered courtyard door, her blood-red lips pulled back in a cruel smile.

She knew.

Panic gripped my gut. The Huldra would destroy not only the school, but every last one of the students inside. "Elin! She's coming!"

The Huldra's smile widened and she turned toward the courtyard. The fear thrumming through my veins picked up speed. She was halfway across the clearing when Signy burst through the door, Finna on her heels. Relief mixed with terror at the sight of the fiercest fighter I knew . . . who also happened to be the being I cared about more than any other. I couldn't lose Signy. It simply wasn't an option.

"Go back inside!" I yelled.

But Signy marched steadfastly forward. "Not on your life. Finna, stay behind me."

"Right." Finna's eyes widened as she took in Viggo's still form on the ground, Dragen holding me at his side, and the Huldra bearing down on her. She stepped closer to Signy. "Elin's in place with Jande. What do I do?"

"Make sure all available *Elementär* are getting that crystal back into the tree," Signy ordered. "Then confirm the queen is on her way and the rest of the students are on lockdown in their common rooms. Nobody is to come out until I give the green light. Go!"

Finna turned on one heel and hurried back toward campus. But before she'd made it five steps, Dragen's invisible tether wrenched her from the gate. While my roommate hovered in the air, my uncle's hold on me weakened. It was the opening I needed, but . . .

How was I supposed to help my friends if Dragen kept controlling us all with some invisible energy weapon?

Energy weapon. The words tickled a memory. Professor Asling had said that true warriors fought energy by shielding themselves—*and others.* That was it! That was how I could help my friends. Only . . .

The flash of excitement snuffed out fast. Professor Asling had also said that shielding took years to master . . . and I had seconds, at most.

But I had to try.

I shoved my panic deep in my chest as Dragen slowly drew Finna toward him. With a breath, I focused in on the space around me and willed it to expand. *Nothing.* In desperation I copied a move I'd seen Professor Asling do, and pressed my palms away from my body. My fingers recoiled in shock as light tingles zapped my hands.

Is that . . . did I just . . . whoa.

For the first time I recognized the tangible buzz of my own energy. It was light, and fizzy, and filled with tiny, powerful charges.

And I was ready to kill with it.

My hands pushed outward against Dragen's hold. The invisible cords that had bound us fell away, freeing me from their control. My heart pounded as I raced to Viggo's side, fell to my knees and cradled his head in my lap. His chest rose infinitesimally, a movement not nearly deep enough to sustain life.

"Breathe," I urged him. "Please."

Viggo's chest expanded again, slightly fuller this time.

"Please!"

With a deep shudder, he drew a singular breath. His eyes fluttered weakly as he drew another. Then another. Finally, he blinked in confusion, teetering at the edge of consciousness.

"Signy, call for more warriors!" I begged.

"I can't. There's a dark blockade around the school." Signy raised a hand and sent a beam of light at Finna. It wrapped around her, pulling her from Dragen's hold.

"No," Dragen growled. He wrenched his hand, making Finna jerk helplessly in the air.

"Aura!" Signy called. "Widen your shield to include Viggo. Once he's strong enough to fight we can take these monsters down together."

"Aura doesn't know how to use her powers?" Dragen chuckled.

"Do it," Signy urged.

Dragen turned a hand toward me and I felt the pressure breach my invisible armor. Tension circled my heart, drawing inward with a decisive tug. But I refused to be crushed. I raised my hands to Dragen and pushed back, sending a surge of light straight for his head. He stumbled backward, releasing Finna as he struggled to catch his balance.

"Finna, go!" Signy ordered. Finna scrambled to her feet and bolted through the ivy-covered gate while my aunt sent a white beam at Dragen. The dark elf fell to his knees, momentarily debilitated.

Come on, Signy. Don't stop.

The Huldra's shriek echoed off the trees in a blood-curdling wail. I tore my gaze away from Signy just as a grey blur leapt from the foliage and flattened the Huldra to the ground. I scanned the area to assess our next threat, but relief coursed through me at the sight of familiar yellow eyes set in a cherubic, furry face.

"Bob!" He'd survived. But the next second, the Huldra wrenched him off her back and flung him into the trunk of a nearby tree with a horrifying *crack.* "Bob?"

I wanted to rush to his side; to help the friend who'd protected me without my ever knowing how or why. But Dragen was on his feet, shoulders squared, and I knew that there would be no second chance. That this time, my uncle planned to kill me himself.

Unfortunately for Dragen, I didn't plan to die.

"Shield up, Aura!" Signy called.

Right.

My mind stilled as I sucked in dust, damp air, and the tang of evergreens. I pulled my hands to my chest, drawing everything inward, then pushed out, expanding my blockade so it protected Viggo, too. Then I angled my hands to the dirt, tucking the invisible protection into the ground. And I waited.

This had better work.

Dragen closed his fingers in a white-knuckled fist. Pressure bumped at the edge of my armor, but it didn't break through—*thank the gods.* Dragen furrowed his brow, trying again. And again. Over his shoulder, Signy drove the Huldra back with beam after beam. And in my lap, Viggo stirred gently.

"Wake up." I shook Viggo lightly. "We have to fight."

Uncomprehending emerald eyes shifted from left to right. "Where are we?"

"We're outside school," I recapped. "Dragen tried to kill you, the Huldra wants to kill Signy, and if we don't get that crystal locked into the tree *yesterday*, they're going to suck my soul then kill us *all*. So, now would be a great time to get up."

My plea worked. Viggo sat upright with a jolt, his eyes moving quickly between Dragen, the Huldra, Signy, and Bob.

"We're going to need weapons," he surmised. "They're too strong for us physically, and that Huldra is *definitely* a better energy warrior than you are. No offense."

"None taken."

Just then, a winged figure swooped overhead. Two sharp objects dropped beside me, landing with a clang to glint in the late-afternoon sun. I looked up to find a hawk flapping back toward the school.

"What the Helheim?" Viggo studied the freshly deposited blades before leaping to his feet. "They're the swords from the marks on our wings. Did the Hábrók hawk bring them?"

Did it? How did it know we . . .

I shook my head. "Fight now. Ask questions later."

Viggo held out a hand to pull me up. We each grabbed a sword, and I tried *really hard* not to freak out when the blades lit up to exchange a glowy, energetic high five. *What. The. Actual. Helheim?*

With a shudder, I turned to face Dragen. His face reddened as he raised one hand, then the other. Each assault bounced right off my shield. Relief coursed through me, but I knew it wouldn't be long before he switched to a physical offense. And even Professor Asling had said an energetic blocker could only do so much against a physical attack. It wouldn't be long before Dragen figured that out . . . if he didn't know already.

"We need to move in on him," I panted. "I can't hold him off much longer."

"You're doing this?" Viggo asked.

I nodded.

"Nice." Viggo twirled his sword in a figure eight. "But I can't let you do all the work. Beta attack?"

"Lead the way."

Viggo sprinted to the left. I gripped my sword in both hands and moved to the right. My armor dipped as I shifted positions, and I swore. Holding a shield while mounting a physical attack was pretty much impossible—no wonder *Verge* and *Empati* had different combat jobs. But so long as Dragen continued to come at us, the block was a necessary defense. The minute he shifted to tangible offense, I could adjust my focus.

I hoped.

"Now!" Viggo shouted. He swung his sword overhead before angling it down at Dragen. My uncle raised his palm to me, but the parry bounced off my stretched-thin shield. Dragen dove on the ground, rolling out of the way as Viggo's sword landed right where Dragen's head had been. Viggo's communicator beeped loudly, but whatever message Wynter needed to convey would have to wait. Dragen demanded our full attention.

And then some.

I took advantage of Dragen's momentary disorientation and charged at his legs. The tip of my blade pierced his calf as he rolled again, leaving thick drops of blood trailing along the mossy dirt. Dragen hissed before turning his hand to the portal. His palm trembled as he withdrew an enormous mace from the other side. Thick, silver spikes rested atop a dull metal sphere, its handle smooth from frequent use. Dragen leapt to his feet, and twirled the weapon in his right hand.

Double skit.

A sharp movement drew my attention back to the Huldra. She held her hands high, fingers bent as if pulling a puppet's strings. Signy's arms dropped to her sides, and her spine straightened as she whirled in a dizzying circle.

Signy swore. "Stay clear, Aura. My mind's clear, but she's got control of my body."

Oh, gods.

Signy raised an arm to me. She fired a blast, but wrenched her hand at the last second to send the shot into a nearby tree. The purple-tipped evergreen had probably spent the last five hundred years standing in that very spot but it now dropped with a deafening boom, landing dangerously close to the academy's back wall.

"Look out!" Signy called as she fired off another shot. This one struck my armor with a vibration so fierce, it resonated through the shield and into the dirt surrounding my feet. I bent my knees to absorb the shock, stumbling as the waves coursed through me. In the distance, I barely made out Bob wrapping muscular paws around the Huldra and sinking his teeth into her shoulder. *Good!* If he could break the Huldra's hold on Signy, I'd stand a *way* better chance of making it out of this forest alive.

Dragen's angry roar pulled my focus back to the mace-wielding psycho coming at me. With a grunt he swung his weapon in a tight circle. The air whistled with each rotation. If that thing made contact I'd be down a limb, and possibly a pulse. I darted to the right, away from where Signy now shot beams at a growling Bob, and positioned myself so my back was to the school. When Dragen charged, I raced for the court-yard wall. I planted one boot firmly on the stones and held my sword overhead, swinging with a decisive swipe as I flipped backward. My weapon struck Dragen in the shoulder, sending a warm, sticky liquid spraying across my face. I wiped the blood from my cheeks with one hand, then gripped my sword with crimson fingers and stepped to the side. Viggo lunged forward. He jabbed his sword through Dragen's back and withdrew it with a thick squelch.

Dragen turned, his expression equal parts anger and agony. He churned his mace in a violent sphere before thrusting at Viggo's leg. My partner cried out as he limped forward, positioning his back to the school. I kept my sword high and moved to his side.

With Dragen's back to the forest, he didn't see Wynter emerge from the direction of The Cloak—she must have decided to deliver her message in person. She held her fingers to her lips, and I distracted Dragen with another jab to his chest. He swung, easily parrying my sword with his mace. My breathing quickened as I struggled to hold the hilt of my weapon while keeping my armor strong enough to deflect the incoming surge. Dragen was throwing both kinds of attacks at me, and I didn't know how much longer I could hold him off.

"If you don't hand yourself over, I will slaughter everyone you care about," Dragen threatened. "Your defiance will cost you everything."

Dragen held up his palm. My armor deflected the blow, but the burn of its impact ricocheted, so white-hot pokers pierced my protection. My shield was weakening. Fast.

Dragen whipped his mace in a circle so tight, it formed a silver blur. He lunged. I jumped to the side, and Viggo stepped behind Dragen. He swung his sword high, bringing it down on Dragen's other shoulder, and sending a fresh splatter of blood onto the courtyard wall. Dragen let out a pained hiss. Behind him, Wynter positioned herself in front of a new portal, its black opening framed by a cerulean frost. She pointed to Dragen, then pointed to the portal.

I focused my attention on my uncle.

"This is *my* home." I moved forward, jabbing my sword through Dragen's thigh. When he limped backward, Viggo swiped at his calf. Dragen stumbled again, closing the distance between him and Wynter's portal. "And *nobody* hurts Alfheim on my watch."

Dragen's angry eyes widened as I threw down my sword. I raised both hands, drawing strength from the moss, the dirt, and the roots of the trees that stretched beneath forest floor. With a sharp exhale, I sent a surge through my palms. It launched Dragen into the air, forcing him through the new portal. His cape waved wildly in the wind as he shot through the darkness. With a final cry, he hurtled his mace out of the portal. Viggo's pained cry tore at my heart, but the chaos to my right commanded my immediate attention. The Huldra had Signy pinned to the ground. Her knuckles whitened around my aunt's throat while Bob lay unconscious on the dirt.

"Signy!" I screamed.

I took another draw from the ground before firing a surge through my palms. The blast threw the Huldra off Signy. My aunt hurriedly lifted her hands overhead, stretched her ribs across the dirt, and raised her palms to her attacker. The Huldra soared backward, her dress tearing on an errant log as Signy forced her through the ice-laden portal. Wynter brought her hands together with a loud clap, sealing the portal and locking Dragen and the Huldra in what I sincerely hoped was an unreachable, icy wasteland.

Exhaustion swept over me as I let my shield drop. I fell on the dirt, gasping as my body finally acknowledged its infinite levels of pain. But the quivering in my arms, burning in my calf, and stabbing in my lungs were accompanied by a deep satisfaction. Dragen and the Huldra were gone. I'd lived to fight another day.

Another groan from behind reminded me that the struggle wasn't over. We'd vanquished the monsters, but we'd been hit. Hard. I whirled to find Viggo hunched on the ground cradling his knee. His leg was bent at an unnatural angle, with Dragen's mace resting inches from his foot.

"It got me twice." Viggo nodded at the weapon. "I need a healer. That thing was probably laced with dark energy, and it's leeching into my bloodstream."

I crossed to Viggo's side and clasped his hand as he sucked a sharp breath through his teeth. I could only imagine the intensity of his pain.

"Signy," I called. My aunt raised her head from her prone position. "Are *you* okay?"

"I'm fine," she called. "Just . . . sore."

"The mace broke Viggo's leg and injected it with dark energy. Where do I find the healers?" I asked.

"I'll get them," Wynter offered. She quickly moved toward the school, pausing at the courtyard door to ask, "Professor Bergen? Is the bobcat all right or should I bring a *Dyr* with me, too?"

My throat clenched. *Bob.* I squeezed Viggo's

shoulder and hurried to my feline protector's side. He lay on the ground, drawing rasping breaths as blood trickled from wounds too numerous to count. I felt awful—I'd let him down so terribly. Bob had looked out for me for years. He'd jumped realms and been turned into a gargoyle just to help me. How had I not protected him during this fight?

"The bobcat is fine," Signy croaked. "The Huldra did a number on him, but he's going to heal."

I nearly collapsed in relief.

"Thank gods!" I gently touched Bob's back. He yowled. "Sorry. I'll bet that hurt."

"You. Have," Bob rasped. "No. Idea. How. Much."

"All of you stay there," Wynter said. "I'll get the healers, and a *Dyr* just in case. When everyone's stabilized, we can check on Finna and Elin. The *Elementär* should be close to reattaching the crystal by now."

"Hurry," Viggo groaned. He bent over his knee, seemingly hit with a fresh wave of pain. I stroked Bob's face, then returned to my training partner.

"You did great out there," I offered as I sat beside him.

"Thanks." His voice cracked as he rocked forward. "This hurts like Helheim."

"I'll bet it does. I'm sorry you got hit."

Viggo winced. "Not your fault. By the way, when I'm not in inexplicable agony, we're going to have to talk."

My heart sank. "Talk?"

"Yeah. About those things on our wings you lied

about? And how we're going to deal with them moving forward?"

"How do you want to deal with them?" I squeaked.

Viggo grimaced before doubling over. A second later, three white-clad healers came running out of the courtyard. They split up, heading to Signy, Bob, and Viggo, individually.

"Was the kneecap the source of impact?" the healer closest to me asked. She carried a set of crutches with her, which she lay next to Viggo.

"Yes," Viggo grunted. "The dark energy already made it halfway up my quad, by the feel of it. It burns."

"I'm sure it does." The healer turned to me. "You'll need to give us some space. I don't want this energy using you as a new vessel." She held her hands over Viggo's leg, and I scooted back. She moved her palms up and down his thigh in a slow line, repeating this motion for a full minute before planting her fingers firmly into the dirt and shaking them. Then she positioned her hands on either side of Viggo's knee and told him not to look. "This is going to hurt."

I squeezed my eyes shut as a horrific crack filled the air. Viggo's grunt was followed by the stretch of unrolling tape. By the time I opened my eyes, the healer had Viggo's leg reset, splinted, and tightly bandaged. His breathing was steady, but I could see the outline of a tear-track along his dirt-strewn cheek. I scooted closer as the healer helped him stand, then propped him up on a set of crutches.

"Are you all right?" I asked.

"I'll live." He grunted. "Professor Bergen and the cat look like they've seen better days."

Near the trees, one of the healers helped Signy to her feet. She limped slowly to Bob, who lay on the ground like a feline mummy, wrapped from neck to tail in bandages.

"I think I preferred being a gargoyle," Bob yowled.

"I'll bet. I'm sorry it's been so—*whoa!*"

I dug my feet into the dirt as a jolt rocked the ground. Seconds later a surge of white light rippled from the front of the school through the forest. The charge sparked every fiber of my being, from my toes to my hair.

Oh, no. Not again. I jumped in front of Viggo.

"I'll cover you," I promised him.

"Stand down, Aura." Signy looked to the sky. "That must have been from the Alfheim Tree. A light surge that powerful can only mean that the crystal has been restored."

"They did it?" I blinked.

"I guess they did," Viggo said.

"Which means . . ." I swallowed hard. With the moment *finally* upon me—the moment in which I prepared to fight my grandmother for the right to rule our people as *I* saw fit—nerves thundered in my ears. What if the remaining *Opprør*—or, for that matter, the citizens—didn't stand with me? What if I was about to confront the Queen of Alfheim with the backing of only a handful of underage students?

What if I was about to fail us all?

"Right. Well." I raked my teeth over my bottom lip. "I'd better get this over with."

"Get what over with?" Viggo hobbled forward so he stood at my side.

"I'm going to find the queen." I picked up my sword, pulled my shoulders back, and drew a determined breath. "And I'm challenging her for the throne. Right now."

CHAPTER 22

"YOU'RE GOING TO DO what?" Viggo's jaw dropped to his chest.

"I'm challenging the queen. If I don't do it now, she'll find a way to make everyone think *she* saved the tree, then use that lie to justify her barrier, or her ban on immigration, or the burning of innocent towns, or gods only knows what else." I turned on one heel and stormed through the ivy door of the courtyard. If I didn't do this *right now*, I might very well lose my nerve. And then we'd be even worse off than we already were.

Just do it, Aura.

"Stop! You shouldn't confront her alone." Viggo's crutches thumped against the dirt as he hastened after me. "Professor Bergen!"

"On it." Signy sounded close, but I didn't bother turning to check. "Aura, the queen could be armed. Or guarded. Or—"

"Or sitting in a corner all by herself?" I stopped halfway across the courtyard at the sight of the Queen of Alfheim perched forlornly on the stone steps leading up to the academy. Her lilac wings hung limp at her back, two wilted appendages devoid of their usual shimmer. She'd wrapped her arms tight around her knees, her normally pristine dress was covered in winkles, and her hair hung in a lifeless curtain around her face.

But Constance was a master manipulator—one who'd played a devastating role in my parents' deaths, and who had stood idly by while her realm was torn apart from the inside. For all I knew, this desolate queen was nothing more than a decoy.

"Where are your guards?" I demanded. When Constance didn't answer, I tightened my grip on my sword. "I said, where are your guards?"

The queen looked up, her eyes an endless, icy void.

"Careful, Aura." Signy's voice was low in my ear.

"I have this," I hissed. My sword vibrated as tension rippled through me. Constance had welcomed darkness and fear and hatred into our world. She'd unleashed a dark elf, and a Huldra, and a political party hell bent on promoting darkness when the entire purpose of our realm was to spread light. She had forsaken not only Alfheim, but its citizens—the very ones she'd taken an oath to protect. She was a monster.

And I would end her reign of terror if it was the very last thing I did.

I stepped closer to Constance, my arm rising of its

own volition. My sword *wanted* to drive through my grandmother; to end Alfheim's tyranny once and for all. But as I stared into those empty, cold eyes, I forced my sword down. I would not become the kind of leader I'd observed. I would be the kind of leader I believed I could be.

No matter how much I wanted to kill the queen.

My fist tightened around my sword as I drew a steady breath. "Queen Constance. As crown princess of Alfheim, I hereby challenge you for the rights and powers accorded the monarch. Under your leadership, our citizens were forced to cede their voice to a regime that silences free speech, undermines progress, and seeks to return the light realm to a dark age inconsistent with the purpose our world was created to serve."

"I know," the queen whispered.

"Your government created a world in which—wait. What?"

"I only ever wanted to protect my daughter. I never intended any of . . . of this." As Constance's gaze swept the courtyard, then rose to study the forest beyond its walls, I caught the vaguest flicker of remorse.

What. The. Actual. Helheim?

Constance closed her eyes. "I've been informed that you orchestrated a plan to recover and return the *Sterkvart* crystal, at great risk to your own life. You were willing to sacrifice your soul for the good of this realm. Why?"

"Because this realm is my home. And I'm not about

to let anyone—" I eyed the queen meaningfully, "—destroy it."

Constance's lids fluttered open. "You believe I am a threat to Alfheim."

"You *are* a threat to Alfheim. Period. Your values go against everything our world stands for. You've destroyed families, broken communities, ruined entire ecosystems. Alfheim is *dying* because of you. And I can no longer allow the degeneration of my realm or my people."

"You believe you could rule more effectively?"

"I don't know," I said honestly. "But if something doesn't change, there won't be a Light Realm for either of us to protect."

Constance held my gaze for what felt like *forever*. Finally, she lowered her chin to her chest. "This isn't what I wanted—not for you, not for Alfheim. I only ever wanted to keep my daughter safe."

"By building a wall to keep her out?"

Signy placed a supportive hand on my shoulder.

"It was never meant to keep her out." Constance looked up, her eyes now desperate. "I authorized construction on the barrier when Lily took up with the dark elf because I truly believed that he was using her to harm our realm. I didn't know he was trying to defect; didn't know his family wanted him dead . . . I didn't even know that they'd had a child."

Wait. What?

Wynter's inky black hair appeared on the terrace. She darted down the stairs, skirting around the queen to stand at my side. The thud-hop from behind let me know Viggo was close. And Signy offered my shoulder a squeeze.

But I couldn't take my eyes off the queen.

"What did you say?" I whispered.

"Shortly before your mother died, my War Minister informed me that an attack party was approaching. Neither of us knew it was Lily the dark elves pursued, nor did we know she carried an infant with her. I agreed to activate the barrier in order to save my realm, never realizing my daughter and granddaughter would . . ."

My gods, was the queen *crying*?

"I didn't learn of your existence until after Signy evacuated you to Midgard. It was the same day my guards discovered your mother's body. I retreated to my summer residence; requested my Minister of Governance rule in my place. It was two years before I returned, and by then Fyrs Narrik had risen to power. He'd stripped the monarchy of substantial responsibilities; funneled many of my tasks to a council comprised of his most ardent supporters. By the time I emerged from my own darkness, I was a figurehead presiding over a shell of my former realm. The *Kongelig* spread hatred where there had been light, and my survival depended on going along with the new law. I should have fought harder; should have returned to governance sooner. And I should have sought the support of the few *Opprør* who managed to maintain power during the transition. But I was afraid. That fear paved the way for so much hatred. And for that, I am sorry."

I shook my head. "That was years ago. All this time you stood by while your realm—and your citizens—were destroyed."

Constance squeezed her fingertips together. "I convinced myself that Narrik's narrative was true—that in order to protect our world, we had to preserve it; prevent any change coming from the outside."

"Did you miss the insanely horrific changes happening from the inside?"

"I allowed myself to believe that the troubles other-worlders would bring would make things even worse. I couldn't face knowing that I'd . . . lost my family." The words came on a breath. "To a barrier that might not serve my realm's highest good."

"It *doesn't* serve the realm's highest good." I held tight to my sword. "And if things don't improve, Alfheim's going to implode. How do we fix this? How do we restore the balance of power that was in place before the *Kongelig* took control?"

"Such restructuring would require a vote."

"That won't work. The last time there was a vote, the *Opprør* leaders disappeared. And last I checked, nobody's heard from them since. What else do you have?"

"Nothing." Constance rubbed her temples. "Under our current governance, the monarch holds one-third of the vote. The remaining two-thirds go to the cabi-net, who, at the moment, are *Kongelig*. If I was able to locate the missing *Opprør* leaders and unite them behind an increased rule for the monarchy, then I could—"

"Nobody will support you," I interrupted. "In their eyes, you and Narrik are the same."

The queen cringed.

"Now me, on the other hand, they'll get behind." My sword vibrated as if in agreement. "Not only did my team return the crystal, saving the tree and protecting Alfheim from an invasion, but I haven't spent the last decade-and-a-half spewing hatred through the realm. I'm sorry you lost your daughter, and I'm sorry Narrik took some of your power. But as monarch, you should have fought harder for your realm."

"And now you want to take on that job?"

"I want . . ." Gods, there were so many things I wanted. But only one really mattered. "I want peace in Alfheim."

A long pause followed my declaration. Behind me, Viggo, Wynter and Signy were so still I barely heard their breaths.

I glanced over my shoulder, seeking out Signy. When our eyes locked, my anger dropped to the ground in a torrent of pent-up tension. In that moment, it hit me: overthrowing the queen would only invite more discord. The only solution—the *only* way to restore light—was to do the unthinkable.

And hope I wasn't making the biggest mistake of my life.

Here goes nothing.

I squared my shoulders and faced my grandmother. "I want peace in this realm," I repeated. "And I believe the best way to achieve that peace is for the two of us to work together."

Air rushed from my friends' lips.

"What?" Viggo blurted, at the same time Wynter interjected, "Are you insane?"

But Signy merely nodded. *Good.*

"Hear me out." I raised a hand. "The realm's lost faith in Constance. But the *Kongelig* won't grant a sixteen-year-old one-third control of their governance. They'll appoint a regent until I'm of age, and Frigga only knows what kind of monster they'll choose—or the damage they'll inflict with complete governmental control in two years' time. If Constance and I are co-monarchs, and if we rally the realm behind us by recovering the missing *Opprør* leaders, we stand a chance of overthrowing the *Kongelig* . . . *before* they completely destroy Alfheim."

Viggo raised a brow. "You think that'll work?"

"It depends." I turned to Constance. "On whether you're actually willing to change—change your rule, change the means by which you govern, change the means by which you protect Alfheim's borders. Change the very fiber of your being, or at least maintain the outward appearance of having done so, for so long as you live. Fear can't rule your heart, and in those moments when it threatens to . . . you'll have to cede to me; hand over decision making so our citizens can be guided with *love.* Otherwise, there's no deal."

I meant it. There could be only *love* to rule the Alfheim, and if Constance was not prepared to embody that love, then there could be only one ruler.

Me.

"I . . ." Constance's features tightened in dismay. "I . . ."

I apprised the woman who'd driven the light realm to darkness. Then I pointed to the school. "Inside that building, they teach us that Alfheim stands for light; for hope; for what's *good* in the realms. The Alfheim Tree exists so we can bring the resonance of those virtues to *all* worlds, even those cloaked in darkness. If we manage to reach creatures in those realms, then it's our *duty* to grant them entry. A true ruler of Alfheim would judge a being by the light in his heart, not the light in his realm. If any part of you still feels that off-worlders don't belong here, then I will not allow you to rule at my side. I will find a way to take down the *Kongelig* myself. And I will *not* offer you my protection." I drew a breath. "Well?"

Constance bristled. "By decree of the Norns, the crown is my birthright for the duration of my lifetime. My *entire* lifetime."

"This isn't a negotiation," I said simply. "Either you take my deal, or I take you down. I won't let you hurt us any longer."

My grandmother stared at me for an endless beat. But I didn't blink—I'd meant every word of what I said.

After a short eternity, the lines around Constance's eyes softened. "When your mother died, the Norns delivered a copy of your prophecy to me, for safekeeping. Do you know all of what it said?"

"I'm a duality, capable of guiding the realms to peace with my light side or war with my dark." I recited.

"That's only part of your prophecy. It also said if you chose to follow the light, you would serve as one half of Alfheim's *Verge* Key—one of two primary guardians of the realm."

"Two?" I asked. "I thought there was only one of each Key."

"Normally, that is true. In the history of our realm, there has only ever been one other set of dual keys. They were my grandparents, and they held the realms in peace for two full centuries as Queen Helena and King Leon."

Jeez, how long was I going to live?

"Who's the other *Verge* Key now?" I asked.

Constance nodded at Viggo, and my mouth formed a small *O*.

Him?

"You will make a strong Guardian of Alfheim," Constance said. "A *Verge* who guides us into a more progressive future."

Sure. If I could figure out how to *be* a monarch. If I could learn how to navigate Alfheim's court and political arena. If whatever army Narrik managed to accrue to resist me didn't *eat me the Helheim alive.*

"Do you accept my terms?" My grip trembled against the vibration of my sword. "To lay down your bigotry, help me find the *Opprør*, and drop your barrier? The *Empati* can evaluate intentions; we don't need a blockade."

Constance flinched, but nodded in defeat.

"Good. We're also going to extend an invitation for my cousin, Ondyr of Svartalfheim to take up residence here. With a dad like Dragen, he's due for a break."

"You have my word." Constance offered her hand, and I closed the distance between us. Her handshake was cold and stiff, but it was a start; something to build on. I'd take it.

"With the tree restored, I demand our current cabinet recall the Midgard party effective immediately." I stared Constance down.

"It will be done."

"And if they're smart, the *Kongelig* will return the missing leaders of the *Opprør* party *before* we start investigating their disappearance . . . and doling out sentences," I pressed

Constance's brows knitted together. "I don't know where the leaders were taken. But I will question the cabinet."

"*We* will question the cabinet," I said coolly. "And *we* will get our leaders back."

"Understood." Constance's eyes dropped to the sword in my hand, its blade still caked in blood. When she looked to my right, her breath caught. "Where did you get those?"

I followed her sight line, and smiled when I realized

Viggo had somehow managed to wedge his sword between his arm and his crutch.

"Your hawk brought them."

Constance's eyes widened. "I haven't seen these since my grandparents' reign. The swords were crafted by dwarves, from the same metal that forged Thor's hammer, Mjölnir."

"What?" Viggo's eyes bulged. "We were holding . . . the bird gave us . . . we used . . ." He let out a low whistle.

I had to agree. Handing two students dwarven-made swords composed of the same metal as Thor's hammer seemed like a very trusting move on the part of the Hábrók. "Maybe somebody should take them back."

Viggo shook his head. "I want mine."

"I want mine too, but I'd imagine so do a lot of creatures. Shouldn't they be in a vault or something? For safekeeping?"

Signy spoke up. "Aura's right. The *Protektors* have been responsible for safeguarding the Light Swords since their inception. When Queen Helena and King Leon possessed them, they were kept in the Treasure Vault for their owners'—and their own—protection. More than a few intruders from Svartalfheim, Muspelheim, and even Helheim, invaded our borders with the intent of stealing the weapons. When wielded individually, the swords are formidable. But when used in tandem, they're nearly unstoppable. As you've seen."

I pried Viggo's sword from his arm, earning a look

of pained despair. Then I held out my hands to Signy. "Here."

She took the swords with a smile. "Don't worry—when you need them again, the Hábrók will retrieve them and bring them to you. She's more than just the royal messenger—Frigga gifted her to our realm for our protection. And as our Keys, the Hábrók will intuit what you require to keep our world safe."

"Okay." Viggo's face was mostly impassive, though the twinge around his eyes left him looking less like an all-powerful *Verge* Key, and more like a little boy who'd lost his new toy.

"And now," Signy carefully nestled the swords beneath her arm, "we should let the school know the threat has been removed. I'll confirm the Council of *Protektors* is aware that the Alfheim Tree has been restored."

Constance pressed her palms to the stone steps, and rose on shaky legs. "I will personally address the cabinet and apprise them of the restructuring of our monarchy. And I will send a party to Svartalfheim to retrieve Ondyr."

"Are you sure his father won't be waiting?" Signy turned to Wynter. "Where exactly did your portal take Dragen and the Huldra?"

Wynter's eyes sparkled behind heavily kohled lids. "I sent them to Hel's icy, inner chamber of Náströnd. There's no way they're getting back to Svartalfheim, or anywhere, ever."

"Well done." Signy's mouth turned up. She

motioned for Wynter to follow before limping carefully toward the queen.

I doubled back to the ivy door, and let the healers, *Dyr,* and Bob, know it was safe to come inside. I pulled one of the healers aside as she passed into the courtyard. "There's a girl inside the school—Britney Blomgren. Long, dark hair. A little shorter than me. She was bought in shortly after the portal opened. Can she be revived, or is she . . . did she . . ." I didn't want to finish the sentence.

"A girl was triaged just inside the entry. She'd sustained multiple traumas, and her physiological systems had shut down." The healer paused. "They were able to revive her, but it will be some time before we can ascertain whether any of her systems incurred permanent damage."

"Okay." My heart tugged. Britney and I hadn't been friends—far from it. She'd shoved anyone in her path below water just to keep herself from drowning, and in the process made the world around her absolutely awful. But I was building a world of infinite possibilities; one ripe with hopes, dreams, and enough love to fill the cosmos. Maybe, one day, Britney would be strong enough to share in it.

As the rest of the healing team filed past me, I made my way back to the center of the courtyard where Viggo was waiting. Wynter had already gone inside, and Signy stood on the steps with the queen. She turned around to apprise my training partner. "I'd ask if you want the healers to escort you to the *Kurera* wing, but I suspect you have healing of a different kind to focus on right now."

"Yeah. I need to talk to Aura," Viggo confirmed.

My stomach lurched.

"Very well. Come with us, Your Majesty." Signy gestured toward the academy doors. "I'll arrange a meeting for you and Aura to discuss transitioning the monarchy. In the meantime, with your *Protektors* soon returning from Midgard, there is at least one *Musa* who will be most pleased to hear her mother is coming home. Do you want to deliver the news to the students?"

The queen nodded at me, then followed Signy through the door, leaving me alone with Viggo.

Alone. With Viggo.

Yikes.

I shook my head, draining the fresh wave of anxiety that flooded my brain. After facing a Huldra, battling a dark elf, and squaring off against the queen, an open, honest conversation with Viggo should have been a walk in the park.

So why did every fiber of my being want to run?

"WE NEED TO TALK." Viggo turned on his crutches. He limped awkwardly toward the ivy door at the back of the courtyard.

"Uh . . . right." Behind us, doors banged open as students streamed out of their residence halls. Most would no doubt be heading for the Alfheim Tree, to see if the report was true, but a few would make their way into the courtyard, and possibly out to the forest. And this wasn't a conversation I wanted to have in front of anyone else. "Do you feel well enough to go for a walk? Or a hobble?"

Viggo chuckled. "I don't think my leg could get me very far. But my wings are just fine. Race you to the waterfall?"

"I don't think a race in your condition is the best— oh!" My heart jumped as Viggo launched himself in the air. He clutched his crutches in one hand and soared through the trees, looking over his shoulder and calling back to me, "You coming, *Glitre?*"

I guessed I was.

With a flex of my shoulders, I leapt off the ground. My wings flapped, quickly pulling me higher as I followed Viggo toward the forest. He soared over the trees, and I stayed close as he headed up the side of the hill that marked the entrance to the waterfall.

"There's the tunnel," I shouted. "Aren't we supposed to go through there?"

"Only if we're walking. I told you we could do things faster if we traveled my way." He reached the top of the cliff and dove over. I pushed harder, reaching the top a few seconds after he did, and flexing my wings so I hovered beyond the water's spray.

"Down here, *Glitre,*" he called.

I followed the sound of his voice to where the waterfall, pond, and artfully arranged vegetation set a pristine scene. Viggo hovered a few feet above the willow where we'd sat before. He tossed his crutches to the ground before carefully lowering himself onto the grass and squinting up at me. "You can stay up there, but it's going to be hard to talk."

Right. I lowered my head and dove for the ground, covering the hundred-plus feet in seconds. With a flap, I pulled up to land. I sat beneath the willow, careful not to get too close to Viggo. I didn't want to accidentally bump his injured leg . . . or freak myself out any more than I already was.

Viggo raised an eyebrow. "When were you planning to tell me about the whole mate thing?"

Yikes. We were jumping right in.

"Um, I don't know. Never?"

"Never?" Viggo frowned. "Is the idea of being with me that awful?"

"No! I mean, I don't know. I'm just not comfortable losing control over *every freaking aspect* of my life. Whoever I marry—mate, whatever it's called here . . . that seems like something I should get to choose for myself. No offense."

"None taken." Viggo studied me thoughtfully. "And I agree."

"You do?"

"Of course, I do. This is as weird for me as it is for you."

Air rushed from my lungs. "Good."

"Come here, *Glitre*." Viggo held out his arm. I cautiously scooted toward him, and he looped his arm around the small of my back. Goosebumps shot up my spine as he pulled me closer and rested his chin atop my head.

It felt . . . nice.

Extremely nice.

As I let my cheek drop to Viggo's shoulder, and breathed in the familiar scent of cedar, my heartrate picked up. I relaxed into the guy who knew me better than almost anyone in Alfheim; the guy *I* wanted to get to know even better, now that we'd saved our world.

Finally.

"For most of my life, I had no voice." Viggo's chest vibrated against my arm. "My parents were stationed in Svartalfheim, and since they wanted us to stay together, it became my home, too. When they died, my *Protektor* and I went into hiding—with good reason, but I didn't have a say in that, either. Then I got here, and I thought I'd finally have a say in how things played out. But I was assigned a discipline, and a training partner . . . and a mate. No matter how much I wanted to take control of my life, every single step was mapped out for me."

"Tell me about it," I muttered.

"But you know what's funny?" Viggo removed his chin from my head.

"What?"

"As much as I hate that the Norns decided how I was going to spend my life, they got the big things right. I like being a *Verge*. I waited sixteen years hoping for the chance to live in Alfheim, and I like that I get to spend the rest of my life defending it. I like being a Key —even if I have to share the job with somebody else. I like knowing that in a few years, I'll have the power to make the decisions that keep our realm safe. And . . ."

Viggo lifted his arm and tucked his fingers beneath my chin. I had no choice but to look him in the eye.

"And?" I squeaked.

"I like *you*, Aura. You're smart, and funny, and you don't let anyone push you around. You stay true to yourself, no matter what the school or the queen or the realm tell you." Viggo's dimple popped. "I may not appreciate that the Norns made my choices for me, but I can honestly say that I'd have chosen this exact path for myself. You included."

My heart thundered against my ribcage. "I like you too," I admitted. "And for the most part, I'd have chosen the path the Norns gave me—except the princess part, that's just . . ." I rolled my eyes, and Viggo laughed. "But I can't spend the rest of my life with you just because we have the same wing tattoo. If we end up together, it needs to be something we choose—not something anyone forces us into."

"I agree." Viggo's dimple deepened. "How do you feel about dating?"

My pulse quickened. "Dating's fine, I guess. Wait, how does that even work here? Does Alfheim even have movie theatres or comic book shops?"

Viggo stared blankly. "What's a comic book?"

"An illustrated, multi-paneled story that . . . hold up. You seriously don't know about comics?" Wing tattoos or no, I was *not* marrying some guy who didn't understand the fundamental difference between Marvel and D.C.

"Svartalfheim and Midgard had different things, I guess." Viggo shrugged. "You'll have to teach me."

"Oh, I will. The first thing you need to know is that there are two main comic franchises—one's lighter, and one's super dark. Obviously, my favorite franchise is—"

"The light," I finished at the same time Viggo said, "The dark."

He shot me a rakish grin.

"What?" I blurted. "No way. The depth of character development, code of honor amongst the superheroes, and of course, the extensively developed female characters within the lighter franchise, make it a far more engaging fandom. You'll see."

"I guess I will." Viggo winked. "So, assuming you have some of these comic books lying around somewhere, is that what you want to do for our first date? Read?"

I arched one brow. "Tread lightly, Sörensson."

"I didn't say it was a bad thing." The twinkle in Viggo's eyes betrayed his lie.

"Never mind. You don't deserve to discover the wonders that are comic books. We'll just have to do . . . whatever it is you did for fun on Svartalfheim."

"Bone carving? Not exactly the best first-date activity."

Ew.

"Come on, *Glitre*." Viggo tugged me closer. His fingertips sent a sea of tingles dancing along my arm. "I'm sure we can think of *something* to do."

"I could always kick your butt in the training center," I offered. "Again."

"Mmm. As fun as that sounds, maybe we could . . ." Viggo lowered his head to mine.

"Yes?" I breathed.

Viggo's emerald eyes darkened a shade. He slid his hand behind my head and gently angled my face upward. My chest trembled with a shaky breath, and

Viggo lowered his forehead to mine. His nose lightly swept my cheek before trailing my jawline. A wave of goosebumps blanketed my skin as he brought his lips to mine and pressed lightly.

Yum.

A pulse shot through me as Viggo pulled me against him. His tongue traced my upper lip, eliciting a surge of heat that ricocheted all the way down to my thighs. My lips parted and Viggo seized the opportunity, sweeping the inside of my upper lip before delving deeper. His tongue moved against mine for an endless, toe-curling beat. Blood pooled just below my navel as Viggo pulled back to nip lightly at my jaw. A jolt shot through me, and I gasped as Viggo slid his hands up the back of my shirt to caress the tender skin between my wings. My hands flew to his chest, my fingertips tugging the thin fabric of his shirt as I pulled him to me. His chest rumbled at the increased contact, and he returned his attention to my bottom lip, sucking with just enough force to send a fresh surge of blood coursing due south. I moved closer, not wanting even an inch between us.

"Mmm," Viggo groaned. He lifted me onto his lap, gripping tight as he lowered himself to the mossy earth and cradled my body atop his. I was careful to keep my weight off his injured leg, but when he lifted his hips to press against mine . . .

Holy. Freaking. Helheim. Screw planning. I just wanted to do *this* on our first date. And on every date after. Forever.

Viggo laced his fingers through my hair and pulled gently, separating our lips in a frustrating display of . . . was he being chivalrous? Now?

"Sorry," he murmured.

Why? In Frigga's name, *why was he sorry?*

"I probably should have waited until our official date to do that." He gently rolled me off of him, turning his head to the side so he could rest his forehead against mine. "After we read all the comic books."

My fist connected with his shoulder, earning a chuckle. "Forget it, Sörensson. You don't deserve them."

"Aw, come on." Viggo nipped lightly at my bottom lip. I barely contained my whimper. "I promise I'll be good."

"Don't make promises you can't keep." I shimmied closer, so our chests were touching. "Or that I don't want you to keep . . ."

Viggo's eyes deepened a shade. "Sure thing . . . Your Highness."

I swatted his arm, and he reached up to grab my wrist. He brought my palm to his lips, kissing it softly. The embers in my heart blazed anew as I moved my hand up to cup his square jaw. His stubble was rough against the pad of my thumb as I pressed my mouth to his and wiggled closer. He groaned before releasing my hand to grip my waist, pulling me tight against him.

To hell with dating. Or ruling. Or any of it. I just wanted to stay in this meadow.

Forever.

When my lips were swollen and my cheeks flushed, I nestled comfortably in Viggo's arms. For the first time in a long time, I felt like I was exactly where I belonged.

"We'd better get back." Viggo stroked my hair. "The *Protektors* have probably returned from Midgard, and I'm sure your friends are wondering where you are."

I sighed. "Plus, we want to be there when Ondyr arrives. Once word gets out he's friends with Key Boy, the *Styra* are going to be all over him."

"Key Boy?" Viggo raised one eyebrow.

"Long story. Jande can explain." I sat up, and Viggo did the same. "Hey, any chance Ondyr's into guys?"

"I never asked." Viggo shrugged. "But I'm sure as Helheim glad you are."

"You are pretty lucky you landed me."

"Mmm." He pulled me in for another delicious kiss. "I am *extremely* lucky to be mated to you."

"Dating me." I blinked up at him. "We're taking this slow, remember?"

Viggo's dimple popped. "Whatever you say, *Glitre*."

He grabbed his crutches and pushed himself up onto his good leg, then offered his hand to help me up. I took it with a smile, not letting go as we soared away from the waterfall and over the forest. I didn't know the first thing about being a princess—or co-queen, *yikes*—or a *Verge* Key or the protector of Alfheim. And I definitely didn't know the first thing about dating my mate-marked training partner. But as Viggo and I made our way back to campus, and I took in the view of the realm that I was destined to rule, I sent a silent thank you to my parents. They hadn't lived to see the fall of the barrier, but the love and light in their hearts had given me a chance to make a difference. And for that, I would be forever grateful.

It took less than five minutes to reach the Alfheim Tree, where Elin's arms were locked fiercely around Larkin, and a very confused-looking boy was surrounded by a swarm of *Styra*. When Finna, Jande and Wynter pulled the boy free from the hormonal horde, his face shone—first with gratitude, then with admiration. He appraised Jande shyly, his cheeks reddening as he shook my friend's hand. My heart swelled. Jande would have his happy ever after. That truth flowed through me with absolute certainty.

As we touched down in the meadow, Viggo arranged himself so he could lean on his crutches while still holding tight to my hand. Soon he'd want to welcome Ondyr, I'd want to meet my cousin, and we'd both want to celebrate with our friends. But for now, he simply smiled. "What do you say, *Glitre*? Are you ready to rule this crazy crew?"

"Not in the slightest." I stood on my tiptoes to kiss Viggo's jaw. "But I'm ready to take on our next adventure. One day at a time."

"One day at a time," Viggo agreed. He lowered his head to claim my mouth in a maddeningly slow kiss that left my heart thundering in my chest. When he finally pulled back, I was flushed, breathless, and completely and totally at peace with my destiny . . . and everything that went along with it.

Once upon a time the Norns decreed I was fated to guide the realms to peace, as princess of Alfheim. But I intended to do something more. I intended to dedicate my life to making sure that everyone with a kind heart had a place where they were free to be themselves, regardless of where they were born or who they chose to love.

And I intended to do it with Viggo Sörensson at my side.

ACKNOWLEDGMENTS

This story has been a long time coming. Over the years it's been through countless re-imaginings, multiple rewrites, and more stops and starts than I ever saw coming. But at its heart, it's always been about the enduring powers of kindness, and compassion, and understanding, and *love*. Things have changed a lot since I first met Aura, and I hope that in reading her story, you're inspired to share *your* light with the world. We need you!

As always, I owe endless gratitude to my beautiful family—nobody spreads love and joy quite like you do! Thanks to my longtime editor, Lauren Clarke of CREATING ink, Antonella Iannarino, and Carmen Jenner—your sharp eyes and thoughtful feedback made this story what it is. Thank you to Alfheim's earliest readers, Alison, Kristie and Stacey—I'm so grateful for you, always. *Takk* to Mariana, Laura and Lorna, who make sure this Viking ship always stays on course. And a huge thanks to the readers who have supported these Norse stories from day one—I couldn't do this without you!

And *tusen takk* to MorMorMa. Always.

Before finding domestic bliss in suburbia, internationally bestselling author S.T. Bende lived in Manhattan Beach (became overly fond of Peet's Coffee) and Europe…where she became overly fond of McVitie's cookies. Her love of Scandinavian culture and a very patient Norwegian teacher inspired her YA Norse fantasy books. And her love of a galaxy far, far away inspired her to write children's books for Star Wars. She hopes her characters make you smile, and she dreams of skiing on Jotunheim and Hoth.

Learn more about the world of S.T. Bende at www.stbende.com.

. . but is their new relationship strong enough to survive the reality of who she is?

In the face of dark magic, powerful enemies, and the unlikeliest of allies, Aura discovers the true nature of her own duality. It turns out that she's more than just the crown princess of Alfheim. She's a dark faerie.

And she's just met her match.

skies, and the only thing more dangerous than the chief who takes her captive is the rival who steals her away. The heir of Norway's most feared tribe is fierce, cold, and absolutely unyielding. With intruders encroaching upon his borders, Erik Halvarsson has little patience for the girl whose ignorance threatens his very existence. He enlists Saga in the magical Valkyris Academy, where she learns the skills she'll need to protect herself from foreign raiders and domestic terrors. But nothing can protect her from falling for the one guy in all the world she's absolutely forbidden to choose . . . or from risking everything to unlock the secrets that haunt him.

When darkness threatens Saga's new home, she must decide whether to return to the life she's always known, or fight for a love she never could have imagined. Her decision will determine a legacy—not only for Saga, but for the world she never knew she was fated to lead.

So nothing surprises her more than catching the eye of Tyr Fredriksen at her first college party. The imposing Swede is arrogantly charming, stubbornly overprotective, and runs hot-and-cold in ways that defy reason… until Mia learns that she's fallen for the Norse God of War; an immortal battle deity hiding on Midgard (Earth) to protect a valuable Asgardian treasure from a feral enemy. With a price on his head, Tyr brings more than a little excitement to Mia's rigidly controlled life. Choosing Tyr may be the biggest distraction—or the greatest adventure—she's ever had.

Learn more about the world of S.T. Bende at www.stbende.com.